To

Thank you for your kindness and for being good neighbours.

x

Ah Boy!

Alan Stevenson

Cover design by Rebecca Cardwell

ISBN: 9781701778740

For Ange

(my amazing, beautiful and supportive wife)

A quick note from the author

Thank you, kind reader, for buying, begging, borrowing, stealing or even just finding this book. I do hope you will enjoy this little comic tale of English country life. Before you turn to the first page though, I would like to point out that in this increasingly 'woke' world that we find ourselves living in, this is merely a work of fiction and the statements, actions, comments and opinions of some of the characters, which may come across as offensive, do not mirror my own, because that's all they are – insensitive outpourings from farcical characters in a humorous work of fiction. So please don't hit me with any of the social justice cards or any cards at all really (you can get a very nasty paper cut off of cards). Try and remember what real life is really like and how monstrously awful some people can be and that this novel is intended to reflect that. So, calm down my friend and read on with assurance, it's just a story.

Thank you

A x

1

On Remand
(September 2000)

Blummin' 'eck, it's funny how things turn out, ain't it? I mean, who would ever have thought that I would have ended up in here, in prison. I would never have thought it in like a hundred years or more and I can't even count that far anyway. I suppose I could feel bad about it, even hold a grudge as they say, some folks would, but you see, I ain't really like that. I mean, it's all come as a real blummin' shock like and I'm as puddled by it all as I could be, but you still have to look on the bright side and try to find the good in everything don't you? Well, I think so. And besides, when you care about someone as much as I do then you just have to see things through. But I'll come to her in good time. For now, I suppose I'll just have to accept what's going on, trust in the Lord and hope for the best.

It's like me mum told me, just before she ran off with that jockey from the stud farm. She said to me 'Joe' she said. She said Joe cause let's face it that's me name, 'Joe, remember this as you go through life my lad. Always try and do people a good turn and if you can't do someone a good turn, then don't do them one at all. And if someone hurts you or lets you down you just turn the other cheek, forgive them and get on with your life. Don't you try and fight them Joe, you must never get into fights, never ever. Or raise your hand to a woman. Go to church every week and say your prayers every night. Keep your life simple Joe, please keep it as simple as you possibly can and always look on the bright side of everything. If you do all these things then you'll be alright my little Joe, I promise.'

That's what she said to me...

...On me tenth birthday...

...And then she went off with that jockey a week later.

Broke me blummin' heart it did, when she went. Still, I suppose she's happy now. She were never really happy with the old man. He were always a bit too handy with his fists and his feet for her liking and what with me mum being such a beautiful looking woman then that weren't right. Were it?

And I ain't one to bear a grudge on anyone really. Least of all me mum. Or me old man for that matter. Mind you, he still says that if he ever finds either one of 'em, he'll kill 'em both. But then again, he spends most of his spare time when he's not poaching sat in front of the telly or down the Pig and Whistle propping up the bar and spending his dole cheque and don't seem to make too much of an effort at looking for me mum. Which is a good thing. I suppose.

Now that's one thing I really miss. The Pig and Whistle, me local pub. Especially Monday nights which is darts night. Alright, so I ain't in the team, down to the fact that I couldn't throw a dart straight if I kept at it all night, but that don't mean that I shouldn't go down there and support the lads, now does it? There's been some great Monday nights down at the Pig and Whistle over the years. They put food on and everything. Most weeks they have a big pot of that fancy curry stuff. It's a bit hot in the mouth but I like it mind, although, it don't half make me fart and stink the next day like you wouldn't believe. Letting off like I don't know what I am the day after. Which is Tuesday of course.

Anyway, like I say, I'm not one to bear a grudge and I always try to look on the bright side, just like me mum made me promise. And a promise is a promise after all.

Although...

It is a bit hard to keep looking on the bright side in here. Especially when I ain't done nothing wrong to be in here in the first blummin' place. At least I think I ain't. In fact, I'm blummin' sure I ain't. But you see, I got so foxed in that courthouse that I ain't sure anymore what's what. I think it's what they call a miss-carry-age of just-his or something like that. Anyway, let me tell you me story, and I'll begin with this place.

They call this place Her Majesty's Prison, after the Queen, although as far as I'm aware she's never actually been here, and I can't think that she'd want to either because the whole blummin' place smells like sweaty armpits on a hot day. It's a huge great place and all but most of the rooms are quite small. Although, the room, or cells as they're called if you want me to use the proper word, that I'm in is considerably bigger than me bedroom back home which is a good thing. I suppose. Then again, at home I've got a bedroom all to meself whereas in here I have to share this room with two other blokes. Still, they're both nice chaps mind you. They go by the names of Rufus and Wendy. I never knew any blokes by those names before but like I say, really nice enough chaps.

And this is the first time that I've ever slept on one of them bunk beds. Funny looking things they are. They're alright, mind you the mattress is a bit thin. I sleep on the bottom bunk and Rufus sleeps on the top, which suits me just fine. It would worry me sleeping on the top bunk. I mean, what if you fall off in the middle of the night and break something. Rufus say's that he never has but me Granddad used to be a terrible one for the sleep walking of a night-time and what if it's heradet... heriraty... hediraraty...

...What if it runs in the family?

We've only got one window in the cell but no curtains so it lets in a lot of light when you're trying to get to sleep. Apparently, that's in case some of the inmates, that's what they call the people in here, try to hang 'emselves with the curtains. Why they would want to do that is anybody's guess but still, it's a funny old world ain't it? I don't know why we can't have one of them venereal blinds like me grandma has in her kitchen. And we're not allowed out of the cell at night either after the door has been locked even to go to the toilet, which I find a bit inconvivi... invonciventry... inceventory...

...awkward.

Because I sometimes wake up in the middle of the night and need to go. However, there is a bucket in the corner of the cell if we need it. It's not too bad, once you get used to it. I suppose it's the same as the old man's gazunder back at home. Mind you, Rufus had the squitters one night last week, which were a bit blummin' ripe I can tell you. We take it in turns to empty the bucket in the morning. This is known as 'slopping out.' Again, I don't really mind doing this because I used to empty the old man's gazunder for him sometimes, if he'd had too much to drink. Mind you, half the time he just pees the bed instead. Some posh folks might call it a chamber pot, but I think gazunder makes more sense because it 'goes under' the bed you see. Still, I had to hold me breath when I slopped out last week, what with Rufus being poorly and everything. Poor Rufus.

We each have a small cupboard to keep all our personal belongings in. I used to have a proper wardrobe back home. Big, old, dark, wooden thing, but we don't have that many sets of clothes in here so I don't suppose there's any need for one. We are allowed to put a few pictures on the walls, which makes the cell look a bit more cheerful. Rufus is obviously a bit of a man of the world because he has a lot of pictures of ladies without any clothes on, on the wall next to his bunk. I tell you what; some of 'em don't half make me blush. And I don't know how they manage to get 'emselves into such fanciful positions. Maybe they're all double-jointed or something, I don't know. I try not to look at 'em mind you. The vicar wouldn't like that. I knew a lad at school who were double-jointed. He could bend his fingers right back. I tried it meself but it blummin' well hurt. I wonder if it hurts those ladies because some of them have a pained look on their faces.

Wendy on the other hand has lots of pictures of men. He must be a real film fan too because a lot of them are actors. He pointed them out to me. He's got that John Claire van Dim, Leonard the Capricorn, Melanie Sibson, Dom Crude, Arthur Schwarner... Schwansan... Schnaw...

...that chap with the big muscles and the funny voice.

There's also a lot of male pop stars who I've never heard of. Maybe he doesn't like any actresses or female pop stars. Still, each to his own I always say. You don't have to like something just because someone else does. And if he wants to look at women then there's always Rufus' ladies to look at. Not that he ever does mind you.

As for me. Well, I've got an old photo of me mum, one of me and me best girl Meg from when we were at school together and a picture of a Friesian cow standing next to a tractor that I ripped out of an old magazine. It reminds me of the countryside. What with the prison being in the middle of the city I don't get to see much of the countryside. Well, never in fact. Although from our window you can see the top half of an hopsital that they call the Royal Infirmary, which is quite interesting I suppose. Not that I've ever been in there or anything, but I should imagine that a hopsital is a very interesting place. Rufus has been in there though. He says he went in for some stitches once after a dealer slashed him down a back alley. I'm not sure what that all means but he's got a nasty scar on his arm so it must be true.

We are allowed out of the cell sometimes, other than for slopping out. We go out to get our meals, which we have to bring back to the cell to eat. I thought the old man's cooking were bad enough, but you want to try the stuff they serve up in here. Dearie, dearie me! I don't know about slopping out, that stuff is more like slopping in! And, every so often, we are allowed out to go for a shower. Wendy always goes for a shower at the same time as me and just recently he has started to offer to scrub me back and me rump for me which is very kind of him as it's so hard to reach, isn't it? I like the showers. Mainly I suppose because the water's hot. Me grandma always says that cleanliness is next to Godliness, which is odd because she always smells of stale elderflower wine, and I've always prided meself on having a bath every Sunday night without fail. The only trouble is that at home the water were always cold. I mean, it's alright in the Summer but by 'eck you want to try the beggar in the middle of December. Brrrr!

We also come out of the cell for what they call reck-ree-ay-shun-all times. I like that a lot. I sometimes go for a walk around the yard because let's face it, that's the only fresh air I'm going to get for a while until I get this malarkey all sorted. They've got one of them ping pong tables here as well and Rufus has tried a few times to teach me how to play. I can't get on with it though on account of the fact that I'm too blummin' slow and I ain't sure whether I should be pinging or ponging, but I enjoy having a go at it all the same.

Wendy has tried to teach me how to play draughts as well, but I'm beggared if I can understand any of it and the board makes me eyes go funny. If only they had a set of dominoes in here. They did have one once they reckon, but someone pinched it. I don't know, some people will steal anything; they ought to lock the beggars up. Anyway, I wish they would get a new set because if there's one game I'm a dab hand at its dominoes. There's not a man in the village who can beat me. If they had a domino team in the Pig and Whistle instead of darts, they'd be the blummin' champions every year with me on the team. But then that's me. Good at dominoes, rubbish at darts, draughts and ping pong.

Rufus and Wendy also go out to work. Rufus works in the kitchen but then I suppose being a foreign chap he'd be quite good at cookery. Rufus you see is one of them West Indians. He came to this country from an island somewhere called Trinidad. Sounds very extocix... ecoxtic... etoxic...

... fancy, don't it.

He's told me all about it. Apparently one of the main pastimes there is smoking the herbs. Now, I've never smoked in me life, the smell of the old man's roll ups put me of it from an early age, but I should imagine that the likes of parsley, thyme, sage and rosemary don't taste none too good when burnt and sucked in. And don't even get me blummin' well started on that blummin' basil stuff. That's what got me into bother in the first place. But I'll come to all that later. Still, Rufus will be able to get his hands on all the herbs he wants working in the kitchens and have a good smoke.

Wendy on the other hand works in the prison laundry. That must be an awful job having to wash all the other prisoners' socks and underpants and things but he doesn't seem to mind. In fact, he says that he would love to do me laundry mine personally. What were it he said now? Oh yes, he said 'I'd love to strip you stark bollock naked Joe and give you a right bloody good seeing to.' That man is just so kind and thoughtful.

They reckon that I'll be given a job soon as well and I know what I'd like to do. They've got a garden here. A lovely ornana... ormana... orneminal...

...a lovely, pretty, little garden.

That's where I want to work. Well, gardening is what I do for a living anyway. It'll be like one of those bus drivers' holidays that you hear about for me. Apparently, the garden here is very useful. Some of the inmates, that's what we're all called remember, are known as sy-co-paffs and they can get very easily provoked, and the garden helps 'em to stay calm. They bring 'em down there to look at the flowers and smell 'em. They feed the big fish in the little pond and sit and listen to the sound of the birds singing and those wind chime things. And they reckon it works as well, although, there were one incident the other week when one of 'em hit one of the warders on the head with a larger than average sized rockery stone. Granite I think it were. Some people just have no respect for the hard work of others. Vandalism I call it.

That reminds me, there were another chap in here got hurt last week. It's a bit of a long story but I'll try and cut it short for you. You see, there's one of the inmates in here, smashing bloke he is, goes by the name of Big Donny. And they ain't joking either, he's a huge great bloke, one of the biggest blokes I ever saw. Anyway, Big Donny is a very popular man in here with most of the inmates and some of the warders too. He's got lots of friends and they're all hulking great blokes as well oddly enough. Big

Donny and his mates are the kind of blokes you'd like to have around because they protect so many people in here. I don't know what they protect 'em from but it's nice to feel safe isn't it? Anyway, for doing all this protecting all they ask for in return is for some of the tobacco allowance of the people whom they protect which is fine by me, seeing as how I don't smoke, so I give half of mine to Big Donny and half to Rufus.

Now, this poor beggar who had the accident last week, who goes by the name of Tony the Greek, had told Big Donny that he didn't want any protection and that he were keeping all of his tobacco to himself, or words to that there effect. There were a bit of swearing as well which I don't want to repeat. Fair enough you may say, it's his tobacco and he can do what he likes with it. But it were only a few minutes after that when Tony accidentally fell from the landing to the ground floor. I mean, call it a happenstance if you will, but if he'd got Big Donny protecting him that might never have happened. Mightn't it? Poor Tony. Still, they say he'll be out of hopsital within six months and that with something called fur-ra-pee he may actually walk again. I bet he'll ask Big Donny to protect him from now on as well. I tell you what, the warders weren't happy with him though.

And that's another thing. The warders.

The warders, or screws as they are known by in here for some reason, are the chaps who look after us and make sure that our doors are safely locked every night. Well, you don't want anyone breaking in, do you? Some of the warders (I don't like the word screws) are thoroughly nice blokes. You know, the sort you can have a laugh and a joke with. They all wear a very smart uniform with really bright, white shirts. Come to think of it, they look a bit like them Mormons who came round the village a couple of years back, the ones whom Her Ladyship made leave by noon under threat of her 'boot up their arses!' Anyway, the warders keep an eye on us all, which is very comforting because let's face it, Big Donny can't be around all the time, can he?. They let us out in the morning and no matter wherever you go in here you're always bound to see one of 'em knocking about. Except in the shower of course. But then, they probably have one at home after breakfast before they come to work.

Some of the warders are more important than the others and the most important of all is a chap called the Governor. He's in charge of the whole blummin' prison, which is a very important job. Apparently, you can ask to see him if you've got anything you want to complain about. I want to see him meself to complain about the dominoes and to suggest that something should be done about making the landings a lot safer. We don't want anyone else falling off now, do we?

Another of the warders who is quite important is Mr Riddle. Mr Riddle is the warder in charge of our wing. The inmates call him Jimmy but only behind his back. That made me laugh that did. Do you get it? Jimmy Riddle? Anyway, Mr Riddle is a fearsome looking man with short grey hair and a tiny grey moustache that makes him look, to me, like an older version of that Hitler fellow I seen on the telly. He's not very tall but he don't half shout loud. The only person I've ever met who can shout louder than him is Her Ladyship. Mr Riddle has this funny walk as well, a bit like one of them cowboys that you see on them old films on the telly. Or then again, like somebody who has just pappered 'emselves but is trying to not let it show. Rufus says that Mr Riddle walks like that to try and make himself look tough but he's really just a tosser. I don't know what a tosser is exactly, but Mr Riddle doesn't look like one to me. To me he looks very tough but then again me granddad used to say that little men were like terrier dogs. Always yelping and trying to make 'emselves sound bigger than they are. Maybe Mr Riddle is a tosser after all. I'm not going to ask him mind, and I'm not going to start calling him Jimmy in case he hears me, and I get into trouble. I wouldn't want that. Mr Riddle were one of the first people to greet me when I came in here. Now that were a right old blummin' rigmarole.

I'll never forget the day I arrived. What a game that were. They brought us here in a big white lorry with writing down the side. I don't remember exactly what it said but it were something or other and then a number, 4 or 5, I forget which. Now counting were never me strong point but I know for a fact that there were more than four or five of us in that wagon. The inside of the lorry had been separated into little rooms not dissimilar in size to the ones you get in pub khazis, and of a very similar smell as well. I don't know about the rest but mine had got writing on the wall, which is like you find in pub khazis as well. I don't read so good but some of the bits I could make out were very rude. Made me blush, some of it. Anyway, we had a very pleasant journey despite all that, and we soon arrived at the prison, which seemed very grand from the outside. Sort of like a big castle or one of them forts like they had in the olden days. It were far more grand than the police station that I had been in before that.

We were then told to get out of the wagon and were taken into a room where I had to sign something and have me photo taken but we weren't allowed to smile and I got told off for doing it which upset me. We were then made to have a shower which were really strange for me as I never had one before because, like I say, we've only got a bath at home. I enjoyed it though and after that we were given our uniforms. Now, I'm no expert on clothes but I reckon for sure that the underpants that they gave me were second hand on account of the fact that there were a, pardon the expression, a what's known as a skid mark in 'em. Still, mustn't grumble. At least they fit. And I were given a blue T shirt, which were nice because I like T shirts and I like the colour blue, and on the front of the T shirt it had the name of the prison printed on it. Just in case anyone loses one I suppose. I got some trousers as well and a jumper, which don't half itch, although I'm starting to get used to it now. And at last, they gave us what few personal bits and pieces that we were allowed and shown to our cells.

That's when I first met Rufus and Wendy. I think they were having some kind of argument when I walked in because Rufus were holding Wendy by the throat and saying that if Wendy touched his ass ever again he would bleed him, slowly, and hide his body in the boiler room. I don't know what that were all about. As far as I know Rufus hasn't even got a donkey. Well, it wouldn't be allowed in here you see. It'd be nice though. I like donkeys. I rode one once when I were a kid.

Anyway, they both made me feel very welcome though, especially Wendy although Rufus keeps making remarks about faggots whenever he's around. Blimey! I wouldn't mind some of them. We haven't had faggots yet since I got here, the closest we've come is liver and onions. I like a nice faggot I do, with mash and peas and gravy. Anyway, do you know what, if it hadn't been for that pair, I don't know how I would have got on. But I'm settled in nicely now.

That were a month ago. To be honest the time has gone by pretty slowly and I must admit that sometimes I do get a bit bored. Wendy says that he would love to show me some hot, hard, sweaty action though, but I don't see how in here. There's not really that much to do. Hardly any chance to work up a sweat.

I suppose I'm bored because I'm from the country. I miss the wide-open spaces and the hills and trees and the smell of silage in me nostrils. Rufus and Wendy are both from the city so I suppose they don't really mind too much. But for someone like me who has never been any further than the cattle market in his whole blummin' life and spent all his time running round Blessham village, I find it so dull. I don't know how people can live in cities I really don't. And I don't know what makes people go and commit crimes so as to get put in here. Blummin' daft if you ask me. I mean, I ain't got much choice in the matter. I know I ain't done nothing wrong, not really, at least I think so, but then I didn't really have much in the way of an explanation about what happened either and I made a right blummin' mess of things in the ma-jee-straights court. Ah well. What's done is done. Only another two months to go before me case comes up and I have to speak to the judge in the big court here in the city. I'm sure he'll sort it all out.

Rufus has got a few years left to do of his prison sentence. He's in here for something called GBH. Apparently, him and some of his friends got into a bit of a fight in a place called a nightclub with these other blokes, and Rufus hit one of 'em over the head with a bar stool. Unfortunately, he then went on to hit him with it another five or six times, which made matters worse in the eyes of the law. I bet that beggar came keen. Wendy on the other hand has only got a couple of months to go before he gets out. Lucky beggar. He's in here for committing an indecent act in a public conveya... conviviance... coveninance...

...a khazi.

I don't know what an indecent act is, but it must be something wrong otherwise he wouldn't be in here. Would he? Still, he's paying his debt to society. He's done his time and paid the price for his wrongdoing so who am I to judge? And Wendy says that he's determined to get into me pants before he leaves. Honestly, I've never known a bloke so keen on his work as him.

I'll tell you something else that I really want to do while I'm in here. I want to learn to read proper. Now, reading is not something that I do too much of at home, because we ain't got no books, and to be honest I'm not that good at it anyway. I can just about manage a little bit if there are no really big words. One thing I would really like to do when I leave here is to read a lesson from the bible in church one Sunday morning. The vicar, Nick, always said that I could but I never had the courage to before because I thought I would feel embarrassed if I made a mess of it, but if I really learn to read, well, then I can do it, can't I?

They've got this place here that's full of books. It's called a lie-brie. What you do is go along to the lie-brie, which is open once a week, and borrow one of the books to take back to your cell to read. Free! No charge! What a blummin' marvellous idea. All you have to do is show the man in charge of the lie-brie what books you are borrowing, then he tells you when to bring 'em back. The man in charge of the lie-brie is one of the warders. I've never seen a bloke with so many muscles. Apparently, he's one of them body builders. The inmates all call him Conan the Librarian. Well, they've got that wrong because I know for a fact that his name is Stewart.

Another thing that puzzles me is why certain of the inmates have to be kept away from the rest of us. The other inmates call these ones nonces. I've no idea what a nonce is but they're not very popular in here. The other inmates don't like 'em one little bit and Rufus says that one of the nonces is going to get it. Big Donny and his boys have taken out something called a contract on him. I think that means that he's going to get duffed up good and proper. I don't know what this nonce chap has done wrong but surely there's no need to give him a knuckling. Oh, I don't know. Part of me says keep your nose out and part of me says that I should report it to the Governor. Maybe it'll all blow over. I can't imagine that somebody as nice as Big Donny would beat someone up, whatever that nonce has done. Nonce! That's a funny sounding word isn't it? Rhymes with ponce. Her Ladyship were always fond of using that word.

Well that's this place. Me home for a little while. I'll get by alright. Things could be worse as well couldn't they? I mean, I could be locked up with a bunch of bad people or for life or something. Or worse still, what if they still had hanging or blummin' hard labour. Blimey, fancy that. Not blummin' likely.

One thing they do still have here is sodialar... sololitry... soladidary...

...this little cell where they lock you up on your own for ages on end.

They put you in there if you misbehave but not me, oh no. After all, like I said, I want to get all this sorted out and I don't want to do anything to muck that up. No, I want to get back home as soon as possible. After all, like I said, I shouldn't even be in here by rights, but they keep talking about this thing called sur-cum-stan-shul-effing-dense. I don't know exactly what that means. And like I say, I mucked things up a bit meself with what I said to the ma-jee-straights. But, I'll try and explain it to you the best I can, and it would be best if I told it all from the beginning.

Oh, by the way, me names Wilkie, Joseph Wilkie, but like I said, everyone just calls me plain old Joe.

2
Growing Up

Now there's a funny thing for you. Not funny as in it'll make you laugh but funny as in... odd! We've got quite a history of jailbirds in our family. Meself of course being the very latest. It goes right back to me great, great, great, great granddad Isaiah Wilkie. He were press-ganged into the navy, took part in a something called a mutiny, got himself locked up and were then hanged by the neck until he were dead at somewhere called Plymouth Dock. Then there were me great uncle Seth and his second wife Hilda who both served twenty years for robbing a post office with a firearm and making off with fifty quid which they reckon were a lot of money in them days. They had the firearm of course, not the post office. Then there were the old man doing a year for poaching and of course me mum getting two months for shoplifting, which I don't remember because I were only about three years old at the time. She told me about it though when I were older and said that I should never get into trouble with the police or break the law. But here I am. They reckon that I might be looking at seven years for...

...Well, that's just it. I'm not entirely sure what for.

But here goes...

I were born at seven o'clock in the morning on the first day of April in the year nineteen sixty-five. Fancy me being born on April Fool's day. What a coincidence that were. Anyway, I were born at home. Home being our little cottage in the village of Blessham. Me mum told me that it had rained all week but just after I came into the world it stopped and the Sun came out from behind the clouds and shone all the rest of the day. The old man weren't present at the birth because that were the time when he were serving his prison sentence. Me mum always said that that were one of the happiest times of her life. I think she means me birth not the old man being in prison. I think. On the other hand…

Me mum called me Joseph. She wanted me to have a name out of the bible, see, and the only ones she could properly remember were Jesus, Mary and Joseph. Well, she couldn't call me Jesus could she because that's the Lord's name isn't it, and you don't take his name in vain, and Mary is a girl's name and I ain't a girl, so by fact of reason it had to be Joseph. But I like it. Joseph, or Joe for short.

Anyway, that's how I came into the world. I were born in Poachers Cottage (which is funny when you think about it what with the old man being a poacher and all), Sheep Dip Lane, Blessham. And that's where I've lived all me life ever since. Poachers Cottage is a quaint, little old place and it holds pride of place of being the smallest house in the village. It's got a thatched roof, stone walls and an outside khazi. The khazi has only got a corrugated iron roof though. Not thatched. Although the walls are stone.

It has got a bathroom but not a very big one and that's why the khazi is outside I suppose as there wouldn't be enough room for your knees when you have a crap if the khazi were in there. There's two bedrooms, mine (the smallest one) and the old man's, a kitchen and a living room. Everything you need in a house really. We ain't got too much in the way of furniture but we have got a telly which of course the old man spends most of the day in front of. That is, when he remembers to put money in the 'lectric meter. We have to have a meter now for the 'lectric because the old man never used to bother with paying the bills and we got it cut off more often than not.

Me mum were very young when she and the old man first got together. Seventeen I think she were, and he were a good ten years older or more than her. I don't know when they got wed but she were such a very pretty lady were me mum. Lovely, soft, brown curly hair and the biggest brown eyes you ever saw. She weren't very tall, but she were slim and she always tried to make herself look nice. As I remember she were always smiling, except when the old man were knuckling her, which were about once a week, usually when he'd come rolling home from the Pig and Whistle with a skinful of ale inside him.

He used to knuckle me quite often as well and sometimes he'd give me the toe end of his boot and all, but I can remember that me mum used to put herself between me and him so that she ended up getting it instead. You know that's one thing I can never understand. How the old man could do that to her. I mean, you can understand him giving me an hammering being so blummin' thick and stupid and all but me mum were such a pretty looking woman. I heard a song on the telly once that were called Pretty Woman. It reminded me of her...

Between you and me, I ain't that fond of the old man, but he's me dad so what can I do?

Anyway, we never had much money, but we never went without really. The old man kept us provided with meat. You know, rabbits and pheasants and trout and such like. When he weren't doing time for it that is. And I can remember me mum used to go out to work sometimes as well. At nights it were. Not every night mind, just when the old man had fallen asleep on the settee, snoring and farting. He used to stay there till morning if he'd had a lot to drink, which were quite often. Anyway, me mum must have worked very hard cause I remember that her hair always looked nice when she went out but were usually all messed up when she got home and one night her dress had got torn. I wish I knew where it were she used to work because after she'd done a night's work, she always had a twenty quid note or more in her purse. I mean, twenty quid were a lot of money for a night's work in those days. Imagine how much she'd be earning now.

I suppose they were happy enough times though, when the old man weren't throwing his fists about. And I grew into a healthy enough young 'un. I can still remember me tenth birthday party. I can remember it really well because it were the only birthday party I ever had. It must have set me mum back a pretty penny because I had a new bike as a present. Well, it were second hand from an advert in the paper but that didn't matter to me, I'd never had one before. I'll never forget it; me mum went out to work every night for a week to pay for it all. I loved that bike. Pity the old man sold it two weeks after me mum went. Still, the rent has to be paid, don't it?

We invited all the children in the village to the party but owing to people being busy and all that, Meg were the only one who came. Me twin cousin's, Ruby and Pearl, came as well so it were alright. We played games like blind man's fluff and pass the parsnip and had party food and there were a great big sponge cake with ten candles on it. I had to blow 'em all out and make a wish. I wished that one day I would marry Meg. It were just a shame that I got too close to the cake and set fire to me fringe whilst blowing the candles out. Luckily me grandma threw a glass of lemonade over me head in time. How we all laughed as the smell of me burning hair filled the room. Aaah, happy memories. It weren't long after of course when me mum left. I can remember that as well.

I remember her coming into me bedroom to tuck me in and kiss me goodnight. She sat on the edge of me bed and said to me 'Joe.'

'Yes mum.' I replied.

'I just want to say sorry.' She said.

'What for mum?' I asked.

'For not being there for you.' She said.

'But you are here for me mum and you always will be, won't you?' I said. I remember that she smiled and began to cry which were odd because people only normally cry when they're sad, don't they? Then she said.

'I love you Joe.'

'And I love you Mum.' I told her.

'I'll always love you Joe.' She said.

'And I'll always love you Mum.' I said.

'Promise me Joe, that you'll never hate me.' She said, which sort of surprised me.

'Oh no Mum,' I said, 'I could never, ever hate you.'

Then she kissed me on the forehead and I remember thinking that she smelled different. All sort of posh and flowery like. I think that she had perfume on. Then she hugged me tight. She hugged me more tightly than she had ever done before in me life. And I hugged her back just as tightly.

She lifted up me head and looked at me. I thought there were something wrong with her eyes because she had this black stuff around 'em, and it were starting to run down her cheeks. She kissed me head again, smiled and got up to leave.

'Goodnight mum.' I said.

'Goodnight Joe.' She replied.

And then she were gone…

And I haven't seen her since...

The next day were a bit mad like. The old man went blummin' berserk. Charging up to the stud farm with an old pickaxe handle and threatening to 'deck' anybody who got in his way. They say he turned crazy when he got there and went for several people, demanding to know where 'that slut and her pip-squeak, paddy lover boy' were. He were talking of course about me mum and that jockey. However, he made the mistake of choosing Alf Ollerthrew, the local farrier, as one of those who he set about. They reckon Big Alf downed him in one with his forehead and then some of the stable lads gave him a proper kicking and carried him out and left him by the side of the road.

I went to live with me grandma and granddad, that's me mum's mum and dad, for a few weeks, which were nice because they had a colour telly. It don't half make a difference when you're watching the snooker I can tell you. They lived at the other end of the village to us and they had a great big garden for me to play in. I had a nice time while I were there, although me grandma got a bit too nifty around me lugholes with the flat of her hand at times if I came in with muddy shoes on the carpet or broke a vase or something.

I went back home again once the old man had calmed down a bit. You know, it's funny, but after me mum had gone, the old man never hit me again. Ever. So at least something good came out of it. Apparently, or so I found out later, some of the blokes in the village told him that if he ever laid another hand on me they were going to put him in hopsital. I don't know about that but he never hit me again although he did start to drink a lot more than before though, which must have took some doing because he drank an 'eck of a lot in the first place. I used to go round me grandma and granddad's house for me tea after school most days but me old man and those two never spoke to each other very much. Truth is, they don't see eye to eye. Never have.

I sometimes wonder where and how me mum is. The old man reckons she's in some place called Ireland because that's where the jockey came from. Maybe one day I'll go to Ireland and try and find her. Of course, I'll have to find out where Ireland is first. I think it's away over the sea somewhere. Anyway, I'll always have fond memories of her and I know that one day I'll see her again.

Me school days bring back memories as well. Not always fond ones mind. They began at Blessham primary school. It were only a small place and there were just eighteen children there, so they tell me. We had two teachers, Mr Rodwell who taught the older ones and Miss Finchley who taught the nippers. Mr Rodwell were also the headmaster and I remember when I were in his class. I never really got on too well with Mr Rodwell but I'll say one thing for him, he knew how to use the stick. I lost count of the times that I had it. Mind you, I can't count that well anyway so it don't matter. Sometimes he would call me out to the front of the class and sometimes I would have to stay behind after school. I remember he used to say things like, 'Wilkie, you damned simpleton, come out here boy this absolute instant!'

I would go up to his desk all of a tremble like whilst all the other kids would sit there sniggering amongst 'emselves. Good job he never heard 'em or they'd of all had a proper tanning and all.

'Touch your disgusting toes you wretched boy!' He'd continue.

'I can't reach me toes Sir.' I once said. 'Me shorts are too tight.'

'Don't answer me back, damn you boy.' He replied.

'Sorry Sir.' I said.

'*Just damn well bend over Wilkie.*' He ordered.

'Yes Sir.' I said.

'Brace yourself, Wilkie,' he said, 'brace yourself now!'

'Yes Sir.' I said.

And then he got stuck into me with it. But I never cried. Oh, it hurt enough to make me want to cry but I didn't want Meg to see me cry so I didn't cry. I just used to clench me teeth, me fists and me cheeks and everything else that I could clench and wait for him to finish. I remember that Jim Booth sat and cried his eyes out that time he had six for bullying in the playground. They had to send him home in the end he were crying that much. Cried like a blummin' big baby he did.

I once tried putting a book down the back of me trousers. It were Jim Booth's idea. It didn't work though because Mr Rodwell found it. Meg said that I should have used a magazine or at least something smaller than the Ocks-Ford English Dick-Shun-Ree. It didn't half make Old Rodwell mad as well and he gave me twice as many as he were going to in the first place. Me rump were tanned red raw when he'd finished and I had to stand in the corner for the rest of the afternoon. I could never quite understand though as to why he used to give me the stick so often, seeing as how I weren't what you'd call badly behaved, so one day I decided to pluck up the courage to ask him one playtime when the other kids were outside.

'Mr Rodwell?' I said.

'What is it you vile, goose-flesh inducing example of a child?' He asked.

'Please Mr Rodwell, I were wondering why I get the stick so often. I'm not a naughty boy and sometimes I don't think I've done anything wrong to deserve it.' I said.

'Is that so Wilkie?' He said with a smile.

'Yes Sir.' I said.

'I beat you so often Wilkie,' he went on, 'because you are a pure, inbred idiot who finds even the most basic of primary school work damn near impossible. You, Wilkie, are a blight on my life, a blot on my landscape, a carbuncle on my horizon and a constant source of irritation to me. I beat you Wilkie because you are a common simpleton and the only thing that your ignorant mind understands and is capable of learning is the feel of my cane upon your despicable hindquarters. Does that answer your question boy?'

'No Sir.' I honestly replied.

'Wilkie,' he said, reaching for the stick.

'Yes Sir.' I said.

'Bend over.' He said.

But for all his faults, Mr Rodwell were a fair and just man and he never gave me any more than a dozen which, when you think about it, weren't so bad as it learned me how to count all the way up to twelve. The sad thing is that we found out later that Mr Rodwell had been very ill for quite a long time. At least, I think he must have been because he's now in one of them special hopsitals. I forget what they call 'em now. Oh, hang on that's it, mack-see-mum-see-cure-ee-tee. Poor old Mr Rodwell.

Still, never mind. Because Meg used to wait for me when I had to go for the stick sometimes after school. I used to carry her satchel for her and we used to walk home together. Meg were, and still is, me best friend. She lived at the other end of Sheep Dip Lane, but her house were quite a good bit bigger than ours and had an indoor khazi. We grew up together. We did everything together, me and Meg

We had some fun I can tell you. Climbing trees were one of our favourite things. Meg could climb any tree better than most of the lads. Mind you she were always very long in the leg and her ankles were good and strong. We must have climbed nearly every tree in Blessham. And fell out of some of 'em too. I remember especially the day we climbed to the top of the big cedar at the Hall. Now, that were a real adventure. Right to the top we went. No kid had ever done that before, mind you, no kid had ever dared to go into the grounds of the Hall before. But me and Meg did. Oh, how we did. It were a Saturday afternoon in the middle of summer. Blazing hot day it were. We were sitting by the old fishpond throwing stones in and talking about all sorts of things when she turns and says to me, 'Hey Joe, want to go and climb a tree?'

'Yeah, if that's what you want to do?' I said.

'Yeah, come on,' she says, 'And I know just the tree.'

'Which one?' I said.

'Guess!' She said and I think she were teasing me.

'I don't know.' I said. 'The oak in the middle of thirty-acre field?'

'No!'

'The wizened old Ash down Fiddlers Lane?'

'No!'

'That big windblown Larch on the edge of the woods?'

'No, no, no! I'm thinking of something much bigger.' She said with a huge grin and her eyes seemed to widen.

'I don't know Meg, just tell me.' I pleaded.

'What's the biggest tree in the village?' She said. And then it hit me.

'You don't mean...?' I said.

'I sodding well do.' She laughed.

'Oh no Meg, not the cedar up at the Hall.' I thought she were off her rocker.

'That's the one.' She said still laughing. She had a lovely, cheeky, little laugh when she were a young 'un. Still has actually.

'You're off your blummin' rocker Meg.' I told her, 'If Her Ladyship catches us on her land, why, she'll skin us alive.'

'Only if she catches us. Come on!' She said.

And that were it. She jumped up and set off for the hall. Well, I had to follow her, didn't I? By 'eck I were scared, shit-blummin'-scared, if you'll pardon such language and I truly apologise for using it. Mind you, anybody would be shit scared if they'd met Her Ladyship. Anyway, we got off the road and crept through the woods until we came to the edge of the big lawn at the front of the Hall. We waited until we were sure that there weren't no one about and then we ran towards the great cedar in the middle of the lawn as fast as we could. And as soon as we reached it Meg shot up it. She must have gone ten feet up before I'd got started. Me heart were pounding, me legs were shaking, and I weren't far from pappering meself with fear. But I just kept climbing. I could see Meg's feet clambering away above me and I just followed 'em. I don't know how long it took, it seemed like forever, but we eventually reached the very top.

It were blummin' amazing. What a view we had from up there. We could see the whole of Blessham and because it were such a clear sunny day, we could just make out the town off away in the distance.

'Do you know Joe,' Meg said, 'we must be the first people to climb this tree.'

'Yeah, I reckon we are.' I said.

'How do you feel Joe?' She said.

'Great,' I said. 'just great.' And then I looked down...

The smell were terrible. I'd never been so frightened. Oh God, it were high up. It took us best part of half an hour to get down and I were blummin' glad to get there. But, as my rotten luck would have it, old Isaac, Her Ladyship's gardener, were waiting for us at the bottom. He grabbed hold of me by the shirt collar but Meg got away and legged it.

'What are you doing on Her Ladyship's land young Wilkie?' He demanded.

'We were just climbing the tree Isaac, honest.' I said and I remember that I started crying I was so blummin' scared.

'Do you know what Her Ladyship says I should do to any of you young 'uns if I catches you on her land?'

'No.' I cried.

'She says that I should I should give your arse a bloody good kicking and cuff you round the lugholes.' He said sternly. I cried some more but then old Isaac started laughing.

'Give over, you soft little sod, I'm not like her. Now go on, get off before she comes out and sees you, you silly little beggar.' He laughed. And then he let me go. He were alright really were old Isaac. So, I walked off to look for Meg. It weren't easy walking either what with having messed me underpants but I found her back at the fishpond and told her what had happened. Ah yes, that were a real adventure that were. And we had loads more. Me and Meg.

And I'll tell you a secret...

If you can keep it...

Meg were the first girl I ever kissed. Actually, she's the only girl I ever kissed. Come to think of it she's the only girl I'd ever want to kiss. I'll tell you how it happened though. It were in the long hot Summer holidays and we had just finished at Blessham Primary before going on to the big school in town. Now, Meg and me had just finished making a den in Farmer Bull's haystack and were sitting in it talking like. Now we had to be really quiet on account of the fact that Farmer Bull didn't take too kindly to kids playing in his haystack. Anyway, as we were sitting there whispering to each other Meg suddenly says to me. 'Joe?'

'Yes Meg.' I said, whispering of course.

'Have you ever kissed anyone before Joe?' She asked.

'Oh yeah.' I says. 'I've kissed me mum, before she ran off with that jockey, and I always have to give me gran a kiss on Christmas day and me birthday. Not that I enjoy it mind because her top lip is all hairy like and...'

'That's not what I meant Joe.' Said Meg.

'Oh, what then?' I asked.

'I mean, have you ever kissed a girl?' She whispered, right in me lughole.

'No, I ain't.' I said and I remember me face suddenly feeling all hot and me voice going kind of shaky. Weird sort of feeling it were.

'Do you want to kiss me Joe?' She said.

Well, I couldn't believe me luck. 'Ooh Meg, not half.' I told her, because you know, I reckon I loved her, even back then.

'Close your eyes then.' She said smiling at me, and so I did.

And then Meg kissed me.

It were the sweetest and most loveliest thing I've ever known. Her lips were all warm and wet and she pressed 'em against mine ever so softly like a butterfly's wings. It tasted delicious, like warm raspberries and I remember thinking that I didn't want it to ever end. Sadly, I ran out of breath so it had to end but I were the happiest person alive. I jumped up and shouted '*I LOVE YOU MEG MORRISON*' at the top of me voice.

'Let's do it again then.' She smiled.

'Yes please.' I said.

Sadly, before I could kiss her again, Farmer Bull appeared, alerted by me shouting. He gave me backside a proper good kicking I can tell you and he kept calling me 'You dirty, filthy, little swine!' as he dragged me out of the farmyard. Still, it were a good job he only had his wellies on and not his hob nailed boots.

Anyway, Meg's parents found out what had happened from Farmer Bull. They gave her a good hiding and told her that she weren't allowed to play with me for the rest of the summer which really upset me. I missed her and wanted to kiss her again. The old man didn't seem bothered about it though. He just told me that there were plenty more fish in the sea. Good of him to try and take me mind off it I suppose but I didn't want to go fishing, I wanted to play with Meg and, you know, kiss her some more and walk about the village with me arm around her waist. But I didn't see Meg again until we went to the big school in town after the holidays. I'll never, ever forget that kiss though. Cor!

Going to the big school were very exciting. We had to travel into town on the bus and I'd never been on a bus before. I used to sit right at the front, behind the driver and pretend that I were driving it meself. Meg used to sit near the back with Sally Firth whom she'd spent the rest of that summer playing with. We were still best friends mind, but her and Sally used to look at pop music magazines and spend a lot of time giggling like a pair of schoolgirls. Of course, that's exactly what they were mind you.

Jim Booth and all his mates always used to sit right on the back seat and show off. Quite often they used to shout down the bus to me. You know, things like 'Oi, Wilkie, how's your mum?' and 'Hey Wilkie, you thick twat.' But I didn't mind, I mean, how were I supposed to know how me mum were, I hadn't seen her for nigh on two years and I didn't even blummin' know what a twat were. Honestly, how stupid can you get? Sitting at the back. I mean, you can't see where you're going if you're sat at the back. Can you?

Anyway, the big school were a very interesting place. I've never seen so many kids in one building before. There were hundreds of 'em. All shapes and sizes. And me new teacher were very nice. Not like old Rodwell. Her name were Mrs Beardsmore, she were quite young, very roundly shaped but very jolly, she had kind eyes, long, dark, wavy hair and smiled a lot. And best of all she didn't have a stick with which to tan me back end.

I were very happy in Mrs Beardsmore's class. It were a very special class. Our classroom were in a separate part of the school to all of the other children and we were known as lower than average learning ability. I think that meant we were a bit slower at catching on than most. But I didn't mind, apart from when Jim Booth said that all the kids who go there were 'as thick as pig shit.' I'll have you know that I made some very nice friends in Mrs Beardsmore's class. Pig shit indeed! Who did he think he were?

And so, I continued through me school years. I were still very close with Meg and after a while her folks forgot about that time in Farmer Bull's haystack. Although, I suppose I began to see less and less of her but then that's life ain't it? She were hanging around with Sally Firth and the other girls more and more. I spent quite a lot of time on me own. I tried to make friends with some of the lads in the village but they all formed a gang with Jim Booth as their leader. They didn't let me join the gang. Not that I minded that but it weren't too long before the main pastime of the Blessham Bulls, as they called 'emselves, became chasing me around the village and throwing stones at me. I didn't mind the chasing so much as I'm quite nippy on me legs and it kept me fit, but some of them stones came a bit keen, especially if they hit me in the head with one.

The Blessham Bulls lasted about four years. I always thought how funny they looked. They all looked the blummin' same. They all wore them denim jackets with the words Blessham Bulls over a picture of a bulls' head on the back, and they all wore jeans and them training shoes all the time. And they all grew their hair really long, like a bunch of girls. I ain't never seen anything look so blummin' daft in all me life I ain't. Sometimes they would carry a big radio around with 'em when they were hanging around on the village green trying to look big and tough and they would listen to something called heavy metal music. Heavily blummin' crap music I called it, if you'll pardon the expression. All screaming and shouting and ever so loud. Some of the locals used to complain and Her Ladyship once threatened to 'Thrash each and every one of them' if they didn't stop lowering the tone of the village. Oddly enough it did stop shortly after that. Her Ladyship does tend to have that effect on people.

Now, that's one thing I never bothered about much - pop music. All a load of rubbish if you ask me. You used to see some sights in them days, them that were into pop music. Silly looking beggars with their hair all sticking up and in different colours, even sillier looking ones with no hair, braces and big boots who looked like council workers, soft apeths in long green coats who must have been really stupid because they had the word 'Who' on the back with an arrow pointing upwards. If they didn't know who they were it's a poor tale. Then of course there were all them longhaired ones like the Bulls. They used to shake their heads about to that music of theirs and called it head banging. It were their way of dancing. Funny looking kind of dancing if you ask me. Blummin' deer don't even go that daft during the rutting season.

No, I never had any time for any of that. I used to like the odd one or two songs if I heard 'em on the radio but the only pop stars I ever really liked much were a group who looked like farmers and had a song about a combine harvester. Now, that's what I call music!

Meg used to love all that pop stuff though and she were really good at dancing to it as well. I remember once they had one of them disco things in the village hall. It were the old vicar's idea. He wanted to start one of them youth clubs or something like that. Anyway, I went along to this disco only because I knew that Meg were going and I were, you know, hoping for the chance of a kiss. A lot of the kids from some of the other villages near Blessham went too. I've never seen the village hall so full in all me life.

Anyway, everything seemed to be going fine at first. Me grandma gave me two quid to spend and I had six glasses of cherryade, which were twenty-five pence each so I had some change, although I did spill one of 'em down the front of me trousers, and there were crisps and chocolate bars and things on sale as well so I had a flake and a packet of cheese and onion. It were really grown up. Meg spent a lot of the night dancing with Sally Firth and some of the other local girls but I told her that they really ought to put their shoes back on because that floor were filthy. They must have thought I were joking or something because they all laughed at me. I weren't though, but I must admit I felt pretty good about making 'em all laugh. There were a funny looking man there who were playing the records. He were wearing sunglasses even though he were indoors and it were dark, and he kept calling us all 'Guys and Gals' and saying things like

'Keep on trucking' and 'Groovy man' and other such twaddle and he had these lights which kept flashing all different colours. Made me feel dizzy after a while it did.

It were a smashing night. Right up until the Blessham Bulls came in. Talk about show off. I remember that Meg and Sally went outside with Boothy and another one of 'em and when she came back in she had a funny smile on her face. I hoped at the time that she hadn't been smoking or anything but then I noticed that one of the lads had his flies undone so perhaps they had all just gone to the toilet at the same time and Meg were smiling at him being so forgetful. I were worried for a bit though I can tell you. Meg's folks would have given her the blummin' hiding of her life if they knew she were smoking. But I weren't going to tell on her though. Not me.

Anyway, it seems that there were another gang there from nearby Stuffham. They were a bunch of them stupid looking, bald headed beggars that I mentioned before and they called 'emselves the Stuffham Scorpions. A bit blummin' daft I thought on account of the fact that you don't see too many scorpions in this neck of the woods. Plenty of wasps, bees and ants like, but no scorpions. Especially in Stuffham. Anyway, Jim Booth started talking to this girl from Stuffham. Nice enough looking lass she were. I reckon he were doing that chatting up business I've heard about. Then one of the Stuffham lads (ugliest, cauliflower-eared, looking beggar you ever saw) runs over and punches Boothy right in the face. He fell backwards over a table. Graham Todd, one of the Bulls, punched the lad from Stuffham and knocked him down. Another Stuffham lad then punched Graham Todd in the back of the head. Boothy got up and punched the second Stuffham lad in the eye and before you knew it the whole place were in a blummin' uproar.

Terrible it were. Lads rolling around punching and fighting, girls screaming and the poor old vicar wringing his hands and pleading for everyone to 'Calm down, show restraint and have some brotherly love.' As for me I did the only right and decent thing. I ran and locked meself in the toilet until it were all over. Well, I figured if I hung around it wouldn't be too long before one of 'em punched me. At least Meg and Sally got out alright. They didn't have any more discos for a couple of years after that. Good job and all if you ask me.

But, on the whole, I suppose that I had a pretty fair childhood. Could have been better, could have been worse. Still, I'm not one to grumble, am I? And I always followed me mum's advice as best I possibly could. I suppose that living in the country helped me along the way. All the fresh air and that. I'd hate to live in the town like some of them kids who I went to the big school with. They all looked chubby and pasty. And they ate too many crisps and chocolate bars which gave 'em these things called zits on their faces. I never had too many meself. Just as well because they're horrible looking things zits are. First of all, they come up this angry, red colour and make you scratch, then they get even bigger and change and go all funny and yellow looking. Then, if you squeeze 'em between two fingers they pop and all the yellow bit squirts out like a blummin' bullet. Horrible they are. But, like I said, I never had that many. Me grandma says that it's because I grew up in fresh air and I never had too many sweets and always ate me vegetables.

Mind you, I did get chicken pox, ringworm, mumps, measles and a rather nasty dose of gastro entritia... enritis... enterniritis...

...I had the squitters for over a week.

Now, I have to be honest and say that me teenage years weren't quite so full of fond memories as me childhood ones. I left school at sixteen with none of them kwal-iffy-kay-shun things. But then, I didn't need no kwal-iffy-kay-shuns because I knew that I were going to work in Blessham and there ain't no jobs there that need fancy kwal-iffy-kay-shuns or nothing. I mean, there's plenty of jobs always going but any idiot can do 'em. And like Mr Rodwell always said, I were an idiot. So that were alright then.

I found the teenage years quite an unsettling time. Especially when things started happening to me body. You know, stubble on your chin and your you-know-what's dropping and your voice breaking and hair in places where you never had hair before. And your armpits start to smell rotten on hot days and you have to spray 'em with that dee-oh-door-ant stuff. I couldn't get on with that spray stuff so me grandma said that I should try a ball dee-oh-door-ant and got me one from the chemist shop in town but I found that it made me underpants stick to me skin so I went back to the spray.

Another thing that I didn't like as a teenager were the fact that I used to wake up in the morning with me... you know... me thingy all stiff and hard like. I asked the old man, but he just laughed, said it were 'Perfectly normal' and told me to 'bloody shut up about it.' I don't know if that's right but if it were then I were perfectly normal every morning throughout me teenage years. And what's even more embarrassing were the fact that whenever I saw pictures of ladies in their underwear or even without any clothes on at all I used to get perfectly normal. The worst time were when some of the local girls were splashing about in the brook and I saw Cathy Baker and Annie McDermott wearing them bikini things. Sure enough, I were perfectly normal. Strange, ain't it?

Sometimes, when I used to wake up perfectly normal in the morning, I'd be holding it in me hand. Can you believe that? In me blummin' hand! Now and again I still wake up perfectly normal but have to run to the khazi. Usually after having had a couple of pints the night before, but the old man calls that being 'piss proud.' Rufus reckons they put something in your tea in prison that stops you from being perfectly normal. I hope so because I ain't too keen on it you see. Especially when you catch it with your flies.

I never bothered with girlfriends though. Me grandma always said that I should let 'em come to me. Not that any of 'em ever did mind but I weren't bothered, there were only room for one girl in me life. Meg!

But I knew that Meg had to have her own life too and she needed friends of the female kind as well. Her and Sally Firth were never apart. You would have thought that they were joined at the blummin' hip that pair. They weren't of course. I mean, how could they have been? Anyway, it were only natural that Meg should start hanging around with other girls.

Then one day, I must have been about seventeen, I were walking across the green when I saw Meg and Sally and some of the other girls talking with Jim Booth and his mates. I didn't want to get involved with that lot but I didn't like the idea of Meg being involved with 'em either. So, I stood watching for a while to see what might happen and the next thing you know Jim Booth puts his arm around Meg's shoulder and kisses her. Kissed her full on her lovely lips. Well, that did it. Something welled up inside me. I saw red. How dare he do that to Meg? I tell you I saw red I did. I should've been the one kissing her, not him. Now, I'm not one for fighting, because me mum told me to never do it and I promised her I wouldn't, but I ran straight over to where they were and I shouted. 'Oi! You leave Meg alone Jim Booth!'

'Get lost Wilkie, you dozy little wank-stain!' He said. I never heard that word before, wank-stain, and I still don't know what it means to this day. I might ask Rufus as I've heard a few of the blokes in here say it about Mr Riddle. Anyway...

'No,' I said standing me ground, 'You can't go around doing that to Meg.'

'It's alright Joe.' Said Meg. She obviously didn't want to cause any trouble, bless her.

'Yeah, now run along thickie.' Said Jim Booth.

'I won't,' I said, 'not without Meg. Now you get away from her.'

'Have it your way then.' He said. 'Get him lads.'

Then all of his mates started pushing and punching and kicking me. I fell over and rolled into a ball but they just carried on. I could hear Meg screaming at 'em to stop. Bless her sweet, darling heart, trying to help me like that. Finally, they did stop. I remember that I had a nosebleed and me guts were hurting but I managed to get to me feet. Boothy put me straight back down again with one good hard punch to me chin - he's got some right hand on him has Boothy. Then he grabbed hold of me by the shirt collar and said, 'You listen here Wilkie, you thick little dickhead.' He snarled, 'Meg's my fucking bird and it's got fuck all to do with you. Right?'

I don't know what he meant by bird but I nodded anyway because I'd had enough by that time. Then he let go of me and pushed me back to the ground and they all went off. Meg stayed for a while to see if I were alright before following 'em. I suppose she didn't want to leave Sally on her own with that lot which were understandable. That's Meg for you though, always thinking of others before herself.

As for the rest of me teens, they passed rather quickly. I started going to the Pig and Whistle when I were eighteen. It's against the law you know to go into a pub before then. Boothy and his mates used to go in before they were eighteen. I were going to tell Bob, the landlord, that they weren't old enough but Meg used to go in as well and I didn't want to get her into trouble. I'm sure she would have been sensible though and not had anything to drink. I overheard one of Jim Booth's mates telling another about how Boothy done her on the pool table one night. That calmed me fears a bit knowing that she only went in to play pool. You would have thought that Boothy would have let her win though. Still, there ain't many of us gentlemen left.

Anyway, by the time I reached twenty I were a regular and Bob let me have me own tankard behind the bar. A fancy looking glass it were, with a big handle and the words '18 Today' on it in big gold coloured letters. Me grandma bought it me for me eighteenth birthday. Sadly, it got broken one night when someone knocked it off the table with the end of a pool cue and it landed on the floor and smashed into pieces. It were full of beer at the time and all

So that's me upbringing. I have to say that the best thing about me childhood were that day in the haystack with Meg and the worst things were me mum leaving, but still, rough with the smooth and all that.

3
Blessham

Let me tell you a little bit about my home village of Blessham. Blessham, in my humble opinion, is just about the loveliest place on God's green earth. I'm not joking either, it's beautiful, especially in the Summer. It's quite a large village although I don't know off hand how many people live there. Quite a few though I can tell you and the village itself sits nestling in the middle of the rolling English countryside. The town is about six miles away (I can never remember its name) and the nearest village to us is Stuffham, which is about three miles away. Mind you there is a very small Hamlet in between Blessham and Stuffham called Dammitt, which consists of four houses and a farm. Me two cousins Ruby and Pearl used to live at Dammitt. They're all grown up now though of course. That's where I used to go for me holidays when I were a kid, Dammitt. Alright, so it weren't much but you know what they say; a change is as good as a rest. So I used to go and stop with me aunt and uncle and cousins for a week every year during the Summer holidays. It were alright I suppose but, Ruby and Pearl were girls and they wanted to play mummies and daddies and dressing up and things while I wanted to play cowboys and Indians. I didn't mind mummies and daddies so much, but I didn't want to play kiss chase with 'em. I didn't want to kiss anyone but Meg. So, they just chased me instead. And by 'eck they could chase could that pair. They chased me all the way back to Blessham once. We got a right rollicking off me aunt when we got back to Dammitt again.

I know a lot of people go to the seaside on their holidays, including Meg. She says that it's lovely but I've never been although I've seen it on the telly and I once saw some pictures of it in a magazine at the general store and it looks nice enough. Maybe one day I might go and see for meself. When I leave here perhaps. Maybe Meg will take me.

Blessham is surrounded by hills and trees and wide-open fields. There's a little brook, called Blessham Brook oddly enough, which runs through the village and actually runs right under Poachers Cottage at one point, which has caused us a few problems with damp during the winter months over the years, but at least it provides us with running water. Poachers Cottage itself is, as I think I already mentioned, the smallest house in the village and is stuck right at the far end of Sheep Dip Lane. Why it's called Sheep Dip Lane is anybody's guess. I've never known anyone to dip any sheep there before. Anyway, our house is a tiny little cottage which sits there on its own. There are four more houses on Sheep Dip Lane but they're all joined together in one big row, known as a tear-arse, which makes our house a bit special don't you think? Meg used to live in the end one of the row when we were kids and if I had a penny for every time that I've walked up Sheep Dip Lane to her front gate and knocked on the door, I'd have about...

...I'd have an awful lot of pennies.

Now, Sheep Dip Lane is, I would say, roughly in the middle of the village which makes it great for getting to all the other parts of the village. If you see what I mean. At the opposite ends of the lane are two other roads. The one at our end is called Fiddlers Lane and the one at the other end is called Cockwright Road, which, of course, leads to the village of Cockwright about four miles off. There are a couple of houses on Fiddlers Lane but the most important place there is Blackthorn Farm, which belongs to Farmer Bull. Now apart from the fact that Farmer Bull has given me a bigger kicking than anyone else in the whole, wide, blummin' world, and that includes the old man, and Jim Booth of course, Blackthorn Farm is a special place to me. Fiddlers lane passes right past our house and the farm is right on the other side. So, the first thing that I see in the morning when I open the curtains is the haystack. The same one where I kissed

Meg on that wonderful Summers' day all those years ago. On hot, sunny days during harvest time I can smell the hay wafting through me open window. Then again on hot, sunny days when it's not harvest time, I can smell the cowsheds but that's life I suppose. I try to keep looking on the bright side just like me mum said I should. Blackthorn Farm is so called because it has a huge great blackthorn hedge at the front of it which looks very pretty when the little white flowers all come out but doesn't feel very nice when somebody pushes you into as the Blessham Bulls once did to me. I were pulling thorns out of me for the rest of the afternoon I were. I wouldn't have minded quite so much but they'd already thrown me into a patch of nettles that morning. I were right blummin' sore that day. The beggars.

If you walk down Sheep Dip Lane towards the Cockwright Road end you come to the village green which is really the very middle of the village I suppose. The Green is a lovely patch of land. It's really...

...green.

It's a very important place as well. For one thing, it's a place where the young 'uns can go and play. You know, football and things like that. I were never much good at football. I like to watch it on the telly sometimes and me Uncle Sid once played on the left wing for Stuffham Rovers but when it comes to playing it meself I've got two left feet. Not really of course. I were talking metacorical... cematorical... mentonophiral...

...Well, you know what I mean.

Apart from kids playing football though there are other things that go on at the green. Every year, on Easter Saturday we have the Easter Fair and on the second Saturday in July, there is the village fete, which I really love going to. Then during the rest of the Summer, the Blessham First Eleven cricket team play on it. They're in the Fartleberrys Brewery Alliance League, they play on Tuesday nights, after which they all troop down to the Pig and Whistle and get 'emselves full of ale and strong drink.

Oh yeah, and they're blummin' hopeless they are and I don't think they'll even mind me saying that. In the last three seasons they've only won five matches but then, I think they're only in it for the beer. Still, they do look nice, all in white with their little caps.

But the most important thing that happens on the village green is without doubt the annual rugby match against Stuffham on New Year's Day. In fact, it's probably the most important thing that happens in the whole village but I'll tell you more about it that later though, and believe me it's worth hearing about.

As well as all this first-class entertainment you've also got the village hall right next to the green. It's used by the Blessham Boy Scout Brigade mostly. I were never in the scouts on account of the fact that it used to take me all me time to tie me shoelaces let alone all them knots they want you to do. I can do it alright now though. Me laces that is. And Bert Roppings who ran the scouts and who they had to call Ark-hay-la-de-da, or something or other, said that I had about as much aptitude for scouting as a half-dead slug.' I never did find out what aptitude meant but I know what a slug is and so I reckon it meant something bad. Anyway, 'Sod the bloody scouts, tain't worth crying over' the old man said when I told him. But then, he also said, 'So stop friggin' whinging you little prick' as well. And that were the end of that.

And of course, the village hall plays host to the annual Blessham Christmas Party when everyone in the village gets together to celebrate the birth of our Lord Jesus Christ. One or two people tend to over celebrate in my opinion. I mean, it's alright getting full of ale to the point where you can't stand up at any other time of the year but not at Christmas. I don't think so anyway.

The Schoolhouse also backs onto the village green on the Cockwright Road and I used to run across it as a short cut sometimes if I were late. I still got a good hiding from Old Rodwell so I suppose it didn't make any difference running when I think about it. The school used to use the green for P.E lessons. I were never that much good at P.E and rounders so Mr Rodwell just used to make me run around the edge of the green while the lesson were on. I used to be proper knackered by the end but that's how I got such good running legs you see.

Opposite the school is what is considered by most to be the very oldest part of the village. The Triangle. The Triangle is a small piece of ground with an old signpost on it. It separates the main roads through the village so that Cockwright Road ends and Main Street begins and in the other direction is a little lane called Dairy Lane. It's a lane alright but there ain't never has been a dairy down it as far as I know. There's a few houses, and one of 'em has a painted up milk churn stood outside with some flowers in it, but no dairy.

Main Street is the main street through the village. I suppose that's why they call it Main Street. Anyway, Main Street is a long, straight road which passes by the end of Fiddlers Lane which, if you will recall, runs past the end of Sheep Dip Lane. So, if you come out of Poachers Cottage, turn right, walk down Sheep Dip Lane, past the green, turn right onto Cockwright Road, keep going till you get to The Triangle, carry on walking down Main Street, turn right again onto Fiddlers Lane, keep going past Blackthorn Farm and eventually you arrive back at Poachers Cottage again. Simple ain't it?

Ah, you might say, but what about Dairy Lane?

Well, I were just coming to that. Dairy Lane brings you out at another triangle of grass but this one only has a signpost and not a name. Anyway, when you get there you've got Blessham Woods slap bang in front of you. Now, the road to the left is Stuffham Road which takes you to Stuffham, handily enough, and also leads to Blessham Hall after about a hundred yards, or so I'm told. I don't know how far a hundred yards really is. I tried counting me steps there one day but I got distracted by a squirrel and forgot where I were although that were probably for the best as I don't think I would have been able to count much further anyway. The road to your right is known as Market Road which takes you into town, which I suppose is handy if you're wanting to go to the market. Which is away off in the town of course.

There are two other roads in the village and they're both on Main Street. The first one and the longer of the two is known as The Crescent. They call it that because it bends round to the left as you go up it...

...It's crescent shaped.

The Crescent is right opposite Fiddlers Lane and a bit further on you come to The Close. The Close is a very short road and only has a couple of houses on it. I suppose they call it The Close on account of the fact the houses are very close together. I don't actually know for sure. Anyway, both of these roads are Cul-de-sh... Cal-de-Sick... Col-di-Sock...

...dead ends.

There are quite a few very important buildings around the village. Apart from the ones that I've already told you about, right, you've got, The Hall, that's where I work, The Stud, where me mum met that blummin' jockey, the Pig and Whistle, the Grange, the Post Office and General Store (that's one building, not two), the Butcher, the Church and the Vicarage. All very self-contained and cosy we are in Blessham.

I suppose me favourite place in the village, apart from the Hall, is the Pig and Whistle. I go there a couple of times a week. It's the best blummin' pub in the county in my opinion. There are others nearby but I don't often go to them. There's the Turned Sod at Stuffham and there's the Inn at Cockwright. The Turned Sod's not bad but the one at Cockwright's a right snooty place. All fancy bar meals and ploughman's lunches. I mean, I've seen plenty of blokes ploughing and their lunch ain't never looked like that. A slice of ham and a noggin of cheese and a tatty bit of lettuce. No, it's not the kind of place I like. I think Meg must go there a fair bit because I overheard her telling Jim Booth one night in the pub that she really enjoys the Cockwright Inn. Still, each to their own I suppose.

The landlord of the Pig and Whistle is a nice bloke called Bob McKenzie. He's a very interesting bloke, always telling loads of stories about what he's done in his life. Been all over the world he has. The old man calls him Bobby Bullshit. I don't know why. The things that Bob comes out with are much too farfetched to be lies. Although, come to think of it, most people call him Bobby Bullshit; behind his back mind. But I reckon he's alright.

Another building that means an awful lot to me is the church, St Mildred's. I go there every Sunday morning without fail, if I can. Just like me mum told me to. Not many people go there mind except for Harvest Festival and the carol service. I think the vicar's usually happy if he gets any more than ten folks in there on a normal Sunday. I don't know why more people don't go; I think it's great. We sing hymns to The Lord while old Mr Cummings plays the organ, then the vicar does his sermon, then we sing another hymn and pass round the offering plate and finally we all say a prayer and then we go home. I'm always the last to go because I help the vicar to put all the hymn books away and straighten up the knee pads. The vicar always says that in doing so I am serving The Lord. Which can't be bad now, can it?

The vicar himself is a really nice chap. He's been there about three years now. Quite a young bloke he is which makes a change from our last vicar the Reverend Everard Menn. He were ninety-two years old when he left us. Bless him. He went to somewhere called the Belle Vue Retirement Home for Clergymen. Wherever that is. Abroad I think, by the sound of it. The new vicar, who just likes to be called Nick, is a very modern thinking vicar with some great ideas. I heard some of the young 'uns calling him Nick the Vic once. Reverend Menn would have gone off his rocker if he'd heard that but Nick just smiled and waved to 'em. What a nice man. His name's actually Nicholas by the way, it's just that he prefers Nick. He's a good man though. Saint Nick I call him.

But church is ever so good because what a lot of people don't seem to realise is the fact that the church is God's house. He owns it. And when you go to church and sing hymns then you're actually singing to God and whenever you pray, you're actually talking to God.

I like praying. Of course, you don't have to go to church to do it, oh no, you can do it anywhere. At home, at work, when you're being chased through the streets of the village by the Blessham Bulls. Anywhere. I've prayed an awful lot since I've been in here. Rufus always says 'You're talking out your ring-piece, country boy, there ain't nobody listnin'' when I say me prayers at night. I'm fairly certain that he means that I'm talking out of me back end. He don't understand though. He thinks that God can't be real or else why would I be in here. But it's not like that you see. God made us and loves us, no matter what we do wrong. We only have to ask and he forgives us. That's why he sent Baby Jesus to us. That's one bit I remember from the Bible 'For God so loved the world that he gave his only begotten son, that whoever believes in him shall not perish but have eternal life.' Wow! Who wouldn't want to live forever? So, you see it don't matter whether you're in prison or wherever you are God still loves you because of Jesus. Nick would explain it a lot better than me. I get me words all wrong. And besides, that's Nick's job really, ain't it?

Then again there's a chap who works in here called the prison chaplain. He's like the vicar I suppose. Only he's called a chaplain. Anyway, every Sunday morning, if you want, you can go along to the chapel and join the Sunday morning service. I do. It's not quite the same as St Mildred's, because they have a guitar instead of an organ but it's better than nothing, ain't it?

Anyway, where were I? Oh ah, Blessham. Now then, next to the church is the vicarage which is so called because that's where the vicar lives. Nick, I mean. A lovely big house it is too. I often go round there for a cup of tea and a chat with Nick. You know, I think Nick is probably one of me best friends. Next to Meg of course. She's me best friend, but Nick and me we get on really well.

Now one of me least favourite places of course has to be the stud farm. Blessham Stud, as it is known, is, if you will recall, where that Irish jockey who me mum ran off with came from. So, I don't want to say too much about the place except that it backs onto the vicarage, you can get to it if you go down Stuffham Road for about fifty yards, it stinks to high heaven of horse manure and they breed racehorses there. And that's all I want to say about the place...

...thank you.

What else is there now? Well, like I said, there are two shops in the village. They're both down on Main Street, opposite the Pig and Whistle. The first shop is the General Store and Post Office which is run very well by Mrs Byamile and Mr Goodnight. She runs the general store side and he runs the post office side. They're not married mind you but then you probably worked that out for yourself what with their surnames being different. What I mean is, they are both married, just not to each other. Mrs Byamile is a very jovial lady, of about sixty, who dyes her hair jet black and I don't mean to appear rude but she's got some sized bosom on her. Like a pair of blummin' rugby balls they are. And she wears these tight-fitting blouses and, well, I just don't know where to look.

Anyway, she sells all kinds of stuff in there. All sorts of groceries and household items and kindling and bottles of beer and newspapers, but best of all she sells loads of sweets and chocolate bars. I'm very partial to a chocolate bar I am. I can afford to buy 'em whenever I want to nowadays, before I came in here that is, but when I were a nipper it were a different story. I never got any pocket money off the old man (I did ask him once but he said he needed all his money for beer) but about once a month me granddad, when he were alive, gave me a fifty pence piece to spend on whatever I wanted. And I wanted to spend it on Mrs Byamile's sweets. I used to buy some for Meg as well. Sometimes I would buy chocolate bars, sometimes I would buy a quarter of boiled sweets out of the big jars on the back shelf and sometimes I would buy a bottle of pop. Mind you, sometimes Jim Booth and his mates used to beat me up and steal the money but then I suppose that's all part of growing up, ain't it?

Mr Goodnight, in the post office, is a short bald-headed man with a little pot belly and a tufty brown moustache. I tried to grow a moustache once but it only really came thick at the ends and everyone said that I looked 'like a sodding walrus' so I shaved it off. Never did find out what a walrus were. Anyway, one of the things that Mr Goodnight does at the post office is a thing called a savings account. I've got one and it's dead good. What you do is, you put money into the account every week and then, after a while, when you take it out you've got more money in the account than you've actually put in. Amazing ain't it? I don't know how it works and to be quite honest I don't care I just like the fact that it does.

Anyway, I don't think Mrs Byamile and Mr Goodnight get on too well at times because a few months ago, I were walking past the shop and the door were open and I overheard her saying to him that he were a very naughty little man and that when they closed for dinner, she were going to take him into the back room and give his bare bottom a good spanking. I never mentioned it to anyone else because I ain't one to gossip. Although, I do think that he's a little bit old for being spanked by Mrs Byamile. Still, she's the one who actually owns the shop so that must make her in charge. It must get very embarrassing for him though, being given a spanking by Mrs Byamile, at his age I mean. Mind you, he didn't seem all that worried about it. Quite the opposite in fact and he said 'Ooh, promises, promises' in sort of high-pitched voice. I found it all a bit strange.

And I also remember that time when Mrs Goodnight came in and had a right old ding dong with Mrs Byamile. Pulling each other's hair and screeching blue murder at each other and everything they were. And then a few days later Mr Byamile went storming in and punched Mr Goodnight right smack on the end of his nose. Made it bleed as well. Honestly, if people can't get on together at work then that's surely up to them. No need for husbands and wives to get involved is there? Funny thing were that a month later Mr Byamile and Mrs Goodnight ran off together and Mr Goodnight moved into the flat above the shop with Mrs Byamile. I imagine he sleeps in her spare room. Honestly, there's some queer goings on in Blessham at times.

Next door to the General Store and Post Office is the butcher shop. The butcher shop is owned by Jim Booth's dad, Mr Booth. They call the shop Booth and Son, Quality Pork Butchers. Why they call it that is anybody's guess because they don't just sell pork in there. They sell joints of beef and lamb chops and chicken and sausages and liver and black pudding and... and...

...well, meat and things, you know.

Anyway, I hear that they do a very good trade and it gave Jim Booth an instant job the moment he left school. Which were alright for him but it weren't much fun for me when him and his mates used to throw sheep's eyeballs and lungs and bits of tripe and things at me. I mean, I'm quite fond of a nice bit of tripe when it's served up with onions but not when a raw lump of it hits you in the mush at high speed. Still, if I managed to catch it before it hit the ground it used to give me and the old man with our dinner. So, it weren't too bad I suppose. Silver linings and all that!

Mr Booth is a very kind man and he's always alright with me. He knew we were always skint when I were a kid so he sometimes put in a bit extra whenever I went in there for anything. You know, a couple of extra sausages or half a black pudding ring or a few slices of corned beef over the weight. He always said that I weren't to tell anyone and that it were because me mum used to do him a favour now and again. Maybe that's where she used to go at nights. To work in the butchers. He's what's known as semi-retired now though is Mr Booth and he leaves the running of the shop mainly to Jim, who ain't kind to me at all so I don't bother using the butcher's much nowadays and leave it to me grandma who does our shopping for us.

Anyway, in between the Pig and Whistle and The Crescent is The Grange. The Grange is a lovely big house which is second in size only to the Hall. It has a long winding gravel drive leading up to it and tall fir trees in the garden. The Grange is owned by Major Brimmish, an old military man. Army, I think. He has two flag poles at the front of the house, one for the Union Jack and one for the St George's Cross which he has flying at all times unless anybody in the royal family dies and then he lowers 'em to half-mast. I think the major is what is known as an eccederent... endecterant... eccenatry...

...he's not the full shilling.

I mean, he's harmless enough like, and you can always be sure to see him in church of a Sunday morning wearing his medals and peaked cap, but it's just that, well, he seems to think that he's still in the army. Don't get me wrong, I mean, there's nothing wrong with that. You see, the trouble is that Major Brimmish still thinks that we're at war with Germany. You know, that Hitler chap I mentioned earlier

Most of the time he goes about in his old uniform and beret and boots and everything and a baton under his arm. He spends half the night patrolling his garden with a large torch, his old service revolver and two blummin' great Alsatian dogs in case of parachuting stormtroopers. Why they would want to be out trooping in a storm is anybody's guess. Other nights he stands at the entrance to his drive shouting at the houses opposite to 'Turn their ruddy lights out!' He salutes everybody he meets which is alright but he expects you to do it back and apparently, I don't do it properly because he pulls me up for it every time and shows me the right way to do it. 'Always, but always, salute a superior officer Wilkie!' He tells me, but I can never seem to get the hang of it. He also says that if we haven't got our Anderson shelter built soon then he's going to report us to the War Office. I don't even know what an Anderson shelter is let alone how to build one. Anyway, like I said, he's harmless enough, most of the time.

Although, there were that one incident when he shot a couple of Her Ladyship's beaters one Saturday afternoon during pheasant season a couple of years ago. They were all wearing them calm-o-flatus jackets like soldiers wear and he thought that 'Jerry' had invaded. He were wrong of course. Neither of 'em were called Jerry. They were alright in the end though, just a few flesh wounds, but the Major don't get invited along to the shoot anymore. You know, for safety reasons.

Some of the local young 'uns used to make up stories about the major. Things like how he once killed thirty German soldiers single-handed at the D Day landings and how he fought against Rommel with the Desert Rats. I never knew the army used rats. I heard that they use dogs and horses but can't see how they would use rats. If they do, I bet the beggars take some training. You get quite a few round here, especially at harvest time, perhaps the army could start training 'em.

So that's me home. Blessham. Some roads, a load of houses, a church, a pub, a stately home, a couple of shops, a farm, a school, a village hall and that stinkin' stud. We've got just about all we need. There's a doctor and a vet if we need 'em at Cockwright but I don't get sick too often really and I ain't got no pets. And they've got one of them little mini mart shops at Stuffham. They sell most things but I think the prices are a bit steep. It's blummin' cheaper to make your own bread than pay what they charge.

I don't know exactly how many people live in Blessham. You know, I don't really care, so long as Meg's one of 'em then that's all that matters as far as I'm concerned. Blessham is where I grew up, it's where I work and you know I do believe it's where I'm going to die and be laid to rest, under the shade of the yew trees at St Mildred's.

Still, it might be a little while yet before I see it again. And do you know the first thing I'm going to do when I get there? If I can pluck up the courage that is. I'm going to go straight round to Her Ladyship and see if I can have me old job back at the Hall.

4
Work

Blessham Hall. What a wonderful place that is. The home of Lord and Lady Stark-Raven. That's one of them double-barrelled shotgun names. His Lordship's family name being Stark and Her Ladyship's family name being Raven. You put the two together, like a lot of the gentry tend to do, and you become Stark-Raven. They're not exactly living in what Nick calls matt-tree-moan-yall bliss. No, there's were what's known as a marriage of con-vee-knee-ants. You see, his family had a title but no money and Her Ladyship's family had loads of money but no title. So, between 'em, they got the best of both worlds. Well, I think that's how it works. Confusing ain't it?

The Hall is without doubt the biggest and most important part of the village. Especially to me because it's where I work. Well, where I used to work before all this happened. Anyway, Blessham Hall were like a second home to me and I have to be honest with you when I say that I were at me very best there. Many a happy day have I spent toileting away in those grounds earning an honest living.

Head gardener I were. Alright, so I were the only gardener but if there's no-one else over you then I suppose that puts you in charge which by rights made me head gardener. Didn't it? I were in charge of meself. Anyway, head or not I were a blummin' good gardener and whatever they say about Her Ladyship, and to be honest most of it's true, I always got on alright with her. Well, sort of. I mean, I were blummin' terrified of the woman, everybody is, but if you played fair with her then she wouldn't have your guts for garters. Mind you, she did have mine a few times. It weren't like you scratch my back and I'll scratch yours. Let's face it, you'd need to use a grass rake to scratch a back the size of hers. But what I mean is you could never really get close to her, even His Lordship could never get close to her. I don't just mean fizzilacy… filazy… phyzololo…

…touching her.

Although, with a women of that size and a man of his frail build it's not really possible and would be dangerous anyway, but what I mean is you have to watch what you say and do with Her Ladyship. If you went a week or more without her threatening you or hurling curses at you in any way then you were doing alright. But I think over the years me and her built up a kind of understanding based on the fact that she were, most of the time, pleased with me work. She used to stop and talk to me some days. I didn't always know what she were going on about but I thought it wise to agree with her anyway. And you know, even if I do say so meself, I were blummin' good at me job and I reckon she thought so too. Like I said before, I didn't pass any exams down to being as thick as two short planks but despite all that I've never been uneplo… unempleen… unoploymo…

…I've never been out of work for long in me life.

Me first job when I left school in the year 1981 were with Farmer Bull. Now that were hard graft I can tell you and he were an hard taskmaster, a right blummin' slave-driver he were. I had to get up at the crack of dawn to go and do the milking and then I'd have to do things like mucking out and stuff. Then the rest of the day would be spent baling hay or fencing or dipping sheep or castrating the young bulls. I used to make meself laugh by saying that I were taking the bollocks off the bullocks, but Reverend Menn told me off and said that were very rude so I stopped saying it. Anyway, we used to work from sun-up until sunset where at last I would go home, have me tea and climb into bed tired out. Still, I got paid a fiver a day and got half an hour for me dinner every day. Farmer Bull were a hard man, you know, knuckles and boots and that, but he were fair. Oh, hang on a minute. No, no he weren't fair at all now I think about it. Still it were a job.

It weren't to last though. You see, Farmer Bull's got a daughter; Desira. Nice enough lass, same age as me, we were in old Rodwell's class together and in a certain light of the day you might even say she were pretty. And a proper country girl she is, all hips, lips and titties if you'll pardon me language, but I don't know how else to describe her. Anyway, I were in the haystack, stacking bales one afternoon and thinking of that kiss like I always did when I were in the haystack. Mid-Summer it were and it were blummin' hot, so I stopped what I were doing for five minutes and sat down to take a breather. Well, the next thing you know Desira turns up in this tiny, little, blue and white checked dress with a bottle of ginger beer.

'Hello Joe.' She said.

'Hello there Desira.' I said back.

'I got something here that I reckon you want Joe.' She said.

'What's that then?' I asked.

'This.' She says putting the bottle right between her legs. Now I've a got something of weakness for ginger beer it has to be said and I could see the little drops of water running down the glass. It must have been nice and cold.

'Don't put it there Desira,' I said, 'It'll get all warm.'

'Oh, it's warm there alright and I'll bet *you're* warm too aren't you Joe?' She said and her voice seemed to go all funny. Kind of hoarse and husky like.

'Too blummin' right I am,' I said, 'I'm sweating like a blummin' pig.'

'Why don't you take that shirt off then?' She said sounding even huskier than before. I thought perhaps she must have had a sore throat. Funny time of year though for a sore throat. Still, I suppose it happens. You know, hay fever and all that.

'That's a good idea.' I said and I took it off.

'Oooh! Haven't you got big muscles Joe?' She said, slowly rubbing me left arm with her right hand.

'Comes from throwing these big old hay bales around.' I said.

'I'll bet you've got nice legs as well Joe.' She said.

'Well, to tell the truth, they're a bit hairy.' I said. 'And I ain't half got knobbly knees.'

'Those jeans must be rubbing Joe,' she said, 'Why don't you take them off as well?' She said, pointing at me trousers.

'I can't do that Desira.' I said in a feeling very surprised at the suggestion.

'Why not?' She asked, raising one eyebrow in a funny sort of way.

'Because I ain't got no underpants on.' I told her. And it were true, I'd got no clean ones that morning so I went what I believe they call Comanche or something or other.

Then, without another word she suddenly pushed me over the pile of bales we were sitting on, jumped on me, popped open the buttons and tried to rip me trousers down. Now, a joke's a joke but what she were doing were a bit beyond a joke in my opinion. And the next thing you know she starts putting her tongue in me ear and saying, 'Come on Joe, I want it, I want it badly, give it to me. Now!' Give her what? I didn't know what the blummin' 'eck she were on about. She'd already got the ginger beer so how could I give it to her? She hadn't even brought any glasses with her. Maybe the sore throat had sent her daft in the head or something, but she just carried on pulling at me jeans and biting me neck like one of them umpires you see in the old horror films. And then, all of a sudden, she's off me. I looked up just in time to see her go flying onto her rump and who should be standing there but Farmer Bull himself. And I could tell he were right blummin' angry. And he's a big, scary bloke and all is Farmer Bull. Especially when he's angry.

'Get in that house!' He snarled at Desira and I swear all the colour from her face just drained away. She ran off crying her eyes out. 'And tell your ma to get the strap out and ready for me!' He shouted after her.

'And as for you, you dirty little bastard.' He said to me in a very low voice that sounded like a growl. 'You're fired. Now get off my fucking land.'

'Yes Farmer Bull, right away sir.' I said and I were just as scared as Desira. I were worried he might fetch his strap to me. 'I'll just get me shirt back on and I'll be off.'

'Not so fast laddie.' He said, crooking his finger and beckoning me towards him.

'What do you mean Farmer Bull?' I asked.

And then he drove his size twelve boot firmly between me legs. Right into me you-know-where. Down I went like a sack of spuds off the back of a wagon. Nearly spewed up I did, and all me wind came up and out of me chest in one loud sort of 'whoosh.' I never knew anything that hurt like it. Then, as I lay there gasping for me breath, he gave me what is without doubt the single most biggest kickings I've ever had in me entire life. And I've had a few I can tell you. He kicked me from one end of that farmyard to the other and then back again calling me some awful names as he went that I don't ever want to repeat. Then he made me put me shirt back on, gave me a couple more helpings of his boot up me back end and told me that if he ever caught me anywhere near his daughter again, he would take an axe to me and bury me in the middle of fifteen-acre field.

To this day I don't know what all that were about but I took his advice and I ran home as fast as I could despite hurting everywhere. As for Desira, I saw her for the last time the next day. I looked out of me bedroom window and saw her walking into the village towards the bus stop with a small suitcase in her hand. She seemed to be walking very slowly as I recall. Never saw her again after that.

But, despite being black and blue all over and having a black eye and a split lip and a badly bruised rump, I knew that I had to do something about getting another job and I soon found one and all. Reverend Menn said that I could mow the grass at the church and look after his garden at the vicarage once a week. It didn't pay much. About a tenner I think it were. But what happened, though, were that I got a reputation for how nice the vicarage started to look. You see, Reverend Menn were getting on in years and he couldn't really do that much about the place but, and I don't mean to boast, I changed them grounds in a couple of months from a right old mess to something that looked like a proper vicarage garden which, if you think about it, is what it were.

Anyway, word soon got round and other folks started asking me to do their gardens and I soon found that I had a different garden to look after every day. I did the church and vicarage on Monday, the Pig and Whistle on Tuesday, the Grange on Wednesday, which meant standing to attention and saluting of course, and old Mr Cummings on Thursday. On Friday I used to mow the grass on the village green, weather permitting of course, which I did for nothing because the Parochial Church Council didn't have a lot of money for it. I were quite proud of that!

It were great. I were working for meself and making about, well, quite a few quid a week, which made up for what old man Bull paid me. Not to mention all the cups of tea people used to make me. When I did the pub on the Tuesday Bob used to bring me out a pint of mild and a plate of sarnies or half a pork pie at dinner time. I blummin' well loved it.

Things were going great. I could save a couple of quid at the post office I were earning so much. Alright, so I used to get the odd bit of hassle with some of the cheeky young 'uns when I were doing the green but I didn't mind. I were happy! I weren't being ordered around and regularly kicked in the back end by Farmer Bull for one thing. Meg said that she were happy for me too which made me feel even more happy than I already were. It's nice being happy, ain't it? Things were soon to change though.

I were in the Pig and Whistle one Monday darts night, in the October of 84 if me memory serves me correct. I think they were playing the Baited Badger from Scuttersby. Or were it the Flattened Ferret over at Scroggleton? No, tell a lie, it were the Dog and Two Cocks at Little Dangleton. Anyway, Ernie O'Dyan comes in, buys himself a pint of best and comes and sits next to me.

'Alright Ernie?' I said.

'Ah Boy, not so bad.' He said and he took a good swallow of his pint. Then he says to me, 'Here Joe, have you heard about Old Isaac up at the Hall?'

'No,' I said, 'he ain't dead, is he?'

'No, he ain't dead you soft looking pillock.' Says Ernie.

'What then?' I said.

'He's only gone and won them sodding football pools ain't he?' Says Ernie.

'Crikey.' I said and I'm afraid I must ask you to forgive me for that kind of talk.

'Yeah and guess what else?' Says Ernie.

'What?' Said I.

'They reckon he's gone and cleared off to Portugal and he's taken old Rosie the cook with him as well.' Ernie laughed. 'I always knew him and her were going at it together, the dirty old bugger!'

'Blimey,' I said, although I didn't know what or where Port-yoo-gull is or what they were going at. 'Her Ladyship'll do her nut over that.'

'Never mind that,' Says Ernie, 'you want to get yourself straight round there in the morning and get your name down for the job.'

'What? Me? Working for Her Ladyship? You've gone soft in the blummin' head so you have Ernie.' I said.

'I don't see why not.' He said, 'Everyone knows how good you are in the garden. You'll get the job no worries.'

Well I thought it over. Things had slowed down a bit with the start of Autumn. And then I thought I'd best ask Meg. Meg works at the Hall you see, in the stables there. So, I went into the games room where she were playing pool with Sally and I told her what Ernie had said. She said that it were true about Old Isaac and Rosie the cook, that Her Ladyship were indeed doing her nut and that if I wanted the job then she would try and put in a good word for me. That were it then. If Meg were backing me up then I were going for it. I finished me beer, got me coat and went home for an early night to get round to the Hall first thing in the morning.

Well, morning soon came. I got up, had me breakfast, scrubbed me face, dragged a comb through me hair and set off for the Hall. I went up Fiddlers Lane, down Main Street to the Triangle then down Dairy Lane, down Stuffham Road and came to the entrance of the Hall in no time. I must admit I felt a fair bit of tripidit... trebedeber... trepititi...

...fear, as I walked along that there drive.

As a child growing up in Blessham you get to hear all sorts of things about Her Ladyship and some of 'em I know for a fact are true. You see, Her Ladyship is a fearsome woman. Local legend has it that she once went ten rounds with the Royal Marines light-heavyweight boxing champion and that she won on points. Oh, but she's a powerfully built woman. If she's any less than three foot across the shoulders then me name ain't Joe Wilkie. And I know for a fact that me name is Joe Wilkie. I reckon she must stand well over six-foot-high and she's got a back on her like a prize-winning Aberdeen Angus and a solid great rump like a pair of beer barrels. I couldn't really describe her face only to say that that Royal Marine must have got a few good jabs in himself. Her face is terrifying when she's riled. Mind you, it's pretty scary when she's not riled. She also has her hair cropped very short and close, which does tend to make her look even more frightening. You don't mess with Lady Stark-Raven let me tell you.

His Lordship on the other hand is a totally different kettle of fish. He stands a good foot or more shorter than Her Ladyship and I ain't no expert but I'd say that he'd be about seven stone soaking wet through. He's got this funny little bald head with a thin ring of fluffy grey hair around the side. And he tends to walk with a stoop most of the time as well and his face always looks worried as if he were expecting that the world were about to end. Bob McKenzie always says His Lordship wears the look of a man with the cares of the world on his shoulders. You know, big, sad eyes with blummin' great bags underneath. His nose looks like the beak of one of them birds that used to be on the black stout adverts and he's got this drooping little moustache that makes him look like an old Airedale terrier that's been left out in the rain. Poor old beggar. For someone with so much money and such a lovely big house he always looks so blummin' fed up. Well, like they say, money can't buy you happiness. Mind you, Her Ladyship never seems to complain. Well, not about money at any rate.

There's not a man in the village who could stand up to her. One or two have tried in the past. Farmer Bull were the last one when they got into a row over her not wanting any more manure off him because she gets enough from her horses. He got a bit too mouthy for her liking and gave her shoulder a push. Laid him flat out with one good upper cut to his chin she did. I tell you I nearly fell at her feet in praise.

And shout, you've never heard anyone shout until you've heard Her Ladyship. That woman can break windows from a good stone throw away with her voice. Deafening it is when you're up close to her. And she tends to spray you with spit when she's screaming a rollicking at you. And I've had a few of them in me time I can tell you. So, it were quite normal I suppose that I should be feeling just a little bit fearful as I approached the Hall that morning. And what a fresh and bright Autumn morning it were. Cool and crisp with all the trees just starting to change colour. Not the sort of day to be afraid of anything. But I were afraid alright. I were blummin' near pappering meself. But the thought of that job were too good to pass up and so I braced meself to face Her Ladyship.

The Hall itself is a magnificent great house. I don't know how old it is but it must be getting on because they don't seem to build 'em like that anymore. It's a huge great sandstone thing. All high, leaded windows and gargoyles and things and a great big oak door at the front with these huge great stone steps leading up to it. It's set in the finest grounds and is surrounded by Blessham woods on three sides with open fields on the other one. And it were that big, heavy, old front door that I walked up to that morning and with a shaking hand I knocked three times on it. I stood waiting there for what seemed like and eterriny… entitty… enrerity...

…A good long time.

Anyway, eventually the door swung open with a loud creaking noise and Her Ladyship's butler, Mr Franks, stood there. 'Ye-e-e-e-e-e-e-e-e-e-s-s-s!' He said in that dead posh accent of his.

'Oh, how do you do?' I said. 'I've come to see Lady Stark-Raven.'

'I see Sir.' He said and I had to try and keep a straight face. Fancy somebody calling me 'Sir.' Mind you he don't say it to me now. 'Do you have an appointment to see Her Ladyship?' I didn't know what an appointment were and didn't want to say yes in case I didn't have one. Then again, what if I did?

'I've come about the garden.' I said.

'The garden?' He said.

'The garden.' I said.

'The garden.' He repeated.

'The garden.' I repeated. I remember thinking to meself that we were going to end up standing there all day at that rate.

'What about the garden?' He said, which were good because it stopped us from repeating each other.

'I want the job.' I told him.

'What job would that be exactly?' He asked.

'The gardening job.' I said. 'Now that old Isaac has gone.' And that seemed to do the trick. He raised one eyebrow, I've often thought how clever he is to do that, then he stared at me for a bit, and closed the blummin' door.

'Good day Sir.' He said.

And he were right. It were a good day. It were a lovely day in fact. But I didn't want to stand there and talk about the weather, I wanted that job. So, I stood and waited for a while. I don't know how long I stood there for because I'd forgotten to put on me watch that morning. Anyway, nothing much seemed to be happening so I knocked again.

After about half a minute the big door opened again and Mr Franks stood there as before but he didn't look none too happy though.

'Oh! It's you again.' He said.

'What do you mean again?' I asked him. 'I ain't gone anywhere yet.'

'I really must ask you to leave Sir.' He said. 'Or I'm afraid I shall have to have the dogs loosed and set upon you. Her Ladyship's instructions, you understand?'

Well, I didn't fancy having the dogs set upon me I can tell you. She's got some terrible big dogs has Her Ladyship. She's got four of them Doberman thingies and two of them great big rottvelli... rovtelli... rottwellies...

...them big nasty looking beggars that you hear about on the telly.

I were just about to leave when all of a sudden, I heard the terrible roar of Her Ladyship's voice echoing around the Hall.

'FOR THE LOVE OF GOD FRANKS! CLOSE THAT BALLY DOOR MAN! THIS PLACE COSTS A FORTUNE TO HEAT AS IT IS WITHOUT LEAVING THE FLAMING FRONT DOOR OPEN!' Her voice were like blummin' thunder. And I must be honest with you; I went very weak at the knees at the sound. The thought of them dogs coming after me down the drive suddenly seemed a blummin' sight better.

'Begging your pardon Ma'am,' said Mr Franks who seemed to start shaking a bit himself, 'there's a young man here who wants to speak to you about the garden. I've asked him to go away Ma'am and I have threatened him with the dogs.'

'BY GOD!' I heard her shout and then I heard the sound of her heavy great footsteps clumping towards the door. 'Stand aside Franks.' She said. 'I'll deal with the blighter.'

Well, I saw Mr Franks brushed aside as if he were a man made of smoke and her massive figure stood in his place and I ain't kiddin' when I say that she blummin' near filled the entire door frame. I ain't kiddin' either when I say that I nearly filled me kecks as I found meself staring into the face of Her Ladyship. And she were right angry I could tell.

'WHAT ON EARTH DO YOU WANT YOU HORRIBLE, POE-FACED, TREMBLING LITTLE TURD?' She shouted at me.

'P-P-Please y-y-your L-L-Ladyship.' I stuttered.

'STOP STUTTERING YOU DRIVELLING IDIOT AND SPIT IT OUT.' She screamed.

'Begging your pardon your Ladyship.' I said tugging me forelock which I thought might help the situation.

'Oh, for crying out loud man,' She groaned, 'it's not the fucking nineteen twenties.'

'What?' I said, not understanding what she meant.

'STOP TUGGING YOUR DAMNED, BONEHEADED FORELOCK YOU BLASTED BLOODY BUFFOON!' She bellowed and I swear I nearly started to cry.

'Sorry your Ladyship.' I said timidly.

'*AND DON'T CALL ME YOUR DAMNED LADYSHIP!* YOU POXY IGNORAMUS. I'M NOT YOUR DAMNED LADYSHIP. WHEN YOU SPEAK TO ME YOU WILL ADDRESS ME AS MA'AM, YOU GREASY, SNIVELLING LITTLE OIK. *DO YOU FUCKING WELL UNDERSTAND?*' She said.

'Yes Ma'am, sorry Ma'am.' I said and I could hear me voice starting to crack.

'And do stop grovelling man.' She said with another groan. I weren't none too sure what grovelling were and didn't like to ask but I think I stopped doing it because I managed to say, 'Please Ma'am, I've come to ask if I can have the job that's going here at the Hall?'

'Job? What job? There are no jobs here. What on earth are you babbling on about man?' She said.

'You'll be needing a gardener Ma'am.' I said, 'Now that old Isaac has upped and left.'

'DON'T YOU MENTION THAT CONFOUNDED, FUCKING MANS' NAME TO ME EVER AGAIN, DO YOU HEAR? WHO DOES HE THINK HE IS? FLOUNCING OFF AND LEAVING ME WITHOUT A GARDENER AND A COOK LIKE THAT? IF THAT OLD FART EVER SHOWS HIS MISERABLE FACE ON MY LAND AGAIN, I'LL STRANGLE HIM WITH MY OWN BARE HANDS, *SO HELP ME GOD!*' She hollered and do you know what, I believed that she really would have done.

'Sorry Ma'am,' I said trying to be as brave as I could, 'But you will be needing a new gardener now though.'

Her Ladyship's eyes glared at me from under that over-hanging great brow of hers and it felt as if they were boring into me very soul. I could hardly stand it. Then she drew her arm back, clenched her fist and were just about to knock me back down the steps when Mr Franks gave out this funny little cough, which I've since heard him do on several occasions. She held the punch back, thankfully, turned and looked straight at Mr Franks.

'I beg your pardon Ma'am but this young gentleman is right.' He said, 'You shall be requiring a new gardener.'

'Hmmm. Yes, I suppose I will.' She said lowering her arm, turning back to me and rubbing that great broad chin with her great broad hand. 'And what makes you think that you're the man for the job you stuttering little pipsqueak?'

'Please Ma'am,' I said, 'If you ask around the village, folks will tell you that I'm about the best gardener there is in Blessham. I work for lots of people and I've never had any complaints from any of 'em.' I can cut grass and weed and prune and dig and I know me plants I do.'

'Is that so?' She asked still rubbing her chin.

'Yes Ma'am.' I said, 'But I'd happily give it all up to come and work here at the Hall.'

'Would you now?' She said. Still rubbing.

I nodded me reply cause I were really on the verge of messin' meself and me mouth had gone awful dry by then.

'What is your name, boy?' She asked me stopping the rubbing and stretching up to her marvellous full height.

'Wilkie Ma'am. Joseph Wilkie.' I proudly told her.

'Ah!' Said Mr Franks all of a sudden. 'I do believe I have heard of the young man Ma'am. He does seem to have acquired something of a reputation in the village for being rather adept at all things horticultural. Quite a green-fingered young man.'

Well, I didn't have a clue what he were going on about because me fingers are sort of pinkish really but it seemed to do the trick. Her Ladyship stood back from the door and beckoned me into the Hall with her finger to enter that great and fearful place.

'I think you'd better come in Wilkie.' She said grinning in a way that made the hairs on the back of me neck stand up and an horrible cold shiver run down me spine.

I were hurried in by Mr Franks, who made me wipe me feet on the mat first, and I followed that magnificent, broad shouldered woman as she had told me to. We entered into her study and she lowered herself into a creaking, great leather armchair that were as big as the settee we've got at home.

'Sit down Wilkie.' She said still grinning and pointing towards a little old wooden milking stool in the corner of the room. I did what she said, still fearing for me life. She then began to bombard me with questions about the gardens that I do in the village and all about plants and things and I think I answered her pretty well. Anyway, the next thing she gets onto is money.

'How much do you earn in a week, Wilkie?' She said.

'All depends Ma'am.' I said. 'Depends on the weather and that. Some weeks is more than others. I ain't too clever with figures like. Never have been.'

'Can you tell me, boy,' she said, 'what seven times eight equals?'

'No Ma'am.' I said. I mean, I don't mind having a go at sums now and again but not when they're that hard.

'No, I thought not.' She said.

There were then a few minutes of silence. Her Ladyship sat with her fingers bunched together and staring at me with those terrible piercing eyes again. I felt like a mouse who has just walked in front of a big old tomcat. The waiting were awful until finally she spoke.

'You'll work Monday to Friday from seven till five, Saturday until Midday except during shooting season when you'll be one of the beaters, you'll get ten days unpaid holiday a year, an hour a day for dinner, two fifteen-minute tea breaks, one in the morning and one in the afternoon, you'll be paid sixty pounds a week and I expect nothing less than perfection as far as my garden is concerned. Failure to do so will result in your employment and possibly your paltry life coming to an abrupt end my uneducated little friend. That's my offer Wilkie. Take it or leave it.'

Take it or leave it? Take it or leave it? Were she blummin' joking? I were going to take it alright. Sixty blummin' quid a week. Imagine how much money I could put in the post office. I could save up for a brand-new bike. And the old man wouldn't need to sell that one because I would be able to pay the 'lectric every week as well.

'I'll take it your Ladyship.' I said.

'MA'AM! YOU SORRY LOOKING, HALF-WITTED LITTLE PONCE! NOT YOUR LADYSHIP!' She screeched with her eyes bulging.

'Yes Ma'am.' I said.

'Very good Wilkie. See you in the morning.' She said, rising and turning her back to me and walking to the window.

Well, I walked home in a daze. Who would have believed it? I got the job. Me, Joe Wilkie. Me, who old Mr Rodwell always said would never come to anything. I were the new gardener at Blessham Hall. Not only that but I had survived a close meeting with the terrible Lady Stark-Raven herself. I were as happy as a sow in muck.

I went to the Pig and Whistle for a few pints that night to celebrate. Only a couple mind you. I wanted to start me new job with a clear head. I told Meg and she were very pleased for me. I said that it would be just like old times with me and her working together at the Hall. Meg smiled. I think she were looking forward to it as well. Bob the landlord were sad that I weren't going to be able to do his garden anymore but he wished me well and he gave me a drink on the house. He then went on to tell me the story about how he once worked as a groundsman for Lord Dallmitey or someone and used to advise his Lordship how best to run the place. He's had some life has Bob. Anyway, I finished me pint and went home to bed. I told Meg that she shouldn't stay up too late on a working night. But she carried on playing pool with Jim Booth and his mates. I told her again but Jim Booth pointed his cue at me and told me to 'Piss off' or he were 'going to ram it up' me nose for me. I didn't want any trouble so I left hoping that Meg would have the good sense to go home soon. I care so much about her you see.

So, sure enough, I were up with the lark the next morning. Have you ever wondered why the lark always gets up at that time? I have. It can't be for worms because the early bird gets those. Anyway, I ate a hearty breakfast of toast and dripping, made some dripping sarnies for me dinner, made sure there were enough dripping left for tea and set off. I were there at ten to seven on the dot. I don't know why people say that. Watches don't have dots on 'em. Do they? Mine ain't.

Her Ladyship weren't there. She'd taken the dogs for an early morning tramp in the woods. Seriously, about once a fortnight she made a point of taking the dogs and a twelve-bore and seeing if there were any tramps knocking about. She catches one now and again and the beggars don't come back afterwards I can tell you.

Anyway, Mr Franks met me at the door and showed me to me quarters. Me quarters were an old brick built potting shed in the vegetable garden. It were full of tools, wheelbarrows, plant pots, hosepipes and all sorts of gardening things. Mr Franks told me that the lawn mowers and the petrol rotavator were in the old garage at the back of the house. I were looking forward to getting hold of that rotavator. After he showed me round he gave me a letter from Her Ladyship telling me what to get on with. He had to read it to me mind you, as I couldn't make out her handwriting. It went like this...

The new fellow/yokel, Wilkie or whatever your damned name is.

Clear all the leaves from off the croquet lawn, carefully mind. Then run the rake over the gravel at the front of the house and level it off. After that start tidying up the greenhouses in the vegetable garden. They're a bally shambles. And make sure you do it all properly by God or I'll set the dogs onto you and feed what remains of your carcass to the crows. Damn your eyes!

Yours sincerely,

Lady Stark-Raven

Well, that all seemed quite simple to start with. So I cracked on and got stuck into the leaves. Every so often I heard the bang of Her Ladyship's shotgun away in the woods. Turned out to be pigeons though and not tramps. I think she were a bit disappointed.

I soon finished the leaves because I don't hang about when it comes to work. Then I got tore into the gravel at the front of the house and I soon got me a sweat on. Mrs Franks, the housekeeper, who were standing in for the cook came out and brought me a big mug of tea and four chocolate digestives at ten o'clock which were very kind of her. Very refreshing too let me tell you.

Anyway, I finished the gravel and made me way down to the vegetable garden to do the greenhouses. What a mess they were in. old Isaac couldn't have spent much time in the vegetable garden due to the fact that it looked like them jungles you see on them Tarbuck the Ape-man films. Still, he were getting on a bit and it were probably too much for him.

So, I started off by pulling up all the weeds in the greenhouses. There's three greenhouses at the Hall. Big old wooden things they are, one of 'em is bigger than Poachers Cottage, and a lot of the glass were at that time either missing or broken. One of Her Ladyship's dogs, the biggest one by the looks of it, had used one of the greenhouses as a toilet quite recently too. Well, I reckoned it were a dog (you never know though do you?). Her Ladyship must want me to start growing tomatoes and cucumbers and the like in the Spring if she wants me to tidy all this mess up, I thought. Anyway, it were just as I started sweeping up the floor of the first greenhouse that who should appear but Her Ladyship herself.

'Morning Wilkie.' She snapped, giving me a start.

'Morning Ma'am.' I said remembering just in time not to call her 'Your Ladyship.'

'Got your work cut out in here Wilkie, eh?' She said standing with her feet apart and her hands on her hips like me P.E teacher at the big school used to.

'Yes Ma'am.' I said.

'And I see one of the dogs has had a damn good crap in here.' She said with a cackle.

'Yes Ma'am.' I said and I were shaking by this point.

'Are you cold Wilkie?' She asked me.

'No Ma'am.' I said.

'THEN WHY ARE YOU SHAKING YOU GORMLESS LOOKING IDIOT?' She bellowed.

'Because I'm scared Ma'am.' I said and in all honesty I were. I really were. Terrified I were. All alone in that high walled vegetable garden with Lady Stark-Raven. I had every reason to be blummin' well scared.

'Scared?' She asked.

'Yes Ma'am.' I said.

'Good, that's good Wilkie.' She said and she seemed to calm down all of a sudden and this funny look appeared in her eye as if she were looking right through me into the distance beyond. 'It's good for a man to be scared Wilkie.' She continued. 'Fear keeps a man on his toes, maintains discipline and prevents sloth. That's the trouble with this country Wilkie, no discipline. Nobody's scared anymore. That's why we're in such a fucking mess. The scumbags get away with everything. Vandals, hooligans, rioters, blackguards, con men, shoplifters, poachers, pickpockets, spineless little creeps who play the system, scroungers, liars, tabloid press, thieves, rapists, murderers, grave robbers, estate agents, muggers, buggers and arse bandits. The whole wretched country is overrun with them. By God I wish I had my way. I'd soon stop them Wilkie, oh yes! The rope, the cat and the birch. That's the only way to put a stop to them. But oh no, the bleeding-heart liberals and the poxy limp-wristed socialists don't want to do that, do they? Mustn't hurt the poor little things, oh no, send them off Scot-free and give them a few hours community service. Ooh yes, slap them on the wrists, that'll teach them. Balls will it! Community flaming service, pah! Hanging and flogging is the only way. Both in some cases, at the same time. That'll do the trick. By God it will. I know it will. I keep telling them Wilkie, I keep writing to them and telling them. But will they listen? Will they hell as like! If you ask me they're as bad. Politicians? Half of them are perverts and cross dressers and the other half are lap dogs and yes men. Rubbish, the lot of them. Lining their own sordid pockets to spend on whoredom, sodomy, all manner of perversion and drugs, filthy drugs that have quite probably been smuggled into the country up some Johnny foreigner's back passage. There's not one real man amongst them. Mrs Thatcher is the only one with a backbone and her hands are tied. By God, if it wasn't for her I dread to think where we'd be. Why can't they see Wilkie? Why can't they understand? The only way to bring about law and order in this once proud nation of ours is to come down hard on the deplorable scum who perpetrate all these foul crimes. Short, sharp, shock. That's the way. Come down hard I say. Give them a taste of the lash then string them up. Make a public example of them. Bring back the rope and the cat. Oh Wilkie, how I wish they would bring back the cat. Don't you agree? Don't you wish that they would bring back the cat Wilkie?'

'Yes Ma'am.' I said nodding. Although I have to confess that I didn't have a clue what on earth she were going on about and as far as I were aware she never had a cat. Lots of dogs but no cat. Maybe she did, I don't know. I've never liked cats meself. Mean, cruel minded things they are in my opinion. Still, it must be quite upsetting to lose a pet. Maybe one day someone will find it and bring it back and then Her Ladyship will be happy.

Anyway, I thought it best just to agree with her. You know, first day on me new job, I didn't want to get on the wrong side of the boss. I wish I knew though what the 'eck she were going on about. I never heard half of those words before. Well, what the 'eck is a blackguard when it's at home? Or an estate agent?

After that Her Ladyship and I seemed to strike up an odd sort of friendship. Well, perhaps friendship ain't quite the right word for it. More like an understanding. I suppose it were born out of the fact that I were always scared of her, she used to pour out her anger on me and I always agreed with her because I were scared of her. I think it were because I always agreed with her that I got on so well in the job. Oh, there were blummin' hundreds of times sure enough when I got on the wrong side of her like, and I would have to duck for cover or keep out of her way for a few days. Like the time when I dropped one of her prize azalea's and broke the big terracotta pot all to beggary in me second week on the job. She went blummin' berserk.

'YOU HOPELESS HALF-WITTED, VACANT, BLOODY MORON WILKIE!' She screamed as I fled across the back lawn, dodging lumps of broken plant pot that flew past me ears. 'I'LL NAIL YOU UPSIDE DOWN TO THE BALLY FLAGPOLE BY YOUR FUCKING TESTICLES WHEN I GET MY HANDS ON YOU!'

She never did it though and I never did find out what testicles were. Probably just a load of old cobblers. Mind you, she has carried out her threats on one or two people over the years so I suppose I'm one of the lucky ones. Although there were the time when I got stuck on the roof but I'll tell you about that later. That nearly cost me me job that did.

Anyway, there I were, at the Hall. I went round to the stables during me dinner break that first day to see Meg and to tell her how I were getting on. When I got there however one of the stable lads who works there, there's two of 'em; Robert and Roger, stopped me. It were Robert and he said that I couldn't speak to Meg just then due to the fact that her and Roger were busy inside the stables mucking out Her Ladyship's favourite charger. It must have been hard work and the stink must have been terrible because I could hear the pair of 'em moaning and groaning and 'oohing' and 'aahing' inside. Poor Meg I thought to meself, she must be having it hard. So, I told Robert to tell her that I would see her later. He said that he would pass the message on and I went back to the shed for me sandwiches. As I left I heard Robert shouting to Roger to hurry up because he wanted a go. How thoughtful of him to want to share the workload. I just hope that they let Meg have a rest as well. I suppose it would have made more sense though if all three of 'em went at it together.

The rest of that first day passed without incident. I got the greenhouses finished although the dogs had again used one of 'em as a toilet whilst Her Ladyship had been talking to me. I wouldn't have minded so much but I don't think one of 'em were very well and I had to get the hosepipe out. In the end though I got 'em all cleaned up and I were quite proud with meself.

I left at five on the dot and I met up with Meg as she were walking home. I told her that I'd come round to see her at the stables but she were busy. I told her that I thought it would be a better idea if she had both the lads in there with her and she smiled and said that she had never thought about it but that it sounded really good and she would 'Suggest it to them tomorrow.' She were sure they would both agree to it. I were pleased to have been able to help Meg out like that. I really do love her you know.

Anyway, so it went on. The days flew by and I became more and more at home in me job. After a while Her Ladyship stopped leaving me notes and let me get on with it. And like I say, for the most part, she were pleased with me work. I were pleased too. I loved it there and, even if I do say so meself, I made those gardens look absolutely immlia... immlacilar... ilmacula...

...look really good.

One of the nicest thing about being a gardener though of course is that you never get bored. Each season of the year brings its own delights, its own surprises and its own challenges. Let me explain if I may.

5
Spring

I love the Spring, don't you? I like all the seasons of the year for lots of different reasons. They sound the same don't they? Seasons and reasons. Anyway, all of the seasons are nice in their own special way but me favourite season has to be Spring. After all, I were born in the Spring weren't I? Spring is the time when the whole countryside wakes up from its long Winter sleep and everything turns green again. It's as if God gives the whole world a little nudge and it suddenly comes into life. Lovely!

Spring were always a very busy time for me at the Hall but I didn't mind; I like to keep busy. I think that's one thing about being stuck in this place that gets me down, spending all me time kicking me heels in this blummin' cell. What I wouldn't give for a bit of lawn mowing or rose pruning or manure spreading. Still, if I get that job in the prison garden things will change, won't they?

Spring is also a very special time for the whole village. It's when the new lambs are born, it's when all the crops start to grow and it's the time of year that we have the Easter Fair on the village green. Unless it's raining of course. Then we have it in the village hall which is alright but it does tend to get a bit cramped. The Easter Fair is always held on the Saturday between Good Friday and Easter Sunday. It's something the village has done for as far back as I can remember and the old man says that they've done it for as far back as he can remember so that must be a long time.

It's dead good though. They have stalls and games and Morris dancers and all sorts of things. It's a bit like the Summer Fete only smaller. I like the Morris dancers. Me Uncle Eli used to be one you know. He once danced all the way from Blessham to Cockwright. They called it the nine-day wonder, on account of the fact that everyone wondered why it took him nine days to do it because it's only a few miles.

Anyway, the whole village turns up for the Easter Fair. Except for Her Ladyship. She goes to the Fete to open it and do some of the judging and she always gives a speech at the Christmas Party but she doesn't go to the Easter Fair.

I once had the nerve to ask her why and she said 'I'll be damned for all eternity before I'm going to stand rubbing shoulders with Johnny Riff-Raff and watch a wandering band of flower wearing nancy-boys in straw hats with bells around their knees jumping about shouting like baboons and waving lace hankies at each other whilst some other mincing buffoon strangles the very life breath out of some knackered old second hand accordion claiming it to be a tune, accompanied by another talentless nobody knocking seven shades out of a tatty old tambourine and some other half dead sack of old guts bellowing out "Hey nonny" in a vainglorious and desperate attempt to try and convince everyone that he can actually sing when in reality he sounds like a lame camel in the midst of a breech birth. Personally, I'd rather be beaten across the soles of my feet with a length of rubber hose pipe for half an hour than endure that blasted, bally racket assailing my ear drums.' That's what she said!

I didn't understand most of it but I get the picture that she don't like the Morris Men. Can't think why, I really enjoy 'em. And there's no one I know in the village called Johnny Riff-Raff. There's a John Dalliard, who lives up the Crescent, but no Johnny Riff-Raff. She must be mistaken, unless there's someone from Stuffham or Dammitt that she knows called Johnny Riff-Raff and maybe he's got that B.O thing that I get sometimes. Anyway, she don't have to stand next to him if she don't want to, does she? There's plenty of other places to stand and watch 'em. Still, it's Her Ladyship's choice and therefore you have to respect it I suppose.

March and April is vegetable sowing time. And Her Ladyship likes her veg I can tell you. She makes me sow all sorts she does. Broad beans, cabbages, carrots, leeks, onions, parsnips, peas and Brussels sprouts. You want to hear her letting rip when she's had a good load of sprouts. Sounds like Farmer Bull's old Fordson Major firing up on a cold morning. She let one rip in me shed one day, came out like a dirty, great drum roll. Fair made me eyes burn it did. And as for the smell... pwoar! You never smelled anything like it. Like sticking your nose in a heap of manure. But I like sowing the vegetable seeds though. I think it's the fact that you're growing something elibi... ebidel... eldibal...

...something you can eat.

The end of March is the time when I have to sow the seed potatoes as well. Now that is back breaking work. I remember once that Her Ladyship said that if I didn't get it done in time she were going to break me back for me. In several places and all. She were cackling at the time, mind you, so it may have been a joke. I got it done in time though. Still, fair play to her, she lets me take as many spuds home as I like, within reason. 'After all,' she says, 'the potato is the staple food of the peasant class.' But, I can't remember if there were any peasants in my class at school. Actually, come to think of it, I don't know what a peasant is. I know what a pheasant is. And you could have one of those with potatoes. I sometimes do if the old man brings one home without selling it. Maybe that's what she meant. The pheasant class.

Now, it's that time of year that the weeds start to shoot up as well. That keeps me busy that does. Her Ladyship has got lots of rose beds and they're her pride and joy they are. I have to take extra special care over 'em. Weeding and pruning and dead-heading and manuring. I must have put tons of manure on them roses over the years. Horse manure of course. From the stables. I were never too keen on the smell of it because of that blummin' stud farm but now I like fetching the manure because it always gives me a chance to see Meg. I push the big wheelbarrow round to the stables and Meg shows me where I can get it from. However, she is rather busy and can't help me. She has to exercise the horses you see. She's good at it too. Roger and Robert told me they've never known a lass who is as good a ride as her. I wondered why they started laughing when they said that. Daft apeths!

Anyway, the roses. Like I said, Her Ladyship is very particular about 'em. And quite rightly so. She's got some lovely bloomers. Flowers I mean. I'm not talking about her underwear or anything. I've never even seen her underwear. Honest I haven't and I don't want to either thank you very much. Ooh, I just made meself shudder then at the thought. Anyway, the only problem with having so many rose beds is that you tend to get loads of weeds in 'em. Takes ages to get rid of 'em it does. Even with a hoe. But Her Ladyship insists that every single one is removed, roots and all. She made it perfectly clear right from the start that if anything happened to just one of her precious roses she would have me 'Damn well hunted down, flayed alive and your filthy, despicable hide turned into an umbrella stand.' Believe me, I take great care with 'em.

Pruning is the worst though. Scary that is. Her Ladyship supervises the pruning personally and by 'eck she gives me a good helping of the sharp edge of her tongue if I make a mistake.

'NOT THERE YOU MORONIC, FUCKING BUFFOON!' She shouts, and 'FOR THE LOVE OF GOD WILKIE! AN OUTWARD POINTING SHOOT, YOU DAMNED, IDIOT BUMPKIN!' and 'ONLY A COMPLETE BASTARD, FUCKING CRETIN WOULD CUT IT THERE MAN! OPEN YOUR DAMNED, BLOODY EYES YOU HOPELESS, USELESS, FECKLESS FUCK-WITTED IMBECILE!' You know, that kind of thing. I'm always glad when the pruning is over for another year.

One of the best things about Spring in the garden though is that it's the time to start mowing the grass again. The lawns at the Hall cover about five acres and take damn near a full day of mowing. Luckily though I've got two of them petrol driven mowers. A small cylinder mower for the croquet lawn and a big old rotary mower for the big lawns. I once suggested to Her Ladyship that perhaps it would be a good idea to buy one of them newfangled sit on mowers. I saw one on the telly. Smashing they are, like driving a little tractor only it's not a tractor it's a lawn mower. Anyway, I asked her about it but she said 'Do you honestly think for one minute that I am going to waste my hard-earned money on an expensive luxury item for the bumbling idiot groundsman. If that's the case then you've got another thing coming. Do you think that I am made of money? Apart from anything else a blasted, blithering halfwit like you is almost certain to either blow it up or crash it into the first tree that you came to and bally well destroy the bloody thing.'

She also said that she wouldn't trust me to walk her dogs across the lawn let alone drive one of those things anywhere near her rose beds and that if I ever mentioned the subject again she were going to slay me by dragging me into the woods, shooting me in the knee caps and then leaving me to the elements. I were then ordered to get me 'stinking hide' out of her sight before she struck me with the poker she were holding at the time. I think perhaps I probably caught her in an off mood because she seemed to have forgotten all about it by the afternoon. I took her advice though and never brought it up again. Still, would've been nice, but no, I just use the other two mowers.

But the best thing about grass mowing is the smell. There's nothing on earth quite like the smell of new mown grass. Especially if you've been spreading that horse muck the day before and your head's full of the smell. I usually do the mowing on Fridays. It's a grand job, especially on hot days. The only drawback with the mowing is that sometimes Her Ladyship's dogs have a nasty habit of doing their toiletries on the lawns. When they're not doing it in the greenhouses or the patio or the paths or in me shed, that is. Anyway, the trouble is that when the grass is quite long you don't always notice it in time. Then, when the mower blades go over it, it all gets flicked up over your boots and trouser bottoms. I've taken to wearing wellingtons when the grass is long although they do make your feet honk in the hot weather. Honestly, those dogs are the bane of me blummin' life. I sometimes think that they do it on purpose. Still, apart from that, the lawn mowing is me favourite job.

Lawn mowing also gives you a good thirst. Which is one of the reasons why I do it on Fridays. I get paid on a Friday and I like to go for a pint in the evening. There's nothing like wandering down to the Pig and Whistle with a dry throat and the smell of new mown grass still in your nostrils and sinking a couple of pints of Fartleberrys Famous Old Mild. Ooh! I can almost taste it. What I wouldn't give for a pint in here.

Spring is also the time when Her Ladyship takes His Lordship to visit her friend in Scotland. Her friend's name is Lady Pavanstones of Kinellphyre and she lives in this big old castle in the Highlands. They say that the castle is haunted but I think that's a right load of old cobblers I do. There ain't no such things as blummin' ghosts except the Holy Ghost of course. That's what Nick reckons. Anyway, if there were such things as ghosts, which there ain't, then they wouldn't hang around very long once Her Ladyship got up there, castle or no castle.

What Her Ladyship goes up there for though mainly is the salmon fishing. And the grouse shooting. And the haggis, although I don't think she shoots them, but maybe they're one of those pro-tek-tid-spee-shees I heard about. And not forgetting the whisky of course. Mr Franks told me that she's quite fond of a drop of the cream of the barley is Her Ladyship. So she has that as well as the whisky. She reckons it's good for the circle-ay-shun. I tried it once, found a bottle of the old man's down beside the settee. He must have left it there when he'd passed out the night before. I don't know about the circle-ay-shun, the only thing that went round in circles as I recall were me bedroom. Spewed me guts up something rotten I did. It burnt me throat both ways. In and out. Never touched it since.

I'll say one thing about Scotland though. It always seems to put some colour into His Lordship's face. He's such a pale looking man most of the time. Meg says it's the whisky that makes his face and nose go red, not the cold mountain air. I wonder if it makes his bedroom spin round. Mind you, Her Ladyship probably wouldn't stand for it.

Anyway, the thing is that Her Ladyship goes up to Scotland for about two weeks at a time. And her being gone for so long tends to have a rather strange effect on the staff at the Hall. Now, there are a good few of us working there. There's Mr and Mrs Franks, who now does the cooking, two maids - Peggy and Polly, Mrs Partridge, a divorcee, who runs the stables with Meg and the two lads, Harvey who looks after the dogs and acts as game-keeper since the last game-keeper, Jack Dittin, drowned himself by accident in the lake having drank best part of a bottle of brandy one night after the shoot, and then there's meself. And it just seems to me that when Her ladyship goes away on one of her trips that a different sort of amophes... atmoseph... astromeph...

...everyone seems all light-hearted and jolly.

It's like they become completely different people. I don't know what gets into 'em I really don't. Mrs Franks walks around the house singing her head off to the radio with all the windows flung wide open. Mr Franks himself rolls his sleeves up and don't wear a tie. And the pair of 'em have to keep going for a lie down. The maids spend half their time giggling and running round the garden teasing me and acting daft. Harvey and Mrs Partridge are seldom seen outside the servant's quarters and every time I go down to see if Meg's there Mrs Partridge answers the door in her dressing gown. Tiny little thing it is and she just stands there with her great, long, muscly legs poking all the way out. I find it quite embarrassing. And fancy staying in bed till that time of day, I ask you. As for Meg and the two lads, they take the horses out for hours longer than usual. Sometimes I think Meg must have fallen off you know because she has bits of straw and stuff in her hair and grass stains on her jodhpurs. She really ought to be more careful.

I don't know. It's as if they've all gone mad. Then as soon as Her ladyship comes back they all start acting normal again. Strange it is. I just get on with me job and try to ignore 'em. That's what I get paid for after all.

Ain't it? Maybe they all act like that because without the steadying hand of Her Ladyship around the place they all feel inserc... incresu... insecru...

...that they can't cope or something.

I can just imagine what Her Ladyship would say if she could see 'em. The air around Blessham Hall would turn blue, so it would. It's poor old Kennedy, the chauffeur, that I feel sorry for. He's the one who has to drive 'em up to Scotland and stay there with 'em. He has to carry on working while this lot all go to pieces. Still, at least I stick to me post. Major Brimmish would be proud of me.

One really good thing about Scotland is the fact that Her Ladyship always comes back in something almost like a good mood. Well, she don't shout for a day or two. And she spends days walking around the estate and the woods in one of them kilt things that the Jocks wear singing 'Flower of Scotland' and 'You Take the High Road' at the top of her lungs. She ain't got what you'd call a good singing voice though it has to be said. To be quite honest it tends to sound more like someone trying to make a tune out of their back end in the bathtub. Still, it makes her happy so the break must do her a power of good.

Mind you, it don't take her too long to get back to her old self. After about three or four days she's screeching blue murder, threatening people and writing letters again. Her Ladyship writes an awful lot of letters. Must cost her a fortune in stamps. Anyway, she writes to all sorts of people. She writes to the newspapers and to the police and to our local MP, whatever he does, and to the houses of par-lee-ment and the prime minister even, he runs the country apparently, and Her Ladyship has even written letters to Her Majesty the Queen of England. Imagine that. The Queen herself. Her Ladyship has met the Queen you know. In London, at the big house where the Queen lives.

The letters that she writes are usually about what we should be doing as a country. You know, things like how to stop crime and bringing back something called National Service and which countries we should declare war on and why and how things were so much better when we had the British Empire and we kept Johnny Foreigner under foot. I've heard that there's a bingo hall in the town called the Empire but I don't think that's the one Her Ladyship keeps going on about. Unless they've got a bingo caller called Johnny Foreigner. Yeah, that makes sense.

As well as the letters, Her Ladyship has written several books on similar subjects and has recently had three of 'em put into print through something called self-publishing. The first is called *'The Rack and its Valuable Place in Modern Society'*, the second is called *'National Service – for pity's sake let's make it compulsory again!'* and the third is a rather more hard-hitting one, called simply '*Hang the Bastards!*'

I didn't know what National Service were so I asked Mr Franks and he reckons it's something we had years ago when you had to join the army whether you wanted to or not. I don't much care for that idea, do you? Having to shoot people and having 'em shoot you just because someone else says so. Still, Her Ladyship swears by it. Mind you, Her Ladyship swears like a trooper a lot of the time. Terrible language she uses when she blows her top. I hope she don't swear when she writes to the Queen.

Another thing that Her Ladyship writes is a diary. She says that she wants to have her life story published posthomo... pomhoustously... posmousedly...

...after she's kicked the bucket.

I don't know what sort of things she puts in her diary but I wouldn't mind having a quick peek at it. Not that I'd dare or anything and besides it's not right reading someone else's diary is it so just forget that I said that. Anyway, I know how Her Ladyship starts her day. Mrs Franks told me.

Her Ladyship rises at six o'clock sharp every morning, brushes her teeth and does fifty press ups on her fingertips with a ten-pound weight balanced between her shoulder blades after which she goes straight into the shower, a cold one mind. When she's in the shower she always sings 'Morning Has Broken.' After her shower (I'd never had one in me life you know until I came in here) she dresses, usually in a tweed jacket and a pair of riding breeches and goes downstairs for breakfast. Breakfast for Her Ladyship takes the form of a large bowl of All Bran (which apparently keep her regular), several pieces of fresh fruit (which apparently keep her regular), six rounds of wholemeal toast and Old English breakfast marmalade, a box of dates (which apparently keep her regular), a pint of fresh orange juice and a pot of tea. While she has breakfast she usually reads the morning papers, which she has delivered from Mrs Byamile's paperboy, to catch up on the news and to see if any of her letters have been printed and if they have it usually puts her in a good mood. If they ain't you have to keep out of her way for a few hours. Then she puts on her boots and takes the dogs for a walk. This means that Harvey has to get up very early as well to ensure that the dogs are ready for Her Ladyship. I'll never forget that one time when he overslept and kept her waiting. She kicked his rump all round them kennels. Yelping louder than the blummin' dogs he were. After the walk Her Ladyship then gets on with any other business of the day or takes one of the horses out for a ride.

She tends to do most of her writing during the long winter months. She spends hours at her desk scribbling away, muttering and swearing to herself. Anyway, come the spring she slows down the writing. It don't stop, she just don't do as much preferring instead to enjoy the trappings of her wealth. She loves her horses and spends a lot of time riding 'em. Of course, finding the right horse for Her ladyship is quite a task. Having one that can actually carry her at a gallop is more important than one that can run fast. She has some handsome great beasts she does. Some of them though she keeps for the sake of it just because she likes horses. I reckon there's close on ten of 'em down there.

'There's nothing like the smell of saddle soap wafting up from between your thighs as you blast along at a gallop.' She always says.

Her favourite horse though and the one that she rides most often is a huge great thing called The General. The General is an ex-army drum horse. Apparently he were a bit too frisky for the army to do anything with so they let Her Ladyship have him for nothing. She soon broke him though, by 'eck she didn't half break him.

Anyway, she takes The General out most days during the fine weather and a more majestic sight you would be hard pressed to see as she gallops over hill and dale. You should hear the snorting and farting and whinnying and the creaking of leather and the sound of a large, heavily sweating beast with great, wild, bulging eyes in the awesome fury of a full charge. The General is quite impressive as well.

His Lordship on the other hand tends to stay in bed until Her Ladyship has left with the dogs. He usually has half a grapefruit for breakfast and a cup of weak coffee. After breakfast he does one or two of them crossword puzzles in the papers (I'm beggared if I know how folks do them things) after which he spends the rest of the morning reading the papers or looking at an old book. He used to smoke a pipe at one time but Her Ladyship has now banned it from the house.

'If I wanted to sit with that kind of stomach-churning stench up my nostrils,' she said to him one day, 'then I'd go and sit in the kennels and inhale the smell of dog shit all day. And apart from anything else it looks positively wet. You look like the worst kind of pansy imaginable. Why can't you smoke cigars like a real man? Now, get rid of that pathetic looking thing and the day I ever see you with it again they'll be holding a funeral for you at St Mildred's the week after.'

But I'll let you in to a little secret, shall I? You mustn't tell Her Ladyship though or she'll have him by the short and curlies, but the thing is, about twice a week, when she's out, he goes down to the vegetable garden and has a smoke of his pipe behind me shed. Been doing it for years he has. But I'm the only one who knows about it, alright? I even get his tobacco for him from the general store. Rough shag is what he smokes. I remember the first time that I fetched it for him. Now that were a funny do that were.

'Hello young Joe.' Said Mrs Byamile as I walked into the shop.

'Hello Mrs Byamile.' I said. 'Are you alright?'

'Ah boy, not so bad. What can I do for you Joe?' She replied.

'A shag,' I said, 'I've been told that I can get one here.'

'Oooh! You naughty boy.' She said making a sort of 'O' shape with her mouth.

'What?' I said.

'I never knew you felt like that Joe.' She said and she seemed as if to go all red and flushed in the face.

'Felt like what?' I asked.

'Well, that a young man like you should be interested in getting it from a much older woman like me.' She said.

'Where else am I going to get it from then?' I asked.

'Well, there's lots of young women in the village Joe. I mean, it's very flattering and everything and if you're absolutely sure then I don't mind at all. You'll have to wait until I close for lunch though, that's when Mr Goodnight is going to the cash and carry.' She were making this kind of panting sound as if she were short of breath and then she undid the top button of her blouse. It weren't that warm in there I know. And I'd never heard of any of the girls in the village selling tobacco.

'Now listen, you come back here when I close for lunch and I'll make sure Mr Goodnight is gone.' She said.

'But, how can I get it if you're closed?' I said.

'How do you mean?' She asked.

'I mean, you're going to have to open up and let me in.' I said.

'Oh yes Joe, I'll open up and let you in alright.' She said and her voice went like Desira's did that day when she started acting all funny with the ginger beer.

'Alright,' I said, 'But I don't want to keep His Lordship waiting. He needs it now.'

'His Lordship?' She said.

'Yes, he's waiting for his tobacco.' I said.

'Tobacco?' She said.

'Yes. Six ounces of rough shag pipe tobacco.' I said.

At that her face seem to turn a brighter shade of red and she seemed to get all flustered and did her top button up again.

'Why didn't you say tobacco in the first place, you stupid boy?' She snapped.

'I thought I did.' I said.

'Here.' She said flinging a packet of tobacco over the counter at me and giving me a rather nasty glare. 'Three pound ninety.'

Well, I paid her the money, picked up the packet of tobacco and walked out of the shop wondering what on earth were up with the woman and why she suddenly changed like that. Maybe it were down to her cycle. Meg tried to explain it to me once. Apparently, women get this thing every month called a cycle. Not like the sort of cycle that you ride on or anything. No, this is a thing where a woman gets a really bad stomach ache and all her oar-moans start playing her up. Then they get this thing called prime-ministerial tension and they start acting all strange and flying off the handle at the slightest little thing. I think that's what must have been wrong with Mrs Byamile. Still, at least I got His Lordship's tobacco so that were alright. I told Meg all about what had happened in the shop and that it fair upset me so it did.

'Oh Joe,' She laughed, and she called me this funny word. What were it now? Oh, that's it, she said that I were nigh-eve. I just smiled and nodded. I'd never heard that word before but I didn't want to let on to Meg that I didn't know anything. And anyway, it were ages yet until evening.

'One day I'll have to tell you about the birds and bees.' She laughed.

Bless her heart. It were very kind of her to offer but I think I know all there is to know on that subject. There's not a single bird in this country that I couldn't name, apart from the puffin. Me granddad, you see, were a keen ornilogo… orthinologo… onthrogolist...

...bird watcher.

And me Aunt Agnes who lives at Dammitt, that's Ruby and Pearl's mum she used to keep bees. Honey bees that is. Now, I'm desperately fond of honey I am and I remember this one time when I were staying there one Summer holiday and me aunt told me that I could help meself to as much honey as I wanted. Of course, what I didn't realise were that she meant I could get it out of one of the jars in the pantry. Anyway, I didn't cotton on like to what she meant and I thought that I would get it fresh straight out of the hive.

One hundred and thirty-seven bee stings me aunt pulled out of me.

Took hours it did using a blue bag and a pair of tweezers. I were sore that day I can tell you. Slathered in calamine lotion by the end of it I were. You'd have thought that something like that would have put me off honey for life but it ain't. It's just put me off taking the lid off of beehives and shoving me head in. Anyway, I think I know more than enough about the birds and the bees thank you very much. Still, it were nice of Meg to offer though.

When His Lordship comes down to the shed for his pipe, him and me often have a chat. You know, about vegetables and things. He always seems to perk up a bit when we do. I have to keep a sharp look out for Her Ladyship though. If she caught us I dread to think what might happen. She's come close to it on a couple of times. His Lordship nearly had a heart attack the last time. I tell you; she'd probably give the pair of us a right proper doing there and then if she found out.

Anyway, back to Spring. Something else that occurs in the garden in Spring that causes me problems is moles. Blummin' things they are. Making dirty great mole hills all over the lawn and making Her Ladyship swear and curse at me. The trouble is you see that the lawns at Blessham Hall are on top of soil that is so rich that it's chock full of earthworms and earthworms are a moles favourite food. So, they charge around under the lawns looking for worms and sending up those mounds of soil and making the grass look a right old mess. I tried putting traps down in the runs that they make but I never caught any. Perhaps I should have used proper mole traps and not mouse traps but that were all I could find at the time. And honestly, every time I clear up one molehill another blummin' one will pop up the next morning. Little beggars they are. They tend to do most of their burrowing at night though and I've spent many a chilly night, under orders, walking around the lawns in the dark with a torch trying to see if they send any molehills up. They never do. I think they must have heard me coming. What I try to do now is get on the lawn early and remove the molehills before Her Ladyship sees 'em. She goes mad if there's any there when she goes out with the dogs of a morning.

'WILKIE, YOU BLUNDERING NANCE!' She shouts. 'WHAT ARE THOSE BALLY MOLEHILLS DOING ON MY LAWNS? IF THEY'RE STILL THERE WHEN I GET BACK I'LL WRING YOUR POXY NECK UNTIL YOUR EYES ARE HANGING OUT OF THEIR SOCKETS! NOW MOVE YOUR ODIOUS, SCRAWNY BACK END AND GET ON WITH IT YOU PITIFUL EXCUSE FOR A MAN!'

'Yes Ma'am, right away Ma'am.' I say to her.

'STOP YOUR JABBERING AND GET ON WITH IT, YOU DISGUSTING LITTLE TOADY!' She says. Mind you, fair do to her, she does calm down when she gets back and finds 'em all gone and the lawn tidied up.

And then there's them grey squirrels. Beggars they are and all. They start coming out in the Spring after they've finished hibraninting... hinbradating... hingbranating...

...when they wake up after their Winter sleep.

They start running around making holes in the lawns to look for the blummin' acorns and hazelnuts they buried in the Winter. Drives Her Ladyship stark raving mad it does. Nasty pieces of work they are too. They're the reason why we ain't got no red squirrels anymore. Killed 'em all off they have. Then there's the rabbits of course and the main trouble with them is that they eat anything and everything in the gardens. The only good thing about the squirrels and rabbits, unlike the moles, is that I don't get the blame for it. And, I don't have to try and get rid of 'em either. Her Ladyship sorts that out herself. She organises regular trips into the woods with Harvey and the dogs. They must shoot dozens of 'em over the year. The beggars keep coming back though. She goes blummin' berserk she does. I sometimes wonder which she hates most. Squirrels or moles. Still, all part and parcel of life in Spring at Blessham Hall I suppose.

But I'll give Her Ladyship some credit though. I mean, even though she lets off enough lead to cover the church roof at the squirrels every year, she don't like that fox hunting and neither do I for that matter. And although she loves nothing better than to charge about on the General, leaping over hedges and things she could never bring herself to ride with the hunt. They're absolutely forbidden on her land. Mind you, that time when they chased that fox across her front lawn and she let 'em have a few warning shots over their heads seems to have put 'em off the idea of doing it again. They always go right the way around the estate now. The grounds of Blessham Hall are a safe place for foxes. Her Ladyship says that they help to keep the 'vermin' down anyway and they won't come anywhere near the house because of the dogs. Personally, I think they're handsome looking animals and I like 'em. Except when you put your foot in a fox hole and twist your ankle but I try and watch where I'm going these days if I go for a walk through the woods.

But what a smashing time of year though, eh? Spring. April showers, daffodils, the return of all the birds that miragted... mitgarated... mignaroted...

...the birds that flew South for the Winter.

I've often wondered where they go. They tell me that London, where the Queen lives, is in the South so perhaps that's where they go. I don't know. Anyway, that's me favourite season, Spring. Mind you, I really like the Summer as well.

6
Summer

Aaah, the Summertime. I heard a song about it once. It reckoned that in the Summertime you could reach right up and touch the sky. Well they're wrong about that because I tried it and got nowhere near. Felt a bit daft afterwards to be honest. I hope no-one saw me. I'd be one of them blummin' laughing stock cubes.

Anyway, I love the Summertime. I always feel happy when the Sun is shining down and turning me skin a lovely shade of brown. Her Ladyship says she can't understand why I 'Want to look like some roaming, bally dago.' I ain't none too sure exactly what a dago is. I think she means dingo, you know, one of them wild dogs that they have roaming around where is it. You know, Arse-Trail-Yeah. I saw 'em on the telly once. Dingoes. They roam around the countryside and get on everybody's nerves. A bit like me, so I suppose Her Ladyship is right in one sense saying that I look like one.

You see, I like to take me shirt off when I'm working in the vegetable garden during the Summer. And I go brown dead quick too. I tan very well. Mind you, so did Mr Rodwell but that were a different sort of tanning. The only problem though is when Her Ladyship comes down. She don't like to see me without a shirt on.

'For the sake of all things decent and proper Wilkie!' she says, 'put your damned shirt back on man. I don't want to see your miserable, stinking carcass in all its naked exposure. Cover it up I say, or by thunder I'll swing for you.' Mind you, I take it off again when she's gone. I were thinking about wearing a pair of shorts once but I didn't in the end because I don't think she'd take too kindly to 'em either and for another thing I ain't actually got a pair.

Major Brimmish reckons too much of the sunshine ain't good for you. He says that it's 'All very well for the Turk, the punkah wallah and the Fuzzy-Wuzzy and the like, Wilkie, but for those of us from dear old Blighty it doesn't do the skin any good.' He says we're white and that's the way we're meant to be. I told Rufus that the other day but he just laughed and said that most honkies he knows turn redder than chilli peppers in the sun and just can't handle it anyway. I don't know, punkah wallah, Fuzzy-Wuzzy, honkies, the Turk, chilli peppers. Some folk talk a right load of old nonsense at times. And I ain't from Blighty, I'm from Blessham. So the major has got that bit wrong, ain't he? And in the Summer I'm brown, not white. Oh, I don't know, we're all the same underneath ain't we?

Anyway, Summertime is also good because of the smells. New mown hay, wildflowers, barbecues. I get invited to quite a few barbecues, especially at the vicarage. Nick's a dab hand with a barbecue. There's always loads of meat - sausages and them burger things and the like, and I eat a lot of it too. Well, you've got to take the chance when it comes along haven't you? The only problem with eating such big amounts of meat is that it can be quite painful when you, you know, go to the khazi the next morning. But I still enjoy it.

Then there's the sounds of Summer too. The insects buzzing around, the birds singing, the sound of leather on willow, the cry of *'HOWZAT!'* And of course, Summer is also the start of the cricket season.

Now Blessham Cricket Club have got quite a repu... reput... respu...

...they're really well known.

The trouble is that they're really well known for being just about the worst team that ever took to a cricket pitch. Honest to goodness, blummin' hopeless they are. If they tried to bowl for dog muck they wouldn't get a smell of it. And as for batting, none of 'em could hit a cows back end with a shovel never mind a blummin' cricket ball. Having said that, I ought to point out that I once had a go at the game when I were at the big school and to be honest with you, I shouldn't really criticize the team. Them cricket balls are rock hard and don't half come keen, especially when they hit you in the face and split your lip wide open. Anyway, all the blokes in the team don't really seem to mind losing so often. After the game they all troop down to the Pig and Whistle and get blind, steaming drunk. Bob McKenzie reckons they'd probably do better if they went in the pub first and then played cricket. Still I must say how nice they all look. All dressed in white.

I'd like to see Meg all dressed in white and walking down the aisle on me arm. I'd be the happiest and proudest man alive. That would be a Summer wedding on a blazing hot day. We'd get wed at the church by Nick and have a great big do at the village hall afterwards with a buff-hay meal and all. And I'd invite everybody in the village to come, except for Jim Booth and Farmer Bull. Sorry, but they're not at all nice to me and it would spoil *our* special day. And I'd get Meg to walk down the aisle to my favourite bit of music, which they always play at the Christmas party. You might know it, it's called the Okey-Cokey. Brilliant song it is and it's got a special dance too, all about arms and legs and putting things in and out. I'd get me grandma to make a lovely big wedding cake and Mr Cummings could take the photos with his instant-matic camera. I can just picture it, everyone throwing spaghetti at us as we come out of the church into the sunshine. And of course, the best bit would be when Nick says to me 'You may now kiss the bride.' Oh, I'd kiss her alright. I'd lift that veil off her pretty face and I'd kiss her right there on her lovely, lovely lips. And I'd say to her 'Meg' I'd say, 'you've made me so very happy. I love you my darling.' That's what I'm going to say...

...one day.

Anyway, Summertime. Now one of the most important events of the whole year at Blessham Hall takes place in the Summertime. I'm talking of course about the open day. Once a year, on the second Sunday in July, Her Ladyship opens up the grounds for the general public to come and have a look. And a very grand affair it is and all. There are refreshments and things laid on and we always have loads of people turn up to see the gardens. All sorts of folk we have. Young couples, old folks, families with kiddies. Mind you, Her Ladyship ain't none too keen on the kiddies. She spends the day patrolling the gardens with her best riding crop in her hands in case as she puts it 'Any of the little beasts think they can turn my gardens into an adventure playground.' She don't like children. 'By thunder Wilkie, if I see any of those young hooligans so much as even touch one of my roses I'll skin them alive, skin them alive do you hear me?' That's what she says and I believe her and all.

And I ain't half busy when it comes to getting ready for the open day. Everything has to be just right. You can imagine what Her Ladyship says if it ain't

'*WILKIE*, HOW THE HELL CAN I CHARGE THE GREAT UNWASHED £4.00 PER VEHICLE TO COME AND SEE THIS BALLY SHAMBLES? GET YOUR UNSAVOURY CARCASS OUT THERE AND SORT IT OUT OR I SWEAR BY ALMIGHTY GOD THAT I SHALL TIE ONE END OF A ROPE TO MY SADDLE, THE OTHER END TO YOUR NECK AND TAKE THE GENERAL FOR A TEN MILE GALLOP!' That's the sort of thing she says. But that's fair enough, she just wants her garden to look nice when people see it.

There's a lot of work to do to get them gardens looking their very best I can tell you. I usually have to work late every night of the week leading up to the open day. I have to work all day Saturday and be there all day Sunday as well which means missing church, which is a shame. In fact, all the staff have to be there. Everybody has to pitch in. We all tear about doing loads of little jobs while Her Ladyship, looking quite splendid in her best breeches and riding jacket stands shouting orders and threats at us with one of them meggy-fone thingies.

No word of a lie, she's had me going round that croquet lawn on me hands and knees on more than one occasion with a pair of small scissors to make sure I got every blade of grass that were sticking up. Took me hours it did, but she wanted it just right. I made a little game out of it to help pass the time. I pretended I were one of them fancy hairdressers that you see on the telly and I were cutting peoples hair instead of grass. Unfortunately, Her Ladyship caught me and she didn't half give me a good, hard kick in the back end.

'What are you pansying around at Wilkie?' She said. 'I don't pay you good money to mince about talking to yourself like some loathsome, little poofter. Now get on with it you fucking halfwit.' Then she gave me another kick in the rump and made me get a move on. And I didn't half get a move on I can tell you. I didn't fancy her toe up me rump a third time. Still, when all's said and done them gardens look absolutely wonderful. Makes me feel right proud it does when I hear people walking around saying how nice it all looks. Her Ladyship takes all the credit mind. Which is only fair I suppose, considering that they're her gardens.

And the open day usually passes without any problems except for all this recent sorry business that I'm caught up in. Oh, and apart from that one time about ten year ago as well, when we had all the rain. Let me tell you about it.

You see, the week running up to the open day had been one of the wettest weeks in July that I can ever remember. Pis..., I mean tipped it down all week it did. Anyway, you know what happens to grass and weeds when it rains. They don't half shoot up. Well, I thought I were going to get a right doing off Her Ladyship due the sorry fact that I just couldn't stay on top of the place. But she were really good about it.

'Damn this weather Wilkie.' She said, 'Damn it all the way to the flames of Hades and back again.'

'Yes Ma'am.' I replied, 'Damn it!'

'I'll say damn it Wilkie,' she said, 'not you. I'll thank you to remember that when you're standing in my presence.'

'Yes Ma'am, right you are Ma'am, just so Ma'am.' I said.

'When you've quite finished simpering Wilkie, I'll continue.' She said. 'Now then, in view of the current inclement conditions I've decided to focus the energies of the entire staff regarding all matters horticultural.'

'Beg your pardon Ma'am?' I said. I mean, inclement, focus, energies, horticultural? What the blummin' 'eck were that all about?

'FOR GOD'S SAKE! YOU KNUCKLE HEADED SIMPLETON! I'M GOING TO GET THE REST OF THE STAFF TO HELP YOU WITH THE GARDEN BECAUSE IT HAS PISSED IT DOWN WITH RAIN ALL WEEK! WHY ARE YOU SUCH AN INCAPABLE FUCKING MORON WILKIE?' She shouted.

'I don't know Ma'am, I just is, sorry Ma'am, thank you Ma'am.' I said.

'Give me strength!' She said. 'Now then, I have decided although I'm certain that I shall regret it, that since you are the gardener here, albeit a slow-witted one, to put you in charge of the whole operation.'

'Oh, that's nice Ma'am,' I said, 'but begging your pardon, what's an operation?

'YOU ARSING, DRIBBLING, THICK-HEADED, FUCKING NUMBSKULL! I'M REFERRING TO THE GARDENS! THAT'S THE FUCKING OPERATION! DO YOU UNDERSTAND MAN OR WILL THE USE OF MY FISTS HELP YOU TO UNDERSTAND IT BETTER?' Ooh, she were ever so riled.

'I think I understand Ma'am. Everyone is going to help me with that grounds.' I said. 'And you're putting me in charge.'

'Finally!' She said staring up at the sky, before adding 'Now get back to work Wilkie, I've had enough of you for one morning. I'll bring the staff out this afternoon.' And with that she began to stomp off towards the house before turning and saying, 'Don't you let me down with this Wilkie. By God don't you dare let me down! Remember that you do so at your living peril. The very fires of hell itself would seem tame in comparison to the flames of my wrath if you let me down Wilkie. Do you understand that?'

'Yes Ma'am.' I said. Although I didn't let on that I didn't understand all that stuff about flames and wrath and peril and all that. Well, I could hardly believe me ears. Her Ladyship were putting me in charge, over everybody at the hall, it were like a dream. Me, Joe Wilkie, in charge of everyone. Mr and Mrs Franks, Robert and Roger, Peggy and Polly (I were going to make them cheeky beggars work and no mistake), Harvey, Mrs Partridge and of course, Meg. I were going to have her working with me.

Anyway, Her Ladyship were true to her word and just after noon she had 'em all lined up at the front of the house for a 'briefing session' as she called it. She even had His Lordship there. Poor old beggar, he looked ill to me. The wet weather always makes his chest play up you see. The rain had stopped and looking at that fine body of men and women stood there, I felt sure that we would sort them grounds out in no time. And we didn't have much time either because it were Wednesday already.

'Now then you bally shower of shite.' She said to 'em. 'As you are all no doubt aware, this coming Sunday is open day. *STAND STILL!* YOU PATHETIC OLD FART!' She suddenly bellowed as His Lordship had one of his coughing fits. 'That's better, I don't want to listen to you hacking your rancid, old guts up when I'm giving orders to the staff. Now where was I? Oh yes, the gardens are not ready. However, I attribute this to the recent bad weather and not to the fact that Wilkie, here, is, a total and utter moron, although he is one anyway, as I'm sure you are all aware.' That embarrassed me that did. I weren't after compliments, but it were nice of her to say so all the same. 'However,' She went on. 'Wilkie *is* the gardener and knows these grounds better than anyone. I have therefore decided to put him in charge of you all and assign tasks to each of you in order to get this place up to scratch. Any questions? No? Good! All yours Wilkie.' Then she stomped off muttering various threats about what would happen to me if I failed in the task.

The problem now were that I didn't know exactly what to do. I'd never been in charge of anyone before, let alone a whole load of people like this.

I looked at 'em and they looked back at me. After a minute or two, and I have to say Robert, Roger, Peggy and Polly were acting very childish and giggling a lot during that time, Mr Franks finally said 'What do you want us all doing Joe?'

Well, I thought about it for a while. What needed doing the most? The weeds! That were it! There were blummin' no end of 'em after all that rain.

'The weeds.' I said with a grin. 'We need to get on with the weeds.'

'Ok Joe', said Mr Franks. 'Where shall we start?'

'Erm, anywhere. I suppose.' I said.

'Why don't you put us into teams of two and give each team its own specific area to work in.' Said Mr Franks. To this day I have no idea what a specific area is but it was kind of him to suggest it all the same. I thought the flower beds would be a better idea though.

'Good idea.' Said Harvey who seemed very keen on the idea. 'Me and Veronica (that's Mrs Partridge) will be one team, where do you want us?'

'Oh yes Joe,' said Mrs Partridge. 'Me and Harvey will make a great team. I can't wait to get down to it.' Well, I were so pleased with their enthesi... emthunis... enthumnisa...

...They were so keen to get on, like.

So, I decided to put 'em to work on the long rose bed at the front of the house. They had to go and get into their old clothes first of course. They were a long time doing that and all, but they seemed so happy and smiling when they finally came back that I thought I wouldn't say anything about it.

As for the other teams, I put Robert and Peggy together, Roger and Polly together and Mr and Mrs Franks together and gave 'em all a flower bed to get on with. This meant of course that I were left to work with Meg. And I'm not ashamed to admit that I planned the whole thing of course. As for His Lordship, I took pity on the old boy and sent him down to the vegetable garden to smoke his pipe and have a bit of a kip.

So, we all got to work. I had to keep checking on Robert, Roger, Peggy and Polly due to the fact that they kept beggaring about and disappearing.

I caught Robert and Peggy in me shed at one point and it didn't end well for them. I went down to see if His Lordship were alright and found him asleep on a bale of peat in one of the greenhouses, so I left him there. Then, as I were walking past me shed I heard a lot of giggling and the like and then Peggy's voice saying, 'Ooh Robert, what a massive great tool you've got.' Well, I had already given 'em all hoes and trowels and such like so what he had got his hands on I didn't know. And then I heard him say that he'd never seen a pair of tits quite like them before. I didn't know he were into bird watching, actually, I didn't know either that tits flew in pairs. Anyway, I went to open the door but the silly beggar had bolted it from the inside. 'Ere!' I shouted, banging on the door. 'What are you doing in there Robert? Open this door.' Then there were a load more giggling and I heard Robert shout 'Hold on Wilkie.' After about half a minute they both came out.

'I'll thank you to keep out of me shed Robert.' I told him.

'Oh, keep your friggin' hair on.' He said. That were a silly thing to say I thought. How could me hair fall off?

'And keep your hands off me tools.' I told him and at that point Peggy suddenly burst out giggling, stuck her tongue out at me and ran off.

'May I remind you Robert that Her Ladyship has put me in charge and I don't think she'd be none too happy if I told her that you and Peggy were skiving off down here.' I said trying to sound as big and as important as I could.

Well, what happened next took me right by surprise. Robert grabbed me by the hair, pushed me up against the side of me shed, shoved his face to within an inch of mine and said, 'If you breathe a word to that fat old bitch I'll give you a right fucking pasting, do you understand thickie?'

I understood exactly what he meant because I know better than most what a pasting is and I didn't want one. However, what Robert didn't understand were that Her Ladyship had come down to the garden to find me and were now standing behind him gripping a very scared looking

Peggy firmly by the arm with one hand and clenching the other tightly into a fist.

'I TAKE IT THAT YOU ARE REFERRING TO ME?' She roared. I don't know whether or not Robert messed himself at that point but I know I would have.

'M-M-M…' He stuttered, letting go of me hair and shaking as he turned to face her.

'MA'AM! YES ROBERT, IT'S ME, THE FAT OLD BITCH, EH?' And blimey her face were blummin' crimson with rage.

'I-I-I…' He began to say. Horrible to see it were. I never saw a man start to shake quite so much as that before.

'SHUT YOUR DISGUSTING MOUTH YOU DISGUSTING WRETCH! I DON'T KNOW EXACTLY WHAT THE HELL YOU AND THIS GIGGLING BLOODY FLOOSIE WERE DOING BUT I'M DAMN CERTAIN THAT IT WASN'T GARDENING! HOW DARE YOU INTERFERE WITH THE MAIDS? HOW DARE YOU THREATEN WILKIE? AND HOW DARE YOU REFER TO ME AS A FAT OLD BITCH? WELL LET ME TELL YOU THIS FOR NOTHING YOU FUCKING, SNIVELLING, LITTLE BASTARD. IF YOU AND THIS SLATTERN ARE NOT OFF MY PROPERTY WITHIN FIVE MINUTES THEN THIS FAT OLD BITCH IS GOING TO KNOCK A HUNDRED DIFFERENT SHADES OF SHIT OUT OF YOU! NOW BOTH OF YOU GET OUT OF MY FUCKING SIGHT AND NEVER DARKEN MY DOORSTEP EVER AGAIN!' *She Shouted so loud and for so long that she had to draw in a great deep breath at the end of it.*

Well, I never seen anyone run as fast as that pair but she still managed to catch him up the rump with her boot as he flew past her. And that were it. They were both sacked there and then. Her Ladyship helped me to me feet, because I'd slid down the side of the shed, and made sure I were alright. I'd never known her to be so caring like that before.

'I've had my eye on him and that other slack-jawed layabout that he works with for some time now.' She said. And that were the last she or anyone else ever spoke on the matter. We were all too scared to mention it again to her. After that she took charge of the garden saying that, 'Although you are quite adept at gardening yourself, Wilkie, your man management skills are at best non-existent and at worst the most pitiful display of leadership that I have ever encountered in my entire life.' I didn't know what she meant by that but to be honest I were glad not to be in charge anymore even though it meant that I were no longer working with Meg. Oh well. That's life I suppose.

Oh, and I forgot to mention that His Lordship got a right rollicking off her as well when she found him laying fast asleep in the greenhouse. Threatened him with all sorts she did.

After that the work seemed to go a lot better and sure enough by Sunday the place were looking as grand as ever. And that Sunday were hot. Not a cloud in the sky. Just glorious sunshine all day. Loads of people came and they all seemed to enjoy the gardens. I got a good telling off at one point after I accidentally broke a window in one of the cars that came to visit. Belonged to a young couple as I recall. I were only trying to help. This big old woodpigeon landed on the roof of the car and you know what a mess them beggars can make. Well, I didn't think straight. It had been a long day after all and when I saw that pigeon I just picked up a pebble and threw it. I reckon you can guess what happened. I never were a very good shot with a stone. Her Ladyship made me apologise and of course the damages, which she paid for at the time, were taken out of me wages and I were given a good and proper dressing down in front of that young couple, although the young lady, who was quite pretty really, did give me a nice smile when they left which was kind of her.

Otherwise, the whole day went very well and one bit of good news were that Her Ladyship gave Peggy a second chance and took her back a week later and I must say, she's been a lot more grown up ever since. You see,

Her Ladyship has got a heart after all. Robert never came back though and I heard he took a job as a farm hand at Stuffham and got a girl in the village pregnant. Also, Her Ladyship didn't take anyone else on and the day after the open day she didn't half get tore into Mrs Partridge and told her that if she didn't 'pull her finger out, spend less time on her back with her legs in the air and her ankles behind her ears and start to pull her weight in the stables' then she could pack her bags as well. I don't know what that were all about and quite frankly it's none of my business either.

Other than that, and of course this year, the open day has always gone well. And like I said. It's always nice to hear the things people say about all my hard work.

Yes, I'm always as busy as can be during the Summer. Her Ladyship won't stand to see weeds in her rose beds for a minute and them lawns have to be mown every week except that blummin' croquet lawn which I have to do twice a week. Her ladyship insists on it.

'Nothing less than perfection with my croquet lawn Wilkie.' She always tells me. 'Nothing less than perfection. By God!'

'Yes Ma'am, right you are Ma'am.' I say.

'Oh, do stop pandering, you lily-livered wimp.' She says.

And she watches me do it as well. Stands there yelling instructions at me she does.

'FOR THE LOVE OF GOD SLOW DOWN MAN! IT'S A CROQUET LAWN NOT A BLOODY RUGBY PITCH!' She says, and *'BY GOD WILKIE IF YOU SO MUCH AS SCUFF ONE INCH OF THAT TURF I'LL SCUFF YOUR ARSE WITH THE TOE END OF MY BOOT!'*

But I don't mind. Her Ladyship is very keen on a game of croquet. Takes it very seriously I can tell you. Anyone would think she were playing for money the way she goes on. Personally, I've never understood the game but then I'm not one of your refined upper classes like Her Ladyship and her mates.

They all get together about once a fortnight during the Summer to have a little open-air dinner party, weather and flies permitting, and then they have a round or two of croquet followed by a few brandies in the drawing room. Of course, when I say a few I mean bottles. I've often wondered why Her Ladyship calls it the drawing room. She never does any drawing in there. She don't even do her writing in there; she's got the study for that. Anyway, at these croquet parties, as she chooses to call 'em, there's usually the same guests every time. There's Her Ladyship of course and sometimes she lets His Lordship take part as well, but not always. Then there's Her Ladyship's oldest friend, Miss Amelia Horton, and she's a blummin' big woman and all. Built like Her Ladyship but a few inches shorter in height. Harvey made up one of them limerick things about her. It goes like this:

There were an old lady called Horton

Who had one long tit and one short 'un

Not only that...

...erm...

...Hang on a sec...

...Da da da da da, da da da da da...

No, sorry, it's gone. Anyway, it's really funny. I just can't remember how it goes off hand. Now then where were I. Oh yes, Miss Horton. Her and Her Ladyship go back a long way. Old public school friends they are, though sometimes you'd think otherwise when the pair of 'em get into a row over something.

Hang on! I've got it now. I can't remember the middle bit but it finishes with - And a fart like a 500 Norton! I don't know what a Norton is but the fart bit always makes me laugh. Farts *are* quite funny aren't they?

Anyway, who else is there now? Well she invites Major Brimmish and he usually comes along but he tends to leave early to go on patrol or night watch. The vicar, Nick, gets an invite too and he always does his best to attend. Him and Her Ladyship don't see eye to eye on a lot of things but she invites him because Reverend Menn used to come and she thinks that it's a good thing to have the clergy in the house now and again. Then there's Mr and Mrs Fagg-Doubt who own a fair bit of land around these parts. Mr Fagg-Doubt is a good deal older than his dear lady wife, by about sixty years, and he quite often falls asleep during the croquet parties. He once fell asleep whilst he were about to take a shot. It took everyone five minutes to realise. They thought he were just being careful. Some reckon that Mrs Fagg-Doubt married the old boy just for his money. I mean, she's got some figure the lass has. Legs like a blummin' thoroughbred racehorse and long blonde hair which she has all piled up in a fancy style. Looks more like his daughter than his missus she does. But why would you marry an old bloke like that just for money? There's more to life than money, some people forget that. But not me! Oh no, I'm going to marry Meg because I love her.

And then finally there's Lord Elppus and his cousin, the ballet dancer Dame Ann Buggarett. She's very small and thin but he's quite a large and loud sort of gentleman is Lord Elppus. Hair the colour of the church roof that sticks up on end like a cockerel and a booming great deep voice. They reckon, although it's just a rumour mind, that Her Ladyship and Lord Elppus were once romantically involved. You know, keen on each other. I find that hard to believe but strange things happen, don't they? Meg reckons that Her Ladyship has still got a soft spot for him. I don't know where though, she's built like a brick wall. There's no soft spots on her. Anyway, that's usually the guest list. And of course, some of us servants have to be there as well.

Now, like I said, Her Ladyship is a real demon with the croquet mallet. In fact, she's threatened to crack me head open with one on more than one occasion when I've not set the hoops out right. Most times it comes down to Her Ladyship and Miss Horton going neck and neck to see who'll win. Gets very intense it does I can tell you. I'll never forget that time Her Ladyship and Miss Horton nearly went toe to toe just cause Miss Horton took an extra shot when she shouldn't have. Her Ladyship called her a 'cheating schemer', which of course Miss Horton took offence to and called Her Ladyship a 'Loud mouthed, flatulent, overbearing bully and always have been.'

Well, they argued and ranted and raved at one another for best part of twenty minutes with the vicar trying to calm them down. Then it got really heated and they circled each other like a pair of old rutting rams before Lord Elppus waded in between 'em to break it up only for Her Ladyship and old woman Horton to both throw a punch at each other at exactly the same time as he got in the middle. Went down like a ton of bricks he did. How his jaw didn't break I'll never know. Took him ten minutes to come back round by which time they'd both calmed down and shook hands. He were alright though. Just a bit of what's known as con-cushion.

Now then, other than the open day and all that croquet, the most important day for the rest of the village in the Summer is of course the annual village fete. Now, *that* is something to look forward to. There's everything you could think off. Flower and vegetable show, which Her Ladyship has won several prizes in. The jam and cake show. I like that one I do. Partial to a nice bit of Victoria sponge cake I am. Then they have all sorts of games and stuff like tombola and raffles and shove ha'penny. All sorts. Even splat-the-rat, although they don't use a real rat of course. And there's welly wanging, that's where you throw an old welly as far as you can and who ever throws it furthest wins a crate of Fartleberrys beer. I had one hit me on the back of the head once. A welly I mean, not a beer bottle. I didn't mind. It were old Mr Cummings and he didn't mean it. And then there's skittles, hog roast, darts, hoopla, bale tossing, you name it, they got it. And, not forgetting, the Morris men again and one time they had a folk singer. I went to listen to him but it sounded like a bunch of blummin' old nonsense to me. Most of his songs were about someone or other dying or were called things like 'Ho! The Roving Beggar-man Now' or 'Ho! The Prancing Peacock Now' or 'Ho! The Leaping Salmon Now.' In fact, most of his song titles started with 'Ho!' and ended with 'Now.' I stuck it to the end though so as not to appear rude.

And of course, Bob McKenzie organises a beer tent. It's great. but we had a spot of bother with some lads from Cockwright a couple of years ago. Got 'emselves well larruped they did. Full of ale they were. Then they went and started a load of trouble at the wet sponge throwing game. You know the sort of thing I mean. They have these wooden stocks with some poor beggar locked into 'em and people pay to throw wet sponges at him and the money goes towards the church roof fund. Anyway, guess who were in it at the time? That's right! Me! Well, these Cockwright lads rolled up, swearing and jeering and creating a fuss and old Mrs Fogarty who were in charge of the stall went off to fetch someone to speak to 'em like and tell 'em to calm down. What she didn't know were that they'd nicked a tray of eggs from one of the produce stalls. By the time Mrs Fogarty got back with Nick and one or two others I looked a right blummin' mess. Plastered with eggs I were. Free range mind you, from the farm at Dammitt. I had to go home and have a wash. Farmer Bull saw me and burst out laughing and called me 'Fucking pathetic' before walking off again but Nick let me out of the stocks so I could go and get cleaned up. Jim Booth took the mickey out of me for weeks over that. Kept calling me 'Eggy.' I'm just glad they hadn't nicked anything from the tombola because all the prizes there were either tins or bottles. A tin of beans would have come keen I know. Still, some of the other blokes found them Cockwright lads and a fight broke out which I'm pleased to say the Blessham blokes won and the Cockwright lads scarpered pretty smartish. Serves 'em right, I say.

The fete is opened of course by Her Ladyship, seeing as how her veg is entered in the show. She gives a bit of a speech to start with telling everybody to 'Damn well enjoy yourselves' but always finishes by reminding everybody that if she catches 'em on her property she will not be held responsible for the consequences. Then she leaves. You know, Morris men and all that. But the rest of us think it's a grand day out.

I remember one year they had a kissing booth. Right blummin' palaver that were. Upset me it did. Now to start with I weren't too sure what a kissing booth were. I thought for a while that it meant kissing one of the Booths and I weren't going to kiss Jim Booth, no way. I mean his sister, Ruth, is not a bad looking lass but I didn't much fancy kissing her either to be honest. It turned out though that it were a little room with a curtain in front where you paid a pound, towards the church roof, and then you got to kiss which ever girl were in there. Now, as you can probably guess, there were only one girl that I wanted to kiss and that were Meg, the love of me life.

Anyway, all the young lasses were taking it in turns to do half an hour each and Meg weren't on till late afternoon. Well, I know it sounds funny and you'll think I'm soft in the head, but I were so excited at the thought of kissing Meg in that there booth that I practised for a while the night before on the bathroom mirror. I wanted it to be just right. Also, I were planning on spending at least a tenner in that booth. I tell you I could hardly wait. Anyway, the next day came around. I reckon I didn't sleep a wink the night before I were so excited. Well, the fete started, Her Ladyship said her piece, hurled some verbal abuse at the Morris men ('Fucking gang of prancing shirt-lifters' I think it were) and left and the fun and games began. I went down to the kissing booth to have a look. Of course, Jim Booth and his mates were there all queuing up to have a go. Sally Firth were the one in the booth giving the kisses at that point. I like Sal, and she's a fine-looking lass, but I weren't going to waste me money. Meg were the one I wanted.

The booth itself were like an old Punch and Judy stand with love hearts painted on it and a curtain across the little window at the front. You got in the queue until you come to your turn, then you rang a little bell, the girl inside opened the curtain, you paid her a pound and then she gave you a kiss. I heard Boothy ask Sally 'How much for a blow job?' What a daft beggar he is. What did he think it were, an hairdressers? All his mates laughed at him and so did I until he poked me in the eye and told me in no uncertain terms what he were going to do if I didn't leave. So, I left.

Sally looked a bit embarrassed and I should think so, she's a vets assistant not a blummin' hairdresser. Anyway, I decided that there were no point hanging around waiting, Meg weren't going to be on until later. I saw her in the beer tent and told her that I were looking forward to the kissing booth. 'Oh, er... lovely... Joe, that'll be er... nice.' She said. That got me even more excited, the fact that she were looking forward to it as well. Can you believe I nearly went perfectly normal as I were thinking about it?

Well, the day really seemed to drag on. I love the fete as a rule but that day just seem to go on forever. I tried me hand at one or two of the games to try and take me mind off the kissing booth. I had a go at welly wanging and skittles and a couple of turns on the tombola. I didn't win anything though. I never blummin' do. Then at long last, I heard the church bell strike four. That were it, Meg were on at four. I ran down to the kissing booth as fast as me legs would carry me. There were a queue forming already. Understandable really what with Meg being such a good looker. There were five blokes in front of me and I tried to remain patient and got me ten quid out ready. We slowly moved forward, each one taking his turn to ring the bell and wait for those lovely lips to do their stuff. Eventually it got to my turn. I have to tell you I were shaking like a leaf in the wind I were. This were it; this were really it. I were going to kiss the beautiful girl I love, ten times.

So, you can imagine me surprise when I rang the bell, the curtain went back and there sat Mrs Byamile.

Now, Mrs Byamile might be a right handsome looking woman for her age and like I mentioned before she's got some set of bosoms on her and all, which she were showing off a bit too much in that dress I thought, but she ain't Meg and I wanted Meg.

'Hello Joe,' she said, 'give us your quid and pucker up.' Then she puckers up herself and leans forward to kiss me.

'Hang on.' I said. 'Where's Meg?'

'Meg?' She said. 'Oh yeah, she said she had to go somewhere urgent so I said I would stand in for her. Come on now Joe, don't be bashful.'

'Well,' I said. 'If it's all the same to you Mrs Byamile, I'd rather not. I were really looking forward to kissing Meg.'

'Oh, come on Joe. Don't you fancy an older woman?' She says.

'No! I don't.' I said. 'I fancy Meg.'

'Right, in that case you little prick you can sod off and it'll cost you two quid for wasting my bloody time.' She said.

I had to pay her of course. But where on earth could Meg have gone? I were very upset and I have to confess that I had a tear in me eye as I walked away. All the other blokes in the queue had a laugh at me and word soon got round the rest of the fete about what had just happened. Thankfully Jim Booth were nowhere to be seen or I'm sure he would have joined in as well. I've no idea where he was. I went straight home and cried me eyes out. Now, I know it ain't right for a grown man to cry, and Her Ladyship always says it's a sign of weakness, but that's what love does to you.

I saw Meg at work on the Monday and I asked her where she had got to. 'I... erm... had to go for a lie down Joe. I... erm... weren't feeling very well.' Poor Meg. She didn't sound very well and I could see that she were embarrassed by it too. Blummin' stupid kissing booth. That were the last time they had it though. The Women's Institute took out one of them campaigns the next year to get it stopped on what they called 'Moral grounds.' Silly really. It weren't on moral grounds at all, it were on the village green. Still, at least Jim Booth didn't get to kiss Meg either. I'm glad about that.

Of course, the other good thing about Summer is that I get two weeks off work. Unpaid of course. Can't expect Her Ladyship to pay me for doing nothing, can you? Anyway, as you may recall me saying, when I were a lad I used to go to Dammitt on me holidays to stay with me cousins, Ruby and Pearl. It were alright but they were always wanting to play girly games. You know, dressing up and dollies and such. But it were a nice house they had and me aunt and uncle were very kind people. I sometimes wished that I could stop there forever but I'm Blessham born and bred.

These days though I don't go to Dammitt for me holidays. Oh, I go to visit 'em now and then but I don't stop there. No, I like to go walking these days. I must have covered every inch of Blessham Hills in me Summer holidays. It's a good place to be on your own. It gives me time to think. I think about the Hall and the gardens. I think about me mum and where she is and what she's doing now. I think about the future and Meg. I think about that an awful lot.

Quite often I spend a lot of time praying. You know, talking to God and that. Nick says that every prayer gets answered and so I often pray that me and Meg will get married one day. But I pray about other things as well. I pray for the old man to change his way, and of course I pray that I'll see me mum again, but not that Irish jockey although, as Nick says is right, I've forgiven him. I pray for Mr Cummings and his half-right-is, which, don't *half* give him some jip at times. I've even prayed for Her Ladyship a few times. Now don't laugh, you want to give it a go sometime. You're never alone when you can talk to God, and he always gives an answer in his own way.

Meg keeps telling me to go to the seaside in the summer. I don't know though. It sounds nice and one day I will but I don't like the sound of all that strange food and stuff. And I once saw a holiday programme on the telly. This big looking, posh sounding, funny orange coloured woman were standing on this beach somewhere and it looked really hot wherever it were and she said that although it were really nice there she reckoned that you shouldn't drink the water. Well, I ask you, that's a fine thing and no mistake. Don't drink the water? What are you going to do? Drink beer all week? Who would want to go off on a foreign holiday and do that? And how are you going have a cup of tea? You make tea with water. And on top of that have you seen how much water there is abroad? No end of it, and they tell you that you can't drink it. No, I think I'll give foreign places a miss until they say you can drink the water, thank you very much.

Meg's been abroad a few times. Come to think of it she goes every year. I don't know what she sees in it meself. What can you get over there that you can't get in Blessham? Mind you she always comes back as brown as a berry. You never saw a suntan like it. Spain or Tenner-Reef I think it is where she goes. Somewhere like that anyway. I don't know where that is. Last year when she came back I heard Boothy in the pun asking her to show him her white bits. The dirty beggar. Mind you, it backfired on him when she laughed and said. 'I ain't got none.' Which of course she must have because you ain't allowed to wander around with nothing on are you?

So, I'll stick to me walking thank you very much. Sometimes I walk to Stuffham or Cockwright and once I walked to the town. Well, not all the way. I got scared after about five miles or so and turned back. They have some very strange people in towns. I've seen 'em on the telly. Pickpockets and the like. No, you're best off not going into town if you can help it. I mean, it were different when I had to go to school in the town and when Farmer Bull used to take me to the cattle market on the back of the tractor when I worked for him.

They have this great big shop in the town called a super-market. What's so super about it is anybody's guess. But you can buy all sorts of things there. Even fancy stuff that you never would see at the General Store. It's where most folk get their food shopping from but Me grandma does that for us though so it ain't a problem.

Anyway, Summertime. Ain't it grand.

7

Autumn

Autumn on the other hand can be a right old blummin' game. I mean, yes, it's nice enough when the trees turn and I ain't one to complain about a good frost or a drop of rain and overall I do like it. But it does get on me wick though when you hear all them townies on the telly oohing and aahing about the leaves falling off the trees and all the reds and yellows and browns. And they bang on about crisp, morning air and mellow fruitfulness. What a load of old cobblers they do talk. That's just part of it. Yes, the trees do look nice (for a while), lovely in fact, and the fruits are nice too (I love a nice russet) but in many ways Autumn can be a right pain in the back end at times as far as I'm concerned. And I'll tell you why.

I spend half of Autumn raking up all them red and yellow fallen leaves off Her Ladyships' lawns and the other half doing beggar all because of the blummin' rain. And then Her Ladyship gets fed up with me pottering about doing next to nothing and sends me out chopping wood for the big open fire in the drawing room or freezing me toes off plucking pheasants in me shed. I hate pheasant plucking. The maids and Roger keep laughing and saying that Meg likes a pheasant pluck now and again but she never offers to help me. Still, I suppose she's busy with the horses. Apparently, in Autumn and Winter they need a good rub down after a hard ride. Meg says that she enjoys a good rub down after a hard ride. Now that's what you call deridiction... dedirection... decerdation...

...being keen on your job.

Of course, Autumn does have good points as well. One being Bonfire Night and another being the Halloween night party at the Pig and Whistle. Other than these two events though, and blackberry crumble and custard, I get fed up with Autumn and it's fallen leaves and it's fallen apples and fallen trees and everything. Apparently in America, or so Harvey tells me, they call Autumn the Fall. I wonder why. Anyway, talking of fall, it were last Autumn that Her Ladyship had one. A fall that is. She fell off the General whilst trying to clear a seven-bar gate. We didn't realise what had happened until the General came back to the Hall on his own half an hour later. She had to walk three miles to get home and by 'eck did she give the General a going over when she got there. She stormed into the house, came out with a stout walking stick and laid into his back end with it. And I'm sorry but I just don't agree with leathering horses. It ain't right and it ain't fair and I'll tell you this, that horse were never the same after that. Although, I know for a fact that she regrets it now. But that's Her Ladyship for you. She tends to do things on the spur of the moment in anger. I mean, she loves her animals really. I reckon she thinks more of her animals than she does of people. Come to think of it she loves her plants more than people so the blummin' animals are much higher up the list. She still rode the General after that, but he just didn't seem to have the same spirit in him as before. Poor old General. You should never let your anger get the better of you I say. You've got to live with the consquinces... consquires... consequarters...

...What happens afterwards.

I took a wander up to the place where she fell the day after which were a Saturday afternoon. Quite funny it were to tell you the truth. The top two bars of the gate were smashed off and because the ground were soft you could see a good, deep mark of where she landed. She must have hit the deck with some force as well and judging by the shape of the mark and I should say that she landed flat on her back with her arms and legs all akimbo. You could easily make out the shape of her great back end in the mud and everything. I bet that beggar hurt you know. Must've took the wind out of her sails.

But, like I say, apart from giving the General that good hiding, which, to her credit, she actually said she'd never forgive herself for and I believe her, she really loves her animals. She's never happier than when she's got her horses or dogs around her. The only thing that she's anywhere as near keen on, apart from her garden and her croquet is her writing. And Autumn sees her writing much more than normal. So much so that we see a whole lot less of her at that time of year. Which I suppose is another good thing about Autumn. But as for the garden. I have me blummin' work cut out. You see, after the Summer and all that loveliness of the flowers and the open day and everything, the garden turns into a mucky, damp, dead leaf covered mess. And I end up doing all the other little odd jobs around the place. I mean, I suppose I mustn't grumble because let's face it a job's a job. And I've always been very grateful for me job. But, I'm not really much of a handyman if you know what I mean. For instance, there were that time when I had to clean out the guttering all around the house. That were a day I won't forget in a hurry. It were perhaps the most terrifying thing that ever happened to me in me entire life.

It all started out well enough. It were me fourth Autumn since starting at the Hall. November it were. A week after the village bonfire party and I were still a bit sore from where one of the local young 'uns had pushed a used sparkler down the back of me trousers as I was bending down to pick up a piece of treacle toffee I'd dropped. Anyway, I were starting to get over the worst of it. It were a very dull day as I recall and there were quite a heavy mist around the village. I'd got meself a second-hand bike by this time although I couldn't ride it just then because of the blister between the crack of me back end. Anyway, it were a right old miserable day and me coat were soaked with the mist by the time I'd walked to work. And I knew that I would be raking leaves up to start with due to the fact that it had been very windy during the early part of the night. I'd listened to it as I lay face down in me bed knowing what I were going to be doing first thing.

Anyway, sure enough there were plenty of leaves on the lawns and so I cracked on with it, if you'll pardon the phrase. Cracked, I mean. Get it? Crack... cracked? Sorry, I never were any good at jokes. Anyway, there I were, grass rake in hand, working away and who should come stamping across the lawn but Her Ladyship.

'MORNING WILKIE!' She called.

'Morning Ma'am.' I replied as she got nearer.

'Lawns are a damned, bally mess this morning, what?' She said.

'Yes Ma'am.' I said, 'I thought I'd better get stuck into 'em right away.'

'Yes, yes,' She said nodding in agreement, 'quite so, and as soon as you've finished that Wilkie I've another little job that I'd like you to do for me.'

'Yes Ma'am,' I said, 'Whatever you say Ma'am. What exactly would that be?'

'The guttering.' She said.

'The guttering?' I said.

'The guttering.' She said.

'The guttering?' I repeated.

'Wilkie.' She said.

'Yes Ma'am.' I said.

'STOP BALLY WELL REPEATING EVERYTHING THAT I SAY YOU PRATTLING IDIOT! IF THERE'S ONE THING THAT I CAN'T STAND IT'S PEOPLE WHO HAVEN'T THE INTELLIGENCE TO SAY ANYTHING ELSE SO THEY JUST KEEP REPEATING EVERYTHING THAT I'VE SAID TO MAKE THEMSELVES SOUND CLEVER! BY GOD WILKIE IF I DIDN'T KNOW BETTER I'D SWEAR YOU WERE TRYING TO EXTRACT THE URINE OUT OF ME!' She bellowed, splashing me face with small droplets of spit as she shouted.

'Oh no Ma'am,' I said, even though I'd never heard of urine before, 'it's just that...'

'IT'S JUST WHAT? COME ON, SPIT IT OUT MAN! WHAT IS IT? I HAVEN'T GOT ALL FUCKING DAY!' She said.

'Well Ma'am, I've... well... you see...' I were struggling for the right words.

'OH, FOR PITY'S SAKE WILKIE GET ON WITH IT. I'M NOT IN THE BEST OF MOODS AS IT IS MAN! NOW EITHER SAY IT OR BY THUNDER I'LL KNOCK YOU DOWN, *WHERE YOU STAND!'* She roared.

I were now feeling somewhat fearful it has to be said. You see the thing were that I'd never had anything to do with guttering before and I didn't want Her Ladyship to think that I were an even bigger idiot than what she already took me for, which were a pretty big blummin' idiot.

'Begging your pardon Ma'am.' I said plucking up all the courage I could muster, 'But I've never had anything to do with guttering before.'

'Wilkie.' She said in that terrible low growl she uses when she's really expasterated... eggsaxpertated... expatriated...

...at her wits end with me.

'Yes Ma'am.' I said.

'You are a bigger idiot than I ever took you for.' She said, pinching the top of her nose between finger and thumb and shaking her head as if in disbelief at what I'd said.

'Yes Ma'am.' Were all I could think of to say. So, she did think I were a bigger idiot than she already took me for after all.

'Is that all you can think of to say?' She asked.

'I don't know Ma'am.' I said. Which of course I have to admit were a complete lie because like I just said that really were all I could think of to say.

'There are times Wilkie,' she said, 'when I really, honestly believe that I could actually throttle the very life breath from out of your lungs with my own bare hands. However, I realise that you are an uneducated ignoramus and little more than the local village idiot so on this occasion I will give you the benefit of the doubt. But by God Wilkie know this, my patience with you this morning is rapidly wearing thin.'

'Thank you Ma'am.' I said although I didn't have the foggiest idea what she were going on about and as far as I and most folks round here are concerned, I were the village idiot! Well, someone has to do it don't they?

'Now.' She said, clenching both fists and teeth (and for all I know her rump as well) at the same time, 'Let me explain to you about the guttering.'

'Right you are Ma'am.' I said feeling somewhat relieved at her calming down a bit although there were a certain something in the tone of her voice that made me think she might go berserk again at any minute and I didn't want to be on the wrong end of them fists if she kicked off.

'It's really quite simple.' She went on. 'All you have to do is fetch the big ladder out of the garage. Prop it up against the house. Extend it until you reach the top of the house. Climb up it. Clear all the leaves and moss and crap out of the guttering as far as you can reach, with a trowel. Then come down. Move the ladder along and repeat the process. Then keep going until you have gone all the way around the house, front and back. Do you understand? Or am I forced into pulverising it into your thick, ugly, clumsy looking head with my knuckles?'

'Yes, I think I understand Ma'am.' I said. 'You want me to get the ladder and a trowel and clean out the guttering.'

'Oh, for the love of God.' She moaned clasping her huge face with both hands. 'Yes Wilkie, that's right. I want you to clean the guttering out with the fucking ladder and a fucking trowel.'

'Righto!' I said. 'But, there is one other thing Ma'am.'

'Yes Wilkie, what is it?' She asked with a sigh.

'Well Ma'am,' I said, 'It's just that, well, I've got rather a painful blister at the moment and I'm a bit worried about bursting it.'

'A blister?' She said.

'Yes Ma'am.' I said. 'In rather an awkward place.'

'Awkward?' She said.

'Yes Ma'am.' I said, 'Very awkward.'

'I see.' She said. 'And where exactly is this awkward place?'

'Well, begging your pardon Ma'am,' I continued, 'it's right between me cheeks.'

She then shoved her great, terrible features to about a hand span away from me face and stared at me as if she were searching for something.

'I see no blister.' She said after a short while.

'Oh no Ma'am.' I said. 'It's not on me face.'

'But you said it was between your cheeks Wilkie.' She said.

'But I didn't mean those cheeks Ma'am.' I explained. 'What I meant were, well, you know, me erm, err, well...'

'Well what?' She demanded and I could tell she were losing her patience again.

'Well, if you'll pardon the phrase Ma'am.' I said. 'I meant me rump cheeks.'

She continued to stare at me for what seemed like ages and then she said, 'Are you referring to your buttocks Wilkie?'

'Buttocks Ma'am?' I said. I'd never heard of the word buttocks before.

'THESE!' She shouted, turning and clasping her own huge great rump cheeks in her huge great hands.

'If that's what you want to call 'em Ma'am,' I said, 'then yes. Me buttocks.'

'Wilkie...' She said.

'Yes Ma'am.' I said, and I knew what were coming.

'YOU'LL HAVE A FINE SET OF BRUISES TO COMPLIMENT YOUR BLASTED BLOODY BLISTER BY THE TIME I'VE FINISHED WITH YOU, YOU VACANT, ECHOING WASTE OF SPACE! I'LL GIVE YOU BLISTERS BY GOD! IF YOU HAVEN'T STARTED THAT GUTTERING BY THE TIME I GET BACK WITH THE DOGS SO HELP ME I'LL SWING FOR YOU! I'M GOING TO CUT MYSELF A GOOD, YOUNG ELDER SHOOT WHILST I'M IN THE WOODS AND IF YOU'RE STILL PONCING ABOUT WITH THESE LEAVES WHEN I RETURN THEN I'M GOING TO DRIVE YOU OFF THESE GROUNDS WITH IT AND THAT WILL BE THE VERY LAST TIME YOU EVER SET FOOT ON MY PROPERTY AGAIN! *DO YOU BLOODY WELL HEAR ME WILKIE?'* She screamed.

'Yes Ma'am.' I said and I started raking them leaves like a madman for I honestly believed she would have done it.

Anyway, off she went for her morning walk with the dogs and I knew that I'd only have about an hour or so to get done with the lawns and get on with the guttering before she came back. I raked like I'd never raked before. Sweat were pouring down me back and I soon had to fling me jacket off. Me blister were throbbing something rotten but I tried not to think about it. It were as if I could almost feel the swipes of that elder shoot and hear her raining curses down upon me along with it. Every now and then I heard the dogs barking and crashing around through the bracken in the woods but I pushed the noise out of me mind and raked for all I were worth. Which weren't much according to Her Ladyship.

I got it done though and got the ladder out and against the side of the house with only minutes to spare. Thankfully Meg got Robert and Roger to give me a hand which were good because it were a great big heavy thing it were. It were like three ladders in one and it were made of that alimio... amiluminim... amolimino...

...One of them ones made of that shiny metal.

And the beggar took some lifting up as well. You have to push all three parts of the ladder up until it makes one great long one. It only just reached to the top of the house. I never realised how high the Hall were until that day. Anyway, I got some bin bags and a trowel and started to climb that ladder. Now, I've climbed loads of trees in my time but I'd never climbed a ladder before. Well, not like that one. Farmer Bull used to have one in his grain store but it were only a short wooden one about four feet high and it were inside of course. This beggar though were something else. It rocked and swayed with every step I took. Three times I had to come back down because the whole thing moved a bit at the bottom. The patio at the front of the Hall, you see, is made of them Yorkshire flagstones and were covered in this green, slimy stuff and were a bit slippery and this made the ladder slide backwards now and then. Me innards began to loosen and I thought I were going to fill me britches a few times I can tell you. I mean, like I say, I've climbed more trees than any other man I know but this were a different blummin' thing altogether. I gripped every rung of that ladder as if me very life depended on it. I must have been as white as a sheet. Although, the sheets that I have on me bed at home tend to be more of an off-white colour. Well, more sort of brownish really which were also what my underpants were close to being. Anyway, I just managed to get to the top of the ladder as Her Ladyship returned. And sure enough she were true to her word and had a nasty looking, thin, young elder branch in her hand.

'That's more like it Wilkie.' She said staring up at me as I clung on to that metal ladder for all I were worth. 'About time you started acting like a man. I want those gutters cleaned out properly now,' She said with a rather nasty grin, 'or else...' And she swiped that elder branch through the air a couple of times as a warning like, which I have to confess made the hair on the back of me neck stand on end even though I could tell that she had calmed down an 'eck of a lot.

'Yes Ma'am.' I answered unable to hide the shaking fear in me voice.

'You should be done by Midday Wilkie.' She said. 'And as soon as you've finished there's another little job that I'd like you to attend to.'

'Yes Ma'am.' I said with me voice all of a tremble. 'What would that be?'

'One of the dogs, I think it was Nero here, has crapped right in the middle of the croquet lawn.' She said with a loud laugh as she patted Nero on the head. 'Be so good as to remove it Wilkie, before it burns the grass.'

'Yes Ma'am.' I said.

'And one other thing Wilkie.' She said.

'Yes Ma'am.' I said.

'I was just thinking about our conversation earlier about that blister of yours.' She said.

'Yes Ma'am.' I said.

'How on earth did you get it man?' She asked with a puzzled look on her face.

'One of the local children put a used sparkler down the back of me trousers at last week's bonfire party Ma'am.' I said.

'BY THUNDER!' She roared. 'The young bastard! How are these children being raised these days? That would never have happened when I was a child. The scoundrel. I blame the parents of course. Let the little brutes get away with murder they do. Oh, if only I had my way with them. Bring back the cane. That's what's needed. The rod! Regularly, hard and unspared! It never did me any harm, never! By all the heavens I'm going to go and write a letter to our Member of Parliament straight away and insist on the return of corporal punishment in the schools. You really ought to get that blister looked at Wilkie.'

'Yes Ma'am.' I said although she lost me with most of except that bit about the cane. I don't know about Her Ladyship but I can remember whenever I got it off old Rodwell it did *me* a lot of harm to me rump.

'Well, I'll get on with that and leave you to it.' She said and then she were gone.

I tell you I breathed a sigh of relief and waited a few minutes to pluck up the courage to start cleaning out the gutter. And what a state it were in. It were full of moss and leaves and bird muck and all sorts of stuff. And stink! It stank something awful. I thought I were going to spew for a minute but I managed to hold it down. Me blister were throbbing really badly too and to be honest I didn't feel very well at all. I think that after all that sweating whilst raking up the leaves I were starting to catch a chill.

Anyway, after a little while I made a start. It were slow going and I began to worry that I wouldn't get it done in time. Midday Her Ladyship had said. The way I were going I'd be lucky to finish by Midnight. It took me the best part of an hour and a half just to go along the front of the house. I were shaking like a leaf going up and down that ladder and every time I cleaned a bit of gutter I had to reach as far as I could which frightened the life out of me. Anyway, it were just as I got to the end of the front of the house that it happened.

Me ladder were about three foot or so away from the corner of the roof and I'd just about got brave enough about being up there. So, I thought to meself, 'If I stretch far enough, I'll get that last bit without having to move the ladder again. Then I'd go and have a quick cup of tea before starting the back of the house.' That were me plan at any rate. So I reached as far as I could and dug the moss and leaves out. Unfortunately, I hit a bolt that were holding the guttering onto the wall and me trowel went spinning out of me hand. Of course, like the blummin' idiot that I am, I tried to catch it. I'm beggared if I know what happened next but all of a sudden the ladder were gone with an 'eck of a great clatter and I were hanging onto the guttering with both hands with me legs going like mad trying to get a foot hold and I swear I don't know how I did it but I somehow managed to scramble up and onto the roof of the house where I laid on me back shaking for quite a while. How I didn't papper me kecks I'll never know to this day.

Anyway, the roof were dead slippery like and after a while I started to slide down it. So in me panic I started scrambling about trying to work me way further up the roof. This worked a treat although it did send a couple of tiles flying off. Good job there were no beggar down below or they'd have been killed, I reckon. But I kept scrambling and eventually, don't ask me how, I reached the very top of the house. I swung me leg over so that I were straddling the roof and I felt sure then that I weren't going to fall. The only trouble were that by doing that I burst me blister and that beggar really hurt I can tell you. And I when I say really hurt I mean *really* hurt. Didn't half make me yelp. I tried to think what I should do next. Sadly, at that point, it started to rain and in no time at all I were soaked to the blummin' skin and there were only one thing for it so I shouted for help. *'HELP!'* I shouted. But no one came.

'HELP ME. SOMEBODY PLEASE HELP ME! I'M STUCK ON THE BLUMMIN' ROOF' I shouted again as loud as I could. But still no one came.

I were blummin' well drenched by this time, so I kept shouting and hoping that someone would hear me. I knew that Meg and the two lads were out with some of the horses and they were always gone for ages. Kennedy the chauffeur had taken the car into town, Harvey would either be checking on the pheasants or with Mrs Partridge and all of the staff inside the house would be busy. I started to think that I would be doomed to spend all day up there but then who should I see out of the corner of me eye but His Lordship, in his coat and Sowester, sneaking down to the vegetable garden for a crafty pipe.

'*SIR!*' I called out. Because that's what we had to call him, Sir. Although Her Ladyship never called him it. I couldn't repeat what Her Ladyship often called him. It were always very dogerity... derugoty... dragoonery...

...not very nice

Anyway, he stopped and started looking around to see who had shouted. *'IT'S ME SIR, WILKIE. I'M STUCK ON THE ROOF!'* I cried.

He looked up and saw me, his mouth fell open in surprise and then he ran back to the house as fast as his legs could carry him. Which weren't very fast it has to be said. In fact, it were more of a sort of funny kind of scuttle really than a run but at least he had seen me and I would soon be saved at last.

'Don't worry Wilkie, we'll get you down.' He said as he drew near and then he disappeared into the house. He came out seconds later with Her Ladyship, Mr Franks and the two maids and by 'eck she were none too pleased I could tell.

'WHAT THE HELL IS THE MEANING OF THIS WILKIE?' She demanded.

'The ladder fell Ma'am.' I said, with me voice trembling.

'BY GOD!' She roared and she stamped over to where the ladder lay and in a matter of seconds her powerful arms had got it back up against the house.

'Right,' she said, 'get back down here you snivelling, little pus-filled wretch.'

'I can't Ma'am.' I said.

'Why not for crying out loud?' She asked.

'Because I'm scared Ma'am.' I said and I burst into tears. You see I were now scared of two things. Firstly, of falling to me death and secondly of what might happen when she got her hands on me.

'Get down I tell you. *THIS FUCKING INSTANT!*' She screeched.

'I can't.' I sobbed. 'I just can't.'

'IF YOU DON'T GET DOWN HERE RIGHT NOW, *THEN SO HELP ME GOD I'M GOING TO COME UP THERE AND THROW YOU DOWN!*' She raged.

'I think perhaps we ought to call the Fire Brigade.' His Lordship suggested timidly.

'WHAT? WHO ASKED YOU?' She bellowed in his face. 'I didn't ask for your whining, wheezing, weaselly opinion did I? No! Right, so, when I want shit out of you I'll squeeze your stupid, pathetic, little head. We don't need the bally Fire Brigade. I'll get the idiot down.' And with that she started to come up the ladder. Came up it like a flaming great gorilla she did, cursing and swearing as she climbed. Anyway, she soon reached the top and she glared at me with such terrible hate filled eyes that I actually thought about throwing meself off and ending it all there and then. They say fear makes men do foolish things, well, I nearly did that day.

'Right, you bumbling bally oaf.' She snarled reaching out her hand. 'Come down here to me and I'll carry you down on my back.'

'I can't.' I cried.

'You'll do as I damn well tell you Wilkie! Now come here.' She ordered.

'No!' I sobbed. 'Please.'

'BY GOD!' She shouted. 'NOBODY SAYS NO TO MY FACE. RIGHT, YOU'VE DONE IT NOW WILKIE, YOU'LL LIVE TO REGRET THIS DAY FOR A LONG, LONG TIME.'

And with that she were off the ladder and crawling up the roof towards me on her hands and knees. I screamed and started to work me way along the roof to get away from her.

'Stay where you are you damned imbecile!' She hissed at me.

'Please don't hurt me Ma'am.' I begged.

'Oh, don't you worry Wilkie.' She sneered. 'I'm not going to hurt you. Not until we get back down and then I'm going to give you the biggest hammering of your despicable, worthless, insignificant life.'

Then something strange happened. Her eyes suddenly seemed to bulge out and her hands started scrabbling away like mad. Then some more of the tiles started to come away and then there were tiles flying everywhere and everyone down below had to run for cover to avoid having their heads caved in. Her legs where going ten to the dozen as well trying to get a grip with her feet on that slippery roof. And then all of a sudden her eyes bulged even further out of her head, she let out this terrible roar of *'YOU FUCKING BASTARD WILKIE!'* and then slid back down the roof. Her hands were clawing at the tiles but she only pulled more of 'em off by doing so. She just kept going and as she went she screeched and swore blue murder and all manner of oaths at me. Then the next thing you know she were at the edge and had hold of the guttering. She took a last few desperate grabs at the roof and then with a blood curdling cry of *'YOU'LL PAY FOR THIS WILKIE! I'LL SEE YOU IN HELLLLLLL!'* she were gone. Down she went. Down to the ground with a loud sort of *'O-O-O-O-O-H!'*

Luckily she managed to keep a hold of the guttering. However, unluckily, I think that when I hit that loose bolt earlier with the trowel it must have damaged it even more because it came away and down she went. Thankfully though the guttering came away piece by piece and therefore slowed her drop a bit. Although Mr Franks tells me still landed with some force and that it knocked all the wind out of her and it were the first time that he had seen her face go white like that.

The fire engine arrived forty-five minutes later and I were finally brought off the roof after several attempts at two in the afternoon.

Mrs Franks were smashing about it. She had me towelled down and wrapped in a blanket in no time, and she sat me next to the big stove in the kitchen with a nice mug of hot sweet tea. The firemen said that I should go to the hopsital to be checked for shock but I told 'em that I would be alright. I hadn't touched anything 'lectric up there so I hadn't got a shock. But I were very wet and feeling very sorry for meself. I would have liked to have had a good look at that fire engine but Mrs Franks tutted and said that I weren't up to it. Anyway, I were just starting to get the feeling back into me fingers when Mr Franks comes into the kitchen.

'Her Ladyship wants to see you now lad.' He said, and he looked very serious.

'Oh, Tom.' Said Mrs Franks. That's his first name you see, Tom. 'He's in no fit state yet.'

'Well she's hopping mad and I can't stop her when she's in this kind of a mood. Come on Joe, best get it over with.' He said.

I nodded, thanked Mrs Franks for her kindness, got up and followed Mr Franks out of the kitchen with me knees knocking. Mrs Franks wished me good luck and I were sure I were going to need it. Her Ladyship were in her study and I have to admit that my legs were all of a tremble as Mr Franks knocked on the door. I could hardly stand up straight I were trembling so much.

'COME!' She shouted. And we entered the room.

Her Ladyship were stood facing away from us, staring out of the window across the croquet lawn with her hands clasped behind her back.

'I've brought Wilkie Ma'am.' said Mr Franks.

'Thank you Franks.' She said in a sort of low growl like a dog makes if you try to take its bone away. She carried on looking out of the window and for ages there were this terrible silence. I could hardly stand it. Finally, she spoke although she didn't turn around and I noticed the big green stain on the back end of her jodhpurs from where she'd landed on the patio.

'Not only have you caused half of the roof to be destroyed, Wilkie, but you have also broken the guttering, caused the Fire Brigade to be needlessly called out and almost brought about my untimely demise. And, furthermore, you have not completed what was, for even the most simple-minded of cretins, a relatively easy task of cleaning out the guttering. What do you have to say for yourself?' She said and I did not like the tone of her voice one little bit.

'I'm sorry Ma'am.' Were all I could say. 'I'm very sorry.'

'SORRY!' She shrieked suddenly wheeling around with clenched fists and a wild look of rage on her face. *'IS THAT ALL YOU CAN SAY? SORRY! YOU PISS POOR, LIMP WRISTED HALF EXCUSE FOR A MAN! I NEARLY DIED TODAY TRYING TO SAVE YOUR POINTLESS LIFE AND ALL YOU CAN SAY IS THAT YOU'RE BALLY WELL SORRY! YOU DON'T KNOW HOW CLOSE YOU ARE TO HAVING ME KNOCK YOU THROUGH THAT WINDOW WILKIE!'* I'd never seen her that mad before. I swear her face were nearly the colour of blackcurrants.

'However,' she said, quietening down 'As much as I would enjoy doing that, believe me, I'm afraid that I am left with no other option but to terminate your employment forthwith over the matter. And I suggest you leave swiftly before I terminate something else. Namely, your life.'

'Beg your pardon Ma'am?' I said because I didn't know what words like terminate and forthwith blummin' meant.

'Oh, for the love of God! You're sacked Wilkie! Fired! Finished! Given the bullet! That's it! Kaput! I want you off my property right now. Do you understand?' She fumed.

'Yes Ma'am.' I said feeling very sorry for meself as it sunk in what she were on about.

'Erm, one moment Ma'am.' Said Mr Franks suddenly.

'Yes, Franks, what is it?' She snapped angrily.

‘Could I have a quick word with you in private Ma’am?’ He asked. ‘It won’t take long.’

‘Oh very well.’ She said, ‘Wait outside Wilkie, I haven’t quite finished bollocking you.’ So I walked out of the study with me mind all in a terrible jumble wondering what were I going to do now?

Anyway, two minutes later and the door opened and Mr Franks beckoned me in again.

‘Right Wilkie.’ Her Ladyship barked. ‘Franks here has persuaded me to give you a chance to prove and redeem yourself. And, to be fair, despite your pathetic and bungling attempt at the guttering, that nearly cost me my life, it has to be said that you do have a good way with the garden, as Franks has pointed out. I suppose it would be a shame to lose you at this point, even though you are the most slow-witted individual it has been my encumbrance to experience, though never let it be said that I’m not without clemency towards yokels, bumpkins, low I.Q’s and people on the lower rungs of the evolutionary ladder and the fringes of decent society. Therefore, you are forthwith re-instated.’

I weren’t too sure what she were on about, and I didn’t want to upset her further by asking, but I rightly guessed that she were giving me me job back again. That were a relief I can tell you.

‘However,’ she continued, ‘this incident cannot go unpunished.’ And with that she stuck her massive chest out, pushed her muscular shoulders as far back as I’ve ever seen her push them and reared up to her full height. And a more magnificent figure of a woman you would be hard pressed to find let me tell you. Anyway, she stared down at me and said ‘Joseph Wilkie, I hereby sentence you to be soundly beaten with a gym shoe. A dozen strokes, to be administered in front of rest of the entire staff. Do you have anything to say for yourself before this sentence is carried out?’

‘Erm, Ma’am!’ said Mr Franks, raising his hand.

'Oh for Heaven's sake, what now Franks?' She snapped at him again. 'Can't you see I'm in the middle of sentencing Wilkie to a damn good thrashing!'

'Erm, yes Ma'am, I can see that, but the fact of the matter is that I'm afraid you can't actually do that to him. Well, not legally at any rate.' He said.

'What? Oh, yes, of course. I forget sometimes.' She said. 'Old habits die hard and all that. Bit of the old public-school girl coming out there. I used to be a prefect you know and sometimes the mind tends to wander and drift back to the good old days. Back then a swift taste of the gym shoe would put any upstart fourth former in their place. Of course, these days the bleeding hearts and liberals...'

'Yes Ma'am.' Said Mr Franks. 'I quite understand.'

'Now then, where were we?' She said. 'Ah yes, in that case Wilkie you shall work two extra hours a day this week to clear up the bally mess you've made and to scrub the green off the front patio and by God scrub it clean, without pay of course, and the repairs to the roof and guttering shall come out of your wages at a cost of, oh let's say, ten pounds a week until it is all fully paid for. Do you agree to this? Or would you rather prefer unemployment? If so, I will, of course, have you seen off the premises by the dogs.'

Well, I could've done without losing a tenner a week but I suppose it were better than losing me job, so I agreed. And before I went home I made a point of thanking Mr Franks very much for sticking up for me. Anyway, it all turned out alright in the end. It took me almost year to pay for the repairs but the whole horrible lot were eventually forgotten by Her Ladyship and things soon got back to normal.

I never forgot it though. I never will. I still have bad dreams about it even now. I suppose that could be one of the reasons why I ain't that keen on Autumn. Because it always reminds of that awful day when I got stuck on the roof of Blessham Hall. And it cost me five hundred quid for the repairs.

Still, all's well that ends well. Me mum used to say that sometimes. She used to say lots of things though. Such as 'Oh for crying out loud Joe get out from under me feet' and 'Come on boy, get out of that bleedin' bed or you'll be late for school.' I remember all of 'em as if it were only yesterday when she said it...

Anyway, Autumn, like I said, has got two main things that stop it from being too blummin' bad. One is the village Halloween party and the other is the village bonfire party. Except when you get a sparkler shoved down your crack but so far that's only happened the once. The whole village turns out for both of these events and what a great time we always have. The Halloween party always comes first. It's held in the Pig and Whistle on the Saturday nearest to the actual day. A lot of people get dressed up for it. You know, ghosts and werewolves and vampires and such like. I don't get dressed up on account of the fact that Sally Firth told me that I didn't need to because I already looked like Frankenstein (whoever he is). Meg told her not to be so horrible but I suppose she were only trying to be helpful. And besides I don't believe in all them ghosts and ghoulies and things. I just go along for a bit of a laugh. And Bob, who always wears this red devil's outfit (which the vicar don't like and to be honest I don't blame him), organises games and competitions. I like bobbing for apples best. I'm rather good at it what with having such strong teeth. Well, I'm good at it when some beggar isn't holding me head under the water so that I can't come back up that is. That Jim Booth has got a very strange sense of humour at times. And Bob makes these fancy drinks called cocktails which are all other kinds of drink s mixed together. 'Cocktails from the Crypt' he calls 'em and he gives 'em these spooky sounding Halloween names like 'Virgin's Blood' and 'Dracula's Drop' and 'Mummy's Ruin.' I ain't worked out what these are all supposed to mean yet but I'm sure Bob will have a reason for it.

Anyway, it's a great night is the Halloween party and everyone thoroughly enjoys 'emselves. Meg normally goes dressed as a witch with this big, black pointy hat and a black cape and wearing black lipstick and nail varnish. She looks very peculiar I think but it's up to her at the end of the day. I let her borrow one of Her Ladyship's besom's as well but don't let on or Her Ladyship wouldn't be none too pleased. She'd probably take the besom to me back end.

Talking of Her Ladyship, she doesn't go to the party herself. She says that she would 'Rather be damned to spend all eternity covered in festering pus-filled sores and burning in agony in Hades than to spend even two minutes engaged in such filthy, debauched, pagan revelry as a Halloween party with a crowd of greasy, malodorous, disease-ridden, ale-fuelled commoners.' I don't think she likes Halloween. And I've often wondered what pagan means.

A lot of the local kids go and do that trick or treat thing where kids get all dressed up like right berks with silly masks and things on and knock on somebody's door and shout 'Trick or Treat!' Then the person has to give 'em something or else they get their windows put through or their front doors kicked or brake fluid over their car or something. I remember once they came round our house and the old man told 'em to 'Piss off!' Well, the next thing you know there were another knock at the door. I opened it and there were a paper bag on the doorstep that some silly beggar had set fire to. Naturally, me first thought, of course, were to stamp the flames out. It were only after I'd put it out that I realised that some dirty little so and so had put dog muck in the bag first. Worst of it were that I only had me carpet slippers on. Little sods they are round here, however there is one house that they don't bother going to and I reckon you can probably guess which one that is. That's right, Blessham Hall. Those kids may be rum beggars but they ain't that daft. I reckon that if they went round there dressed as witches and warlocks and wearing silly masks and the like, Her Ladyship would probably have 'em burned at the stake, like they used to in the olden days.

Then of course, a week later, it's bonfire night. And bonfire night means the village bonfire party. Now, apart from that episode with the sparkler being shoved down me crack, I really enjoy the bonfire party. I didn't always though. When I were a kid I were constantly bombarded for about two weeks before bonfire night with bangers and jumping jacks and roaming candles and all sorts of fireworks by Jim Booth and his mates. I don't think they were deliberately trying to hurt me, just frighten me. If that's the case then it worked a treat. It frightened the life out of me. Especially when you get one through your letter box at night when your old man is out poaching. But as I grew up they eventually stopped it. Still, I suppose having fireworks thrown at you ain't as bad as the time when they pushed me round the village in a wheelbarrow asking everyone for a penny for the Guy. I wouldn't have minded so much but they said that if I moved or spoke then I were going to get a pasting and on top of it all they made over seven quid and out of all the people they asked only three of 'em realised that it weren't a real Guy Fawkes. I were dead embarrassed I were.

These days though I really enjoy it. We hold the party on the village green where some of the local men have built the bonfire out of whatever scrap wood they can get their hands on. Old Mr Cummings always makes the real Guy for the top and Farmer Bull has the job of lighting it. Which I should imagine to be a highly dangerous job. Well, it were that time when his trousers caught fire. But then, that's the risk you take when you go chucking petrol on a bonfire after eight pints of scrumpy at the pub first. But apart from that it's always good amtoseer... amsopeer... amosphate...

...everyone gets on really well.

And we have loads of food too. We have jacket spuds and hot dogs and baked beans and mugs of soup and of course me very favourite, treacle toffee. Oooh, it makes me mouth water to even think about it. I'm going to ask Meg to bring me some if she visits me after the bonfire party. You see, it's the simple things in life that I miss the most. And I'm going to miss the fireworks too, not the sparklers mind, but all the others though. I love to see the rockets and the roaming candles and the Catherine wheels. I wonder who she is, this Catherine woman. And why does she make firework wheels? Perhaps I'll never know.

So, this will be me first Autumn in nigh on sixteen years where I've not had to rake leaves up, and do you know what? I think I'm going to miss that as well. I do wish that I weren't in here. It's dull and boring and a bit scary at times and I miss Meg and me friends. Mind you, they got heating in here so this place might be a sight warmer than Poachers Cottage in Winter.

8
Winter

You see, Winter can be a very hard time in the country. Especially in our house. We ain't got any of that fancy central heating stuff. They've got it at the Hall and like I say, they've even got it in here, which quite surprised me. I were expecting this place to be as cold as Poachers Cottage. But, it's really warm in here. Poachers Cottage on the other hand is like a blummin' ilgo – oogli – oolgi...

...one of them ice houses that them folk with furry coats live in.

Except the front room, which is the only room with a fireplace, although that means me having to spend endless hours getting firewood and chopping logs for it. The old man says he can't do it because of his back. Me mum used to say that the only thing wrong with his back were that he spent so much time on it. That used to make me laugh that did, she were a card were me mum. I miss her little jokes. Anyway, that open fire in the front room is a real blessing in the Wintertime.

We've got a 'lectric oven in the kitchen and years ago, if the old man were out poaching or down the pub, which were most nights, me mum used to turn it on full blast and we'd sit in front of it with the door open and drink big mugs of hot tea. Of course, doing that does use an awful lot of 'lectric and in the end we had the 'lectric cut off. The old man were none too chuffed when he saw the' lectric bill. He gave me mum a right helping of fist that day I can tell you. Blackened her eye the blummin' rotten old so-and-so did, never forgiven him for that I ain't. Still, we got the 'lectric back on after me grandma paid the bill for us and me mum's face cleared up quick enough so we soon got back to normal. I always make sure we pay the 'lectric bill these days. It's horrible when you come home after a hard day's manure shovelling and you can't switch the lights on.

The other problem with the 'lectric is that we ain't got one of them im-her-shun heaters for the water. I have to have cool, shallow baths with maybe a kettle of two of hot water in it you see and I'll tell you what, you don't hang about in there, I can tell you. In and out, sharpish like. Not so bad in the Summer though. Quite refreshing on hot days if I've got a sweat on at work.

I used to have a little 'lectric heater in me bedroom once. Meg gave it to me; it were one she had when she were a little girl. I'd put it on when it were really cold. Just for ten minutes or so before I got into bed. It were alright were that heater and then, one day, it just vanished. I don't know where it went. The old man said he knew nothing about it. Mind you, he had drank best part of a bottle of scotch when I asked him. How he managed to afford that I'll never know. He told me that morning that he were skint because he were waiting for his giro and some money for a brace of hares that he'd got for someone. I suppose I could have gone and bought a new one but I don't like to go into town and besides, that one had semtinel... setinam... senmental...

...that one were special because Meg gave it to me.

Anyway, you get hardened off to the cold when you live in the country. You have to. That don't mean that I ain't looking forward to being warm in here though. It'll make a nice change not to have to scrape the frost off the inside of me bedroom window first thing in the morning. Rufus says that where he comes from it's really warm all year round and that he never even saw snow until he came to this country. Imagine that, spending your whole childhood without building one single snowman. He says that he spent most of his time as a kid playing cricket and selling something called soo-ven-ears to some people called tourists. Maybe when we get out of here I can get him in the Blessham team. They could do with a decent spin bowler. And a batsman. And a wicketkeeper. And a fielder... They could do with a decent everything I suppose. Maybe even a tourist, whatever they are.

But, apart from the cold, I quite like Winter. It's got a certain kind of magical feeling about it. Especially on snowy days or when it's really frosty. And, believe it or not, I'm usually very busy throughout the Winter months. It's the time when I get to do all those little repair jobs around the garden and best of all it's the time when I get to do the digging. I blummin' love digging I do. I think Her Ladyship does too on account of the fact that she seems to want an awful lot of it doing. It's hard, sweaty and back breaking work but to me there's something so good and honest about working the soil over and being close to the earth itself. And of course, doing the digging means that I have to work plenty of manure into the ground and that means that I have to make regular trips to the stables which means I get to see Meg quite often.

Well, when she's not busy like. She works really hard that girl does I can tell you. Roger says that he can hardly keep up with her when she's on the job. Harvey says that she's a right blummin' goer, Mr Franks always says that when it comes to a ride she's a match for any man and even Mrs Partridge reckons that Meg is the best woman she's ever had under her. I think she means that Meg is the best female stable hand she's ever had. She must think an awful lot of Meg because she's always inviting her into her quarters for coffee and cake.

What a lovely looking lass Meg is as well though. She's grown from that happy go lucky tomboy, who used to climb trees with me, into a fine figure of a woman. She's the prettiest thing as well, and I mean really pretty. Oh so pretty. And her dark, chestnut brown hair shines like a new penny and comes half the way down her back with a long fringe at the front. And she ain't half got some shape to her. You know, curves and all that and a nice round bum like a couple of small balloons, if you'll pardon me crudity. I can't understand why any of the local blokes don't ask her out for a date, not that she'd lower herself to go out with any of those yobbos of course. I've asked her plenty of times but I've always had the rotten luck to ask her on days when she's been busy. Sods' law they call it. Still, we've had a few drinks together in the Pig and Whistle often enough, so that's sort of like a date, ain't it?

Anyway, where were I? Oh ah, Winter. Another thing that I really enjoy in the Winter, oddly enough, is the snow. I remember when I were a kid and me mum and me used to make snowmen in the garden. Before she left of course. We'd spend hours out in that garden and our hands would be frozen stiff when we'd finished. Me and Meg used to make snowmen as well. We'd sometimes make one each and I used to pretend that they were us and that they were married and…and…

…Oh, I know. I'm talking daft.

And then there were that time when we had really bad snow, ever so deep it were and we couldn't get to the big school because the bus couldn't get through. Two whole days off school we had. Mind you, Boothy and his mates jumped on me on the way back from the bus stop and put a load of snow down me back. Then they rolled me around on the ground until I were plastered with it and then they chased me home with snowballs. Every time it snowed that lot would use me for target practise. Now, I don't mind snowballs normally, but Boothy used to put stones in the middle of his and they hurt, you know.

Anyway, another thing Meg and me used to do as kids were to make a great big ice slide down sheep dip lane. That were great fun that were. First we'd get an old fertiliser bag and Meg would sit her on it whilst I pulled her up and down a few times to pack the snow down. Then we'd take it in turns to run like blazes and slide along on our feet. And the more you do that the harder and more slippier it gets until you have a really good slide. I remember once right, we made one that ran halfway down the lane and I said to Meg 'Here, watch me Meg!' and I ran right from the far end of the lane as fast as I could. I weren't half motoring by the time I reached the slide and I shot down it like a ferret down a rabbit hole. Of course, I hadn't seen the vicar walking up the other way had I?

He had that plaster cast on his leg for six weeks. Poor old Reverend Menn.

The bad thing about the snow, apart from stones in snowballs, is that I have to clear it all away from the drive up to the Hall and all the footpaths around the Hall as well. Her Ladyship insists that all of the paths are cleared and gritted. 'I don't want to slip and break my bally neck Wilkie. And if you don't want yours breaking by me then you'd better get rid of all this blasted snow.' She says. She did slip over once, a few years back. By 'eck I had to scarper smartish that day I can tell you.

'YOU USELESS, FUCKING, LAME-BRAINED, ARSE-WIPE!' She called after me as I ran. 'CALL THAT SNOW SHOVELLING? YOU COULDN'T SHOVEL SHIT IF YOUR LIFE DEPENDED ON IT! BY THUNDER WILKIE I'LL HAVE YOU BY THE BALLS FOR THIS, *SO HELP ME GOD WILKIE!'* They tell me she calmed down a bit by the time she'd had a couple of stiff brandies.

Of course, there's more to Winter than just beggaring around in the snow. There's a lot more. There's all sorts of things going on in the Winter in the countryside. Let me see now, there's the pheasant shooting, the Christmas party, the New Year's Day rugby match against Stuffham and like I said, there's plenty of jobs to do around the garden. You know, it's a common misconsentrip... mysogenisty... massconscription...

...A lot of people think...

...That there ain't nothing to do in the garden during the Winter months. But they're wrong. For a start I have to clean out all the greenhouses and repair any broken glass. I cut meself once, on the hand and Meg said that after that I ought to ask Her Ladyship for a pair of thick gloves. So, I did. She told me to 'Stop being a mincing ponce Wilkie and get on with the damned job or I'll cut you myself. By thunder I'll cut you, I'll cut your bally manhood off so help me God. Are you trying to waste my valuable time Wilkie? You'd better not by God. If I find out you're trying to waste my time I'll have you larched off the premises. Now get out of my sight.' I think she were having a bit of an off day because a few days later Mrs Franks came down to the vegetable garden and brought me a pair of gloves. Nice, new, thick, hardwearing ones that Her Ladyship had ordered out of the gardening catalogue. That was kind of her.

I like to do the greenhouses on bright, sharp, sunny, frosty days. You know, when your breath comes out in clouds. Sometimes I pretend I'm His Lordship smoking his pipe. Just for a bit of fun like, you know. I'd never smoke in real life. It's bad for you. Meg smokes these days. I told her it wouldn't do her any good but she just laughs and says that she does it to be socio… solocio… socolocial…

…because other people do.

I wish she didn't though and I tell you one thing. There'll be none of that when we get married. Anyway, I couldn't get angry with her, not Meg. I'm sure a sensible, responsible person like her will pack up one day. Yes, I'm sure of it.

Anyway, the Winter. Every Saturday throughout the Winter the air around Blessham is filled with the sound of shotguns letting rip at pheasants. Make a right old row they do. Bang, bang, bang all day long. Still, I don't mind. I go bush beating sometimes to drive the pheasants out of the wood, when I don't have much to do at the Hall that is. It's a hard job but somebody has to do it. There's usually about, well, I don't know how many because I ain't too clever with numbers but there's at least enough of us to fill at least two cricket teams. We all stand in a long line a few yards apart from each other and then we walk through the woods shouting and hollering at the top of our voices and banging sticks together. This makes the pheasants fly out of the wood where upon Her Ladyship and all her well to do mates blow 'em out of the sky with their shotguns. Now, it might sound simple but believe me it's a lot harder than it sounds.

For a start, most of the woods around Blessham are full of brambles and you get scratched and snagged on the blummin' things all the time. The woods are also full of rabbit holes and fox holes and such like and you trip over 'em. Because it's Winter all the trees and bushes are soaking wet and you end up getting it in your wellies. And all that shouting don't half make your throat sore. You want to hear the noise we make. Hooting and bellowing at the top of our voices we are. No wonder them pheasants want to beggar off and take their chances with the guns.

Of course, it's only the gentry that do the shooting. I don't mind, I reckon I'd be dangerous with one of them things in me hand. But, it's not a bad day all the same. We get paid five quid an hour, get a bottle of beer at dinner time and now and then we get a brace of pheasants to take home. So that makes it all worthwhile.

I always try and make sure that I don't stand anywhere near Jim Booth or his mates when we go through the woods. You can imagine what sort of things they do to me. Beggars they are. They once pushed me into the brook. They often push me into bramble bushes. They put things down me wellies and they once tied me to a fir tree with some baler twine and left me there. No-one noticed until dinner time and then they all laughed it off. I didn't think it were very funny though. Although, I did mention it to Her Ladyship and she said 'The bastard, bally bounders! By God, who do they think they are? They should be horse-whipped for that.' And she wouldn't let 'em do any more bush beating for the rest of that Winter.

And I say it served 'em right. Mind you, they did give me a couple of good right handers in the car park of the Pig and Whistle for telling on 'em. But I didn't mind. It were only a few and they didn't knock me down and besides, I could go bush beating for the rest of the season without having 'em picking on me. But to tell you the truth, I'm going off it really. You see, I heard one of Her Ladyship's friends, a certain Duke Aire, saying one time at the end of a day's shooting 'Thank you Lady Stark-Raven. Jolly good sport today, what-ho?' Now, I ain't never been no good at sports but I reckon sport should be fair where both sides have the same chance as one another, like the rugby match. And them poor pheasants ain't got shotguns, so it ain't fair is it. You know, I don't think I'll bother this year unless Her Ladyship makes me. Oh, hang on a minute! I can't anyway, can I? Sorry, ignore what I just said.

The worst bit about pheasant season though is plucking the blummin' things. I don't like that job. For one thing half the poor beggars have still got their eyes open and it makes me think they're looking at me even though they're dead. And they must be dead because they're all full of buckshot. And before you can pluck 'em they have to hang up in me shed for a week to trenderiff… tendagise… tenremeriderise…

…to make the meat softer

And this also makes 'em taste better they reckon. I don't know about that. When the old man ever brought one home it were plucked and in the pot before you could say… 'pheasant.' Never around long enough to hang. But Her Ladyship insists on hanging 'em. 'Gives them a nice tang Wilkie!' She says. Well, I pluck 'em and I ain't ever seen any tangs on 'em. Mind you, I don't know what a tang is so I ain't too sure what I'm supposed to be looking for.

And so I have to sit in me shed in the freezing blummin' cold and pull all the feathers off 'em. And they have to be done right or it's a round of F's and B's for me off Her Ladyship. I've got to get every feather off. And it's harder than you think. You see, because they've been hanging so long the skin gets soft and then tears which I find really horrible. Turns me guts it does. Then there's all the blummin' feathers everywhere, which I have to pick up and burn. Get all over the place they do. In me hair, down me wellies, in me pockets, everywhere! And blimey, you want to smell the beggars when they burn. I'd rather smell the old man's farts after a night on the stout. But I've got to do it every week throughout the season. Pheasant, you see, is Her Ladyship's very favourite. I reckon she'd have it every day if she could. Which she probably could actually. And she also insists on a brace being given to each player on the rugby team if they win the annual match against Stuffham on New Year's Day.

Aaah! The rugby match. That's a really big thing in the village. A very important event. They have it every year with both villages altnertating... alterating... anlegating...

...taking it turns to host it.

Of course, when I say rugby match, what I mean is a right blummin' good punch up poorly disguised as a rugby match. There's no love lost between Blessham and Stuffham at the best of times and the rugby match is a time for everyone to let off steam and get stuck into each other. I mean, there's rules and all and there's a referee of sorts. They always get Wilf Hartigan from Dammitt to do that. He's a huge big bloke he is and about the only one who stands a chance of keeping some kind of control on the game. Not much mind you. Still, he gets a brace of pheasants as well so he's happy enough.

Blessham have won it for the last two years on the trot and they're hoping for a hat-trick this year. Daft really. Who's got time for blummin' conjuring tricks and pulling rabbits out of a hat during a rugby match. Anyway, Blessham are the current champions and we want to keep it that way. I always go along and cheer for our lads. I did play once, in 1989 it were, but I got laid out cold in the first minute before I'd even touched the blummin' ball. I only said I'd play because Graham Todd were injured after falling over on New Year's Eve and breaking his nose. I don't even know how to play it really. I know you have to catch that funny shaped ball and then run like beggary but apart from that I ain't too sure what to do. But I'll tell you one thing, that game has gone down in local legend. To this day they still call it the Battle of Blessham Green. Blummin' free-for-all it were.

Like I say, I were put in the team at the last minute, and I must admit I were feeling a bit nervous due to the fact that the whole village had turned out to see it and I wanted to do well in front of Meg. Anyway, at two o'clock sharp the whistle went and Stuffham kicked off. There I were, minding my own business when one of our lads catches the ball and our team started running forwards. I didn't know what to do but Farmer Bull, who were watching the game, shouted 'FOR CHRIST'S SAKE WILKIE, RUN YOU HOPELESS FRIGGIN' TWAT!' So I started running, despite the fact that I don't like hearing the Lord's name taken in vain like that. Well, I hadn't gone very far when there in front of me were this huge bloke from Stuffham; great, big beggar he were. I stopped in me tracks and said, 'Excuse me Sir,' to him as politely as I could, 'can I get past you please?' Well, the next thing I remember is coming round on the touchline with a black eye and a nosebleed and Meg asking me if I were alright. Which I weren't to be honest. Far from it. But the game carried on and we had to find a sustibute... bustitute... prostitute...

...someone to take my place.

Everyone were stood there wondering what to do as punches flew on the pitch when all of a sudden the crowd parted like the Red Sea did with Moses that time and who should walk through but Her Ladyship. She looked down at me and shook her head. 'Get this hopeless article out of my way,' She said, 'and damn well get me a shirt.' A gasp went through the crowd. 'What are you all gawping at?' She demanded. 'I was a prop forward at University. By God, just get me on that pitch.'

Well, it took a few minutes but they managed to find a shirt big enough for her and she pulled it over her head. It were a bit tight it has to be said. Her bosoms were straining it at the front and it clung to everything as her muscles bulged out underneath it. By 'eck, she were a magnificent sight to behold. Anyway, the referee stopped play for a moment, although there were still some punches being thrown, and on she went, barking orders at our team and hurling abuse at the Stuffham lads about what she were going to do to 'em and that. And it sounded very painful to me.

Wilf blew his whistle again and that were it, both sides piled into each other once more. There were punching, kicking, gouging, head-butts, knees in groins, stamping, elbowing – you name it, Her Ladyship were doing it. She stood there like a rock in the middle of the pitch and knocked down every Stuffham player that got anywhere near her. The rest of the team were having a right old go at it as well, and all the while that ball just got hoofed from one end of the pitch to the other with no-one really trying to try (if you know what I mean). There were even a bit of fisticuffs on the touchline between rival fans and there were poor old Reverend Menn with his hands in the air calling for everyone to 'Show the spirit of Christian fair play and sportsmanship.' I'd picked meself off the floor by this time but I had a right shiner I did.

And that's how it carried on until half time, a right blummin' set to. Most of the players came tramping off the pitch with one or two scuffles still going on here and there and they all cracked open a can of beer each which Bob McKenzie had provided and a pork pie each from Mr Booth's shop. Bob gave me a can of beer too saying, 'There you go Joe, I reckon you need this boy.' It were that lager stuff though, which I ain't keen on so I didn't finish it. The pie I had were nice though. Her Ladyship didn't have any beer though. 'The abominable beverage of the brawling Luddite!' She calls it. Actually, she didn't have anything to drink although she did have three pork pies and then she were first back on the pitch for the second half, clapping her hands together and shaking her fists in front of her and shouting, *'COME ON THEN YOU FUCKERS!'* to the Stuffham players.

Well, they all went back on with Wilf Hartigan pleading with 'em all to actually play some proper rugby rather than just hoofing and fighting. Anyway, he blew the whistle and off it went again. A Stuffham lad caught the ball and set off towards our end like a rocket. He didn't get too far though as Her Ladyship stopped him with a move that I believe is known as a 'clothesline.' Rolling around clutching his throat he were whilst she grabs the ball, tucks it into the crook of her arm and sets off in the other direction with a great cheer from the Blessham crowd. She hadn't gone far when who should try to tackle her but that big beggar who gave me the shiner. Came bearing down on her he did, like a bear, with a loud roar. *'FUCK OFF YOU PISS-ANT!'* She shouted at him as her left fist crashed into his jaw and down he went. I never felt so proud to be her gardener as I did right then. Well, with two Stuffham players on the deck the odds were well in our favour and soon she were surrounded by Blessham players who were fighting off the advances of that Stuffham lot. It were truly marvellous to behold, it really were. They just kept going and battling their way forward. One of their lads eventually got through but she put her hand into his face, pushed him to the ground and ran over the top of him and then she were there and over the line. She dropped to the ground and touched down, the whistle blew, the crowd went berserk and Blessham were in front. Sadly, Jim Booth failed to convert it, for which Her Ladyship called him 'You fucking limp-wristed fucking pile of fucking rubbish!' and the score stayed at 5 - 0.

Well after that it got serious with Stuffham trying everything to pull level. But we never let up for a moment. Every time a Stuffham player got the ball a Blessham player would lamp him one or kick him between the legs. And there were Her Ladyship, right in the middle of it all, swinging punches like crazy, and receiving a fair few too now and then. Them Stuffham lads were giving as good as they got. It were powerful stuff to watch and to be honest I were blummin' glad not to be involved anymore. Blimey! I'd have had the pasting of a lifetime if I'd still been on there. And then suddenly, old Wilf looks at his watch and blows his whistle for the final time. It were over. Blessham had won by one try. Mind you both teams carried on fighting for a couple of minutes until they were all eventually separated by friends and family members. Her Ladyship had one Stuffham lad in a headlock with her left arm and kept swinging right hooks into his face and telling him what a terribly effeminate gentleman he was (or words to that effect). But eventually they all came off the pitch to a round of applause from the crowd. Now, I ain't a great one for stastics... sitasters... sacsictics...

...facts and figures like.

But they reckon that between the two teams there were no fewer than 9 broken noses, 15 missing teeth, 12 black eyes, 4 cracked ribs, 3 dislocated shoulders and a rather nasty looking broken jaw. However, do you know what? They all blummin' well shook hands when it were all over and then went down the Pig and Whistle and got a skinful. Well, all except Her Ladyship who stamped off back to the hall saying that she 'Never, ever will sup with the proletariat' and that she were 'Going home for a salt bath and a stiff whisky.'

I were going to go along to the pub meself for a pint of two of mild but I weren't feeling too good and me head hurt. Meg went along though and I heard her telling Polly the next day that she 'Had a right good doing.' I'm sure she meant to say, 'It were a right good do.' Anyway, I went home and got into bed. Seems strange, don't it though? All that friendliness after they'd been kicking seven bells out of each other. Still we'd won the game and that were the main thing. The Battle of Blessham Green were over.

I'll tell you another good thing about Winter – snowdrops. The flowers I mean, not the, you know, snow that drops out of the sky. We got loads of 'em at the hall and they come out in February and it just makes you feel better when you see them little flowers poking out the ground. I picked some once to take round to Meg but Her Ladyship caught me doing it and said that if it ever happened again then I would live to regret that day for the remainder of my life and that if I wanted to 'Present flowers to the local tart' that I should 'Fuck off into town and damn well buy them out of your own money.' Now I know for a fact that you don't put flowers into tarts. You use jam instead. I mean, I didn't want to put 'em in a tart in the first place, I wanted to give 'em to Meg. Also, If I wanted a tart I would ask me grandma to make some because she makes the best pastry I've ever had. And jam. And she don't put no flowers in 'em either. And if she did I don't think I'd have to pay for 'em. I think Her Ladyship must have been confused. Come to think about it, so am I about the whole affair. Still, I've never tried to pick any of her flowers since.

So, Winter, you see, in Blessham, is a special time. The rugby were never as bad again as it were that day on account of the fact that Wilf made sure there were a police presence every year after that. Of course, Winter has its problems, you know, burst pipes in Poachers Cottage, waking up in the morning and breaking the ice in the khazi before you can do your business and power cuts and the like but I don't mind the Winter really because you see, one of the best times of the whole year happens in Winter. And I'm talking, of course, about Christmas!

9
Christmas

I heard a song on the wireless once about Christmas. It were called 'The Most Smashing Day of The Year.' Or something like that. Well, I reckon they weren't far wrong if you ask me. I blummin' love Christmas I do. Always have, right back as far as I can remember. The first Christmas I can remember properly were when I were about five years old. I remember it because I had a new pair of slippers and in me excitement I accidently kicked one of 'em off and into the fire. The old man went mad but seeing as how he had most of a bottle of rum inside him me mum just managed to push him back into his armchair before he could land one on me. It didn't spoil the day though because me and me mum went to me grandmas for a lovely big turkey dinner whilst he slept it off and when he woke up he'd forgotten about it.

I always go to me grandmas for dinner. She's a dab hand in the kitchen she is and there's always a big turkey and loads of veg and stuff. And we have crackers to pull and beer to drink and, well, you know, all the Christmas day stuff. I always invite Meg every year because she shares a rented house with Sally Firth up the Crescent these days and she don't seem to bother much with all the trimmings and what-not so I thought it might be nice for her. Maybe one day she'll accept. Apparently her and Sal had a cockerel from Booth's for Christmas dinner last year. Well, I think that's what they meant. I overheard Meg telling Jim Booth in the pub on Boxing Day that they'd 'Both loved having your cock inside of us yesterday' and he said that he were 'Happy to oblige.' I remember that Ernie O'Dyan said 'For fuck's sake, they couldn't be more bloody blatant if they tried. Fucking slapper!' I wonder what blatant means. And I'd never slap her! That's the very last thing I'd ever do. And I told Ernie that and he told me not to be so bleedin' wet. Then I got confused so I went home and watched the two Jonnies on the telly.

Now Christmas is a very, very special time for a very, very special reason. The twenty-fifth of December is the birthday of our Lord Jesus Christ. And you can't get much more special than that can you? And that means that there's loads of things going on at the church. There's Christingle – that's the start of advent, the children's nativity play and the carol service. I go to 'em all and I help Nick out as much as I can. I were in the nativity play when I were a young 'un. I played the donkey every year. Jim Booth said that were the ideal part for me. Don't know what he meant but I always enjoyed it. Although, really, I suppose I should have played the part of Joseph as that's who I'm named after ain't I? Trouble was that when I mentioned it to the old man he said that 'the only acting you could do is acting the bloody fool.' I mean, that's all well and good but there ain't a part called the fool in the nativity, is there? Never mind. Meg got the part of Mary a few times and she also played an angel once. She'll always be my angel though, any time of the year.

Anyway, I remember this one year, I reckon I'd be about 8, and I asked if I could be a shepherd or one of the wise men for a change. Miss Finchley, who were a teacher at Blessham primary, remember, and who used to organise the nativity, said that me playing a wise man would be 'Bordering on gross hypocrisy and an insult to the performing arts.' However, she said that I could try for the part of a shepherd but I would have to 'Refrain from any form of speech whatsoever and merely stand there watching the sheep.' She were always very wordy were Miss Finchley and to be honest, between you and me, a bit hoity-toity like. I mean nice enough woman and all, and she never leathered anyone's rump like Mr Rodwell, that were his job, but she were a bit stuck up at times. She claims to be what's known as 'something of a thespian' which I think means that she's rather keen on other women.

So anyway, there I were at resherals… rehorses… hersharals…

...practice night...

And me mum had got me done up in me dressing gown and put a tea towel round me head and fastened it with a length of baler twine so that I looked like a proper shepherd from bible times, and we had to fall on the floor in fear and dread when the angel of the Lord, who were being played by Meg that year, suddenly appeared to tell us that the baby Jesus had been born in Bethlehem and all that. Well I fell down alright, like we were told to, but I banged me nose on the floor and we had to use the tea towel to stop the bleeding which made one of the other shepherds cry because he didn't like the sight of it. We eventually stopped me nosebleed though and I tried to carry on without me head scarf. We made our way to the stable by walking around the church as Mr Cummings played 'While Shepherds Washed Their Socks by Night' on the organ and we then had to go and kneel in front of the manger where the baby Jesus lay. Problem was, me nose started bleeding again at that point and I had to wipe it on me dressing gown sleeve and I weren't watching where I were going. I tripped over the manger, knocking it off its stand. The doll they were using as baby Jesus fell out of it and I fell as well. I reached out to stop meself but in doing so I pulled Joseph's false beard off, which made the lad playing Joseph cry because it hurt his ears when the 'lastic snapped, and I landed on top of the manger and squashed it flat. Miss Finchley screamed and then all the other children started crying except for Jim Booth, who were playing King Herod, and Meg, who were the angel of course. Boothy were laughing and Meg just smiled at me.

'You stupid, stupid boy!' Said Miss Finchley, pulling me to me feet. 'Just look at what you've bloody well done!'

'Ere you!' Said me mum who had been watching. 'Don't you talk to my son like that, you uppity bitch.' She then grabbed me by the hand and said, 'Come on Joe, we're not staying here to be spoken to like dirt.'

'Yes, go, get out.' Shouted Miss Finchley, 'you're a disgrace to both the nativity and the acting profession!'

'Piss off you stuffy, wrinkled up old bag.' Said mum over her shoulder. I didn't know where to look. Dead embarrassing it were, me mum swearing in church like that.

I apologised to Miss Finchley at school the next day, after Mr Rodwell had warmed me backside for it of course, and she said that she forgave me but next year I would be back to playing the donkey again. Ah well, I tried didn't I?

They still do the nativity these days but it's the carol service I like most. Now like I say; I can't sing for toffee but I give it me best at the carol service. I love a nice carol I do. Me favourite one is Silent Night. I think that's me favourite because it were me mum's favourite and it reminds me of her at Christmas. There's loads of really good carols though. Her Ladyship goes to the carol service. It's the only other time of the year that she goes to church other than Easter. And blimey, you want to hear her bellowing out them carols. She sings like a blummin' old heifer she does. Right at the top of her voice. You can hardly hear the organ for her. 'If you must sing to the Lord, vicar', she once said to Nick, 'then sing loudly and lustily.' Ooh, I don't know about that. You know, lust and all that. Not in church at any rate. I mean, there's a time and place for such things surely. It's making me embarrassed just thinking about it.

I remember once, years ago, that Reverend Menn asked Her Ladyship if she wouldn't mind inviting those that attend the carol service round to hers afterwards for sherry and mince pies as a gesture of peace and good will to all men at this special time of the year.

She replied 'My dear, good Reverend. If you suppose, for one second, that I would invite the hoi polloi of Blessham into my living room with their muddy boots on my Axminister and their greasy trousers on my furniture then you can think again my pious, white-collared friend. And as for good will to all men. Pah! I think I show enough of that every year when I open my grounds to the nosey blighters. No sir, there'll be no sherry being poured down their greedy little throats by my hand. I have dogs Reverend.

Big dogs, that are not averse to sinking their teeth into a man's leg should they come trespassing at the hall. I'm therefore hardly likely to *invite* rabble onto the premises of a night-time in the very depth of Winter, now am I? I'll be on my way now. Good evening to you vicar!' To this day I have no idea what hoi polloi or rabble or Axminster means but we must have 'em in Blessham or she wouldn't have said it, would she? And besides, we go to the village hall for sherry and mince pies now anyway. I'm not keen on the sherry though.

The other service we have is Christingle at the beginning of the month. It starts advent off you see. I ain't too sure what advent is. Nick tried explaining it to me but it went over me head. What I do know though is that advent is when you get one of them special calendars with little doors that you open every day all the way up to Christmas Eve. I get mine from the general store and last year it had a little bit of chocolate behind each door. I enjoyed that I did. I don't know if they have advent calendars in here and I bet if they do they don't have chocolate in 'em. I remember one year, when I were a young 'un, me mum bought an advent candle instead. I were dead excited as she said that I could light it and up to then I'd never been allowed anywhere near matches for fear of burning the blummin' house to the ground. And after them times with the cake and the slippers I were always a bit wary with anything to do with fire. But I were so excited about that candle. Anyway, the first of December came around and when it got to evening time me mum helped me light a match and put it to the candle and then placed the candle in me bedroom window with the light off. It looked truly magical it did.

'Now listen carefully Joe,' she said to me, 'You make sure you blow that out as soon as it gets down to the 2nd.'

'Yes mum.' I said.

'And don't you go buggering about with it, do you hear me?' She said.

'No mum, I won't.' I said.

'Alright then,' she said, 'I'm off out to work now so if you have any problems then wake the old man up. Hopefully you won't.'

'I will mum,' I said, thinking that it should be alright as I could hear him snoring and farting in their bedroom. He'd been on the stout in the Pig and Whistle all afternoon you see and came home well drunk. Then she gave me a kiss on the forehead and went off out to work.

Well, I sat in bed and stared at that beautiful candle for ages and I don't know how it happened but I remember waking up and thinking I best blow it out. So I got out of bed and went to do just that. Imagine me surprise when I looked and saw that the candle had burnt down as far as the number 1 and 8. Erm... 18. I must have been asleep for a good while. I remember that I started crying because it meant that I'd have to wait another... hang on a minute... another... 1, 2, 3... 5... 9... 4... 10... erm...

...a good few days before we could light the blummin' thing again.

'Whada ya bloody bawlin' about!' Shouted the old man, which to be honest didn't help.

'I had a bad dream.' I called back, which were a lie I know but I were scared he'd give me a good hiding if he knew what I'd done.

'Well bloody well shurrup!' He slurred. 'I've got a head like it's been friggin' kicked in and a mouth like a soddin' cesspit. Now get back to sleep ya whining little bastard or I'll give ya somethin' to cry about!' And I reckon he meant it.

I were right upset I were. I loved that candle and now it were nearly all gone. I didn't know what to do but then I had an idea, and I don't have too many of them I can tell you. I put me slippers on and I tip-toed out of me bedroom and went downstairs trying to be as quiet as I could. One or two of our stairs creak you see when you step on 'em. But I made it down without waking him up again and I crept into the kitchen and opened the cupboard under the sink. Sure enough there were a box of candles under there. We always kept some for when the 'lectric got cut off. Anyway, I took one out of the box and the matches off the top of the cooker and then I went back up to me room. Once I got there I found the felt tip pens me gran had bought me for me birthday and I set about marking that candle as best I could so that it looked like the one that had burnt down. I were quite chuffed with meself I have to say; I'd never had such a great idea before. So, I took the matches and I lit the new candle I'd made and I stayed awake watching it until it burned all the way to the 2nd and then I blew it out. It took a while and I were ever so tired but I forced meself to stay awake this time. Then I hid what were left of the old candle under me bed and got in and pulled the covers up to me chin.

Me mum woke me up for school the next morning and I jumped out of bed. She didn't seem to have noticed and I were pleased that me little trick had worked. I brushed me teeth, had breakfast and got dressed and tried to act normal. Everything were going great. And then, just as I were going out the door she says to me, 'Is there anything you want to tell me Joe?'

'Don't think so mum.' I said.

'Oh!' She said. 'That's odd. I thought there would have been.'

'No.' I said.

'Well,' she said, 'Was everything alright last night?'

'Fine,' I said, 'just fine, why mum?'

'So nothing was amiss last night then?' I were getting worried now so I thought I'd better keep going and bluff it out.

'Well,' I said, 'I did have a bad dream, but the old man told me to get back to sleep and so I did. Apart from that though it were all ok.'

'No problems with your candle then?' She said.

'Don't think so.' I replied with a gulp.

'You see Joe,' she said, 'it's just that this morning your candle seems different.'

'How do you mean mum?' I were desperately trying to think of what to say.

'Well,' she went on, 'for one thing the numbers on it aren't in the proper order. You see, 7 usually comes after 6, not before, 11 has two ones in it not 3, the number 4 is the wrong way round and for some reason the number 13 is missing completely.'

'Oh right!' I said. 'I hadn't noticed.'

'But that's not all.' She said.

'Why, what else is there?' I asked.

'Well, last night the candle was red and this morning it's white.' She said sternly, folding her arms and looking very cross with me.

I admit that I started sniffling at that stage and I looked down at me feet feeling very ashamed of meself for lying to me mum. But she put her hand on me chin and lifted me head up and looked me in the eye.

'Do you know what Joseph Wilkie? I ought to box your ears for you.' She said and I sniffled some more. But she just sighed and said, 'I suppose it's my fault for leaving you alone with that bloody candle. Let's say no more about it eh?' I nodded and smiled and she wiped a tear off my cheek.

'But don't you ever lie to me again Joe. Don't you ever do that.' She said.

'I won't mum, I promise.' I said drying me eyes. 'I'm sorry mum.'

'And I'm sorry too.' She said. 'I shouldn't have left you in charge of a lighted candle. 'I'll tell you what, I made a few bob last night. Why don't I meet you after school and we can go down the shop together and get a calendar? What do you say to that?'

'That would be great mum.' I said.

'Right. Off you go then and I'll see you later.' She said giving me a peck on the cheek.

And she were as good as her word. We went and got that calendar and we never mentioned the advent candle ever again. She must have worked very hard that night because she did have a good few quid in her purse, but when we took the calendar to the till Mr Goodnight just winked at me mum and said, 'It's alright Sarah, have this one on me.' Very kind of him I must say. That's the true spirit of Christmas right there that is.

So that's advent for you. And like I say; it leads right up to Christmas Eve. Ah, that's a magical day that is. For one thing, if it falls on a weekday I get to finish at twelve and go home early. Then I get Christmas Day and Boxing Day off too. I wander home on Christmas Eve with all sorts of things in me head. Thinking about presents and Christmas dinner and the like. And I've always found it hard to get to sleep on Christmas Eve as I get so excited. When I were a young 'un I used to try and keep meself awake and look out for Santa Claus through me bedroom window. Of course, eventually I came to find out that he weren't real like. Ruined me early twenties that did.

Mind you I still get presents without him so I ain't too bothered now. I always get socks, underpants, soap-on-a-rope and a chocolate orange off me grandma and Ruby and Pearl always get me a little something each. The old man always says he's getting me the same thing as last year but as I remind him he never got me anything last year. He's dead forgetful he is. And besides, he's always full of ale at Christmas and what with being busy, poaching and thieving and the like, I suppose he ain't got time to go shopping. I buy him something though each year. Last year I got him a new woolly bobble hat from the general store to keep his head warm when he's out in the woods of a night time. Bright yellow one it were. Don't know what happened to it because he lost it soon after. I don't think we'll get many presents in here though. Still, it would be lovely if I'm out of here for Christmas. I wouldn't want to miss me grandma's Christmas dinner now would I?

It's a great day. All the family go, except the old man, who always says he 'Can't be arsed.' But Ruby and Pearl and their folks are always there and they're both married now to decent blokes with young 'uns of their own. Uncle Joe they call me. I heard 'em singing a song about me once. It went:

'Uncle Joe, he's really slow,

But he can make your garden grow!'

Well they're right about the gardening but I think I'm pretty fast at it really. Still that's kiddies for you. Pearl's got two young lads and Ruby has got three kids, one of each. Little beggars they can be too. Always playing tricks on me. Mind you, that's not hard.

But anyway, Christmas dinner. It's a grand affair. There's always a large turkey the size of a... really big chicken! And there's roasties and sprouts and parsnips and red cabbage and sprouts and gravy and stuffing and sprouts and that cranberry sauce and carrots and not forgetting of course...

...sprouts!

Afterwards there's a great big pudding. Like a blummin' football it is and me gran always puts a coin in it. When I were a young 'un it were a shilling but it's more than that now what with infartation... inflatulation... inflagration...

...the cost of living and all that.

Nowadays it's a shiny new pound coin and whoever finds it gets to keep it. I only found it the once. Chipped a tooth on it I did. Still, it were a quid in me pocket weren't it. Tooth blummin' well hurt for a day or two though. Anyway, after dinner I always help me grandma with the washing up and then we play games like hide and speak and blind man's fluff. I ain't too good at that one to be honest. I walked into the wall once and got a bigger nosebleed than that day in the church. How we all laughed as I had to sit with me head tilted back holding a towel. And as for hide and speak I only ever get to hide due to the fact that I can't count up to fifty. But I'm ever so good at hiding though and I always win. They never find me. I always hide in the airing cupboard you see and for some reason no-one ever seems to look in there. Can't think why. Trouble is, I'm always soaked wet through with sweat by the time I come out what with spending an hour huddled up next to the hot water tank. But I win though don't I?

Now Christmas is a time for something else as well and the woods around Blessham are full of the blummin' stuff. I'm talking, of course, about mistletoe. They sell it in the general store in little bunches for a couple of quid but I go and pick me own. I mean, why pay for it when you can get it for nothing? I said that to Mr Goodnight once and he said that he couldn't agree with me more and Mrs Byamile giggled and called him naughty again. That were strange. She's always telling him he's naughty. And what's naughty about mistletoe? I use it to decorate Poacher's Cottage with a bit of holly here and there as well. We ain't really got room for a tree. But there's another use for it which you may or may not know about. Mistletoe is for kissing under and you know what that means don't you. It means that I'm always trying to get Meg under it every year. I've not had any luck so far as there's always something that gets in the way of it. I tried it at work, but she were worried about Her Ladyship seeing us. I tried it in the pub, but she said people might start talking. I tried it walking home one dark evening on our way home from the hall, but she said it where neither the time nor the place what with being outdoors and all that. It makes me smile to think about it though. Meg is a real lady to not do things like that in public. Oh, if only I could get her back in that haystack, I'd give those lovely lips a right good going over I would. And I suppose with her being such a classy lass then no-one else gets to kiss her either which is good. One day though, one day...

Her Ladyship won't have it in the house. Mistletoe I mean, not kissing. Although she probably wouldn't allow that either. As for the mistletoe, she always says it's 'A filthy, pagan symbol of lust and debauchery, propagated by the immoral society that is prevalent in our country. I would rather the house burn down around my ears than have that accessory to whoremongering brought in.' I ain't got a blummin' clue what she means. She does have a bit of holly though and a tree so she's not too down on Christmas and she does give all the staff a little present each to show her app-ree-shay-shun. Last year I got a new penknife. I thanked her for it of course and she said, 'Just try not to decapitate your idiot self with it Wilkie. I don't want your wretched blood on my conscience. Merry Christmas, and now get out of my sight before I knock you to the ground. See you on the twenty-seventh.' Very thoughtful of her I think.

And we have a Christmas party as well at the village hall. It's usually about a fortnight before the big day itself and everyone gets full of ale and Bob makes a big bowl of that punch stuff. It's alright but it leaves a funny taste in me mouth. Jim Booth told me one year that if I didn't get out of his way at the bar then he were going to give me a punch in the mouth. I'd had a few pints of mild by this time and I thought he meant he were going to get me a glass of punch which made me think that the spirit of Christmas must be in him so I said, 'Thank you Jim. I don't really like it but go on then.' And then he smacked me right in the teeth with the back of his hand. So much for the spirit of Christmas. Old Mr Cummings saw it and told him he were a 'rotten bloody thug' but that just made Boothy laugh and walk off. Mr Cummings said he were a bully and that I ought to stand up for meself and fight back, but it weren't a hard hit and besides that's not what the good book tells us. We're meant to turn the other cheek. Mind you he'd probably hit me there as well if I did. And besides, I just ain't one for the fighting, especially at Christmas time.

There's always a lot of dancing at the party but the only ones I know are that Okey-Cokey one I told you about and the conga. That's where we all stand behind each other with our hands on the hips of the person in front and then we go all around in a big long line. I were lucky enough to be at the front one year so I had to lead everyone. I got a bit carried away though and by the time we were halfway across the village green I were the only one left. A bit embarrassing it were.

Then there's New Year's Eve where everyone piles into the Pig and Whistle and gets properly larupped with ale, except the old man who always says it's one of his busiest nights of the year. Bob has to order in a load of extra barrels of ale and we all get very merry. This means that there's a lot of thick heads the next day for the rugby match but them Stuffham lads are in just as bad a way so it probably evens it out. Then at midnight we all link arms and sing that 'Auld Lang Syne' song which means we're all supposed to be good to each other for the next year. I don't think it works though, do you?.

Last New Year were a special one though as it were the start of a new mill-hen-yum. That's when we've had like a billion years or something and we start counting again for another billion. I think. The New Year Eve party were really something I'll tell you. There were fireworks and that blummin' folk singer again (singing 'Ho The Prancing Reindeer Now' and other twaddle) and loads of food and when the clock struck twelve everyone were kissing each other. Of course, as you can guess there were only one girl that I wanted to kiss but, in the crowd, I couldn't find her, which were a shame. I were right gutted about that. But drink? Blimey! There were some ale supped. People were crawling home on their hands and knees at the end of the night. Well, when I say end of the night what I mean were about six in the morning. I've never been so tired. They cancelled the rugby match this year for the first time ever.

I saw Meg at work on the day after New Year's Day and she said she were sorry she didn't see me at midnight but she had to meet her cousin who had come to stay with her and that she had got high with him. I told her that I hoped she hadn't been climbing trees in the dark which made her laugh and say that she would explain it to me one day. It made me feel better though, knowing she'd been with her cousin. She said she wanted to introduce me to him, some fellow by the name of Simon and that he were a hippie. I asked her what a hippie were, but she said it were too difficult to explain. Anyway, don't matter what he is I suppose. 'Any relation of yours Meg is a friend of mine.' I told her. I were quite looking forward to meeting Simon. He sounded like a nice enough chap. Although, now, I wish I blummin' hadn't ever clapped eyes on him. Anyway, I finally met Simon about a week later.

10
Simon

It were a Friday night and I'd spent the day doing some heavy digging in the vegetable garden, getting the ground ready for the spuds. And I'd worked me up a right thirst and all so I went home, had me tea which were tripe and onions, washed me armpits (which were a bit ripe), put on a clean shirt, well, cleanish and then went down the pub. There weren't many in at that time but Ernie O'Dyan were in his usual place at the corner of the bar chatting to Bob.

'Alright Ernie! Alright Bob!' I said as I walked in. 'Pint of mild please.'

'Ah boy, not so bad.' They both said at the same time and Bob set about pouring me a pint of that delicious mild.

I paid him and said, 'Sounds lively in there!' nodding towards the pool room where there were a lot of laughing going on.

'Oh, Meg's in there with that cousin of hers and a few others.' Said Bob.

'Is she?' I said. 'Really? In there?'

'I just bleeding well said she was, didn't I?' Said Bob looking at Ernie and turning his eyes upwards towards the ceiling.

'Yes, you did Bob.' I said. 'I remember you saying it.'

'For the love of...' Said Bob and he wandered off down the cellar to get a new box of cheese and onion crisps.

'If you'll excuse me Ernie,' I said, 'I'll go and say hello. Meg wanted to introduce me to her cousin.' And I went to walk into the pool room. Then Ernie grabs hold of me arm which were odd because he's never done that before.

'Joe, just be careful lad.' He said.

'How do you mean Ernie?' I said.

'Don't get yourself mixed up in things that you shouldn't.' He said.

'I won't.' I said, thinking that he must have thought I were going to have a game of doubles or play for money or something. To be honest, I ain't too good at the game so I tend to just watch the others play. 'I'm just going to say hello!' I told him.

So, I took me pint and went into the pool room. Well, the first thing I noticed were a funny smell. Sort of sweet smelling like but unusual, a kind of a cross between the incense at church and me granddads' chilblain ointment, and there were a lot of smoke in the room. Now, I don't like smoking as you know and I could see that Meg had one of them roll-up cigarettes in her hand and I weren't too happy about it. I didn't want to make a scene though. I looked round and there were Polly and Sally and Graham Todd in there as well and some strange looking fellow who I'd never seen before. Now, I know I ain't a bright spark like, but by the process of emulsion... emulation... elmagration...

...I worked out that that must be Simon.

You know, drink does some strange things to people. Polly started cackling when I came in like she were off her head and Graham Todd looked like his face had dropped and he didn't recognise me and Meg were rocking her head from side to side with her eyes closed and a smile on her lovely face like she were away with the blummin' fairies. But I thought, I'm here now! So I said, 'Hello Meg!'

She opened her eyes and smiled again and said, 'Hey Joe!' and giggled. 'you want some blow?' She said with the strangest look in her eyes and offering the cigarette she were holding towards me. Then she giggled again.

'No thank you.' I said. 'I don't smoke. I've come in here to meet your cousin. What's his name? Simon?' Then Polly cackled again. Sounded like some blummin' old witch she did.

'Simon,' Meg said, 'come and meet my old mate Joe, who I was telling you about.'

So, I were right then. That fella *were* Simon. Funny looking beggar he were and all. He were quite tall and he had light brown hair that were in... well... clumps is the only word I can think of. Long sort of clumps. And he had one of them beards that make you look like a billy goat and he had I don't know how many earrings in both ears. Major Brimmish once said to me that 'Only two kinds of men wear earrings Wilkie! Pirates and poofters!' Well, I don't know what a poofter is and were too shy to ask but I know what a pirate is and this Simon character didn't look like a pirate because they have patches on their eyes and carrots on their shoulders, so he must have been a poofter. Well, that's the way I saw it. I might ask Wendy if he knows what a poofter is because he's dead clever with words. He's ever so integregant... illegerent... intillergrunt...

...a real brainbox.

Anyway, Simon were wearing this long coat that looked a bit like an inside out sheepskin with long fur at the edges even though it were warm in there and he had these trousers that looked like they were made from about five different pairs and on his feet he had blummin sandals with no socks and his feet looked like they'd never seen soap and water! To top it off he had a T shirt that said 'Grateful Dead' on it. I know because I asked Meg the next day what it said. All seemed very strange to me but he were Meg's cousin so I weren't going to say anything. I were going to ask him if he were a poofter but I thought I better not. And who'd be grateful to be dead. Not me that's for sure. Anyway, Simon put his pool cue on the table and walks over to me holding out his hand for me to shake. 'Hey there man.' He said. Well, he were right there. I'm a man ain't I? 'You ok Joe?'

'Ah boy, not so bad.' I said, shaking his hand. 'You must be Simon. I'm Joe.'

'Cool man, cool.' He said.

'It is,' I said, 'and it's going to get a lot cooler. There's going to be a right good frost tonight, you mark me words.' That made him laugh.

'No man, what I meant was that you seem cool.' He said.

'Well I were when I were walking here but I'm much warmer now.' I answered.

'Forget it man.' He smiled. Well, he seemed like a really nice friendly. 'Do you like ganja Joe?' He then said.

'What's that then?' I asked.

'You know, man,' he said, 'grass!'

'I do Simon,' I said. It takes me a full day to mow it like but it looks great when I'm done.'

Simon laughed again and he gave me a sort of gentle punch on the arm which were alright as it didn't hurt compared to all the other punches I'd had in me life.

'You're alright Joe.' He smiled.

'How long are you staying in the village for?' I asked him and at that point Graham Todd passed his cigarette to Polly, slid off the table he'd been sitting on and lay sort of sprawled on the floor for a while murmuring some load of old cobblers. I don't know, some people just can't hold their drink. But do you know what, I were starting to feel a bit light-headed meself by then. Fartleberrys Mild ain't normally that strong. I felt that I needed some fresh air and I were starting to feel dizzy.

'I'll be around for a while. Hey! Do you listen to the Floyd man?' He said.

'What's that?' I asked feeling even dizzier.

'Pink Floyd, man.' 'You know, Dark Side, Atom Heart Mother, Ummagumma.' He said but I don't know what had come over me. He weren't making any sense and I were feeling blummin' strange.

'Excuse me.' I said and I ran out of there and into the gents khazi and nearly threw me guts up but just air and spit came out. Horrible it were. Ooh, I did feel queer. I could still hear Polly cackling and I just wanted to get out of there and go home. Me eyes were all funny and blurry and I felt really ill. I reckon I'd picked up some kind of bug. I wiped me mouth on me sleeve and went out to the carpark. Me head were spinning by now and I were worried I wouldn't be able to go to work the next day and would get a rollicking off Her Ladyship. I ran home. Ran I tell you, all the way to Sheep Dip Lane without stopping. I'd never felt so ill and I just wanted to get to bed. And that's what I did. But here's the funny thing, the next morning I were as right as rain. I felt fine. How strange is that?

I saw Meg on the way to work and apologised for running out like that but she said it were alright but that I missed a really good night. I'm glad she enjoyed herself but I wish she wouldn't blummin' well smoke. Still once we're married...

I were still feeling a bit puddled though. I mean, I get puddled a lot but some of the things that Simon were going on about were just strange. Her Ladyship came down to the vegetable garden to see how I were getting on with the digging and to tell me that if it weren't done right that she would take the spade to the back of me head and I were thinking of asking her what an Ummagumma were but then I thought better of it. She weren't in the best of moods anyway because the local paper, or 'rag' as she calls it, hadn't printed her latest letter about crucifying fly tippers on telegraph poles. It got me thinking though. He'd been on about something called a Floyd that were pink and a dark side of something or other. It made me wonder if he were right in the blummin' head. So I left it at that.

Anyway, I didn't speak to Simon again for a week or two although I did see him quite often walking around the village. He never seemed to do any work though. I mean, there are jobs to be had in Blessham if you want one. I'm sure Farmer Bull could've done with some help. But he just seemed to spend his time drifting about the village, calling people 'man' and doing beggar all. Still, I suppose he weren't making a nuisance of himself so that were alright. In fact, it weren't until the end of March that I had what you'd call a proper chat with him.

I were in the big greenhouse getting ready for planting time when I heard a noise, looked up and there he were in the doorway standing next to Meg and that beggar Jim Booth (of all people) were with 'em too. I've got to be honest with you, I don't really like Boothy. He's picked on me all me life but this time he were alright with me. Friendly like. That were really odd that were.

'Alright Joe.' He said. Well, Boothy has never said that to me before. Never called me Joe. But I answered and said, 'Ah boy, not so bad.'

'Hi Joe.' Said Meg with that lovely smile of hers.

'Dude!' Said Simon nodding his head up and down like one of them little toy dogs you see in the back of cars. Then they all walked in and Boothy closed the door behind 'em.

'Ere,' I said. 'You can't all come in here like that. Her Ladyship will have your guts for garters. Mine and all.' I said. 'She'll have the dogs set on you. You don't want that.'

'It's alright Joe,' said Meg smiling, 'Kennedy has taken her into town in the Rolls. She'll be gone for hours. We need to have a little chat with you.'

Well, the last person I wanted to chat with were Jim Booth. It were only a few days earlier that he'd called me a 'thick knobhead' as I walked past his shop which weren't very nice. But me beautiful Meg were smiling so sweetly that how could I refuse. 'Alright.' I said. 'What about?'

'Plants man,' said Simon, 'plants.'

'Oh no,' I said, 'I can't give you any of Her Ladyship's plants. If I gave you any of her plants she'd drag me through the village by the...'

'No dude,' he said, 'We don't want *her* plants man. We want to grow some plants. Here, in your greenhouse man.' To this day I'm beggared if I know what a dude is.

'Ooh,' I said, 'I don't know about that. If Her Ladyship found out I'd get into an awful lot of trouble.'

'We'll make it worth your while Joe.' Said Boothy.

'How?' I asked.

'What would you like in return man.' Said Simon.

'Nothing.' I said, 'I got everything I need thank you. And I really don't want to rile Her Ladyship. You don't want to either if you've got any sense.'

'There must be something Joe.' Said Boothy and I've got to be honest, it were giving me the creeps him being so nice to me. That's how odd it were.

'The only thing I want in this life,' I said, pointing at Meg, 'is to marry that beautiful girl standing there.' Well, they all looked at each other and that Simon gave a bit of a silly laugh. But I were dead serious. 'So unless you can promise me that,' I said, 'then I ain't going to let you have any plants in here.' And they all looked at each other again. I were worried that Boothy might start getting busy with his fists but he didn't. It were Meg that spoke next.

'Tell you what,' she said, 'you two step outside and let me have a word with Joe.' They both agreed and they stepped outside. Meg turned to me, looked me straight in the eye and said, 'Joe, we've known each other a long time ain't we?'

'We have that, Meg.' I said. 'Since we were young 'uns.'

'And we've always been friends Joe. Ain't we?' She said.

'Oh Meg,' I said to her, 'you've always been more than a friend to me. Remember when I told you I loved you in Farmer Bull's haystack? Well I meant it Meg. I've always loved you and one day I'm going to walk you down the island in church.'

'You really do love me don't you Joe?' She smiled.

'More than anyone.' I said. 'More than me mum even.'

'Well, in that case,' she said, 'won't you do this one thing for me and let Simon grow some plants in here?'

'What sort of plants?' I asked.

'Oh, just some, erm, herbs, you know.' She said.

Well, I didn't know about that. Her Ladyship ain't too fond of herbs. 'Vile organisms whose only purpose in this world seems to be to disrupt, alarm and inflame the taste buds.' She says. 'The only herb worth having Wilkie is the humble parsley and only then in a sauce, as an accompaniment to fish and boiled potatoes. And perhaps a little mint now and again; to aid digestion and dispel flatus. But nothing else! Nothing else, do you hear me? By God if I catch you growing any other herbs than that I'll break you Wilkie. Break you I say.' I didn't understand half of what she were going on about but I got the gist. So, with that in mind I were really hoping that Meg were just going to say, 'parsley and mint.'

'What sort of herbs?' I said.

'Well, nothing you've heard of Joe. They're sort of foreign herbs.' She said.

'Foreign?' I said gawping at her.

'Yeah, erm, kind of like basil.' She said.

'Basil who?' I asked. There hadn't been anyone called Basil in the village since as long as I could remember.

'No Joe,' she laughed, 'basil is a kind of herb. A foreign herb.'

'Ooh no,' I said feeling my guts starting to loosen at the thought, 'Her Ladyship don't like foreign things. If she knew there were foreigners in her greenhouse she'd give me a right, proper pasting.'

'But she needn't know.' Said Meg. You could keep it secret. Our secret Joe.'

'She said she's break me Meg, break me, if there were anything other than parsley and mint,' I cried, 'and I don't want breaking.'

'Oh, come on Joe, there's got to be some little spot where she won't see,' said Meg, 'and besides, she's starting work on a new book soon so she'll be too busy to come down here that often.' She were right and all. Her Ladyship were writing a new book, bit of a long-winded title called - 'The Thumbscrew and It's Limitless Possibilities in Helping the Police with Their Enquiries.'

'Well,' I said, shuffling me feet about and looking down. 'There's a couple of spare cold frames on the far side there that she said I could grow me own radishes or whatever in. You could have them. But you mustn't say anything to anyone about it or she'll have me off the premises before you could say 'Jack Frost.'

'That would be fine.' She said, her gorgeous, big eyes lighting up. 'And I tell you what Joe. When the herbs are all grown, I'm going to give you something in return.'

'What?' I asked, and then she leaned in close to me and whispered right in me ear.

'I'm going to kiss you over and over and over again Joe Wilkie.' She said. 'Over and over and over again. In private and full on the lips!'

Well do you know what, I could feel meself starting to go perfectly normal when she said that. I couldn't hold back any longer. 'Alright Meg, my darling Meg,' I said to her with my voice shaking, 'you can have them cold frames. Blimey Meg. You could have the whole blummin' vegetable garden and beggar the job if you kissed me over and over again.'

She smiled and said, 'Thanks Joe. I'll call the lads back in.'

So, Simon and Boothy came back in and we began to make plans about Simon growing his herbs and how he could come up to the vegetable garden when Her Ladyship were out. It felt wrong to be honest, being sneaky like that, but I couldn't get the thought of kissing that beautiful girl of mine out of me head. And I figured that Her Ladyship probably wouldn't find out because she said I could have the cold frames and if she did find out I could say they were my herbs and that would be alright. It felt a bit like lying though which ain't right and I thought I better pray about it when I went to bed that night.

Now, an even stranger thing happened the next time I went down the pub on the Friday night. Boothy blummin' well offered to buy me a pint. And that ain't never happened before. I mean he's drank me pint before and he's spilled me pint before and he's thrown a pint over me before but he's never wanted to buy me a pint. I were so surprised I didn't know what to do at first but he were so friendly and persoovive... perusive... perversive...

...cajoling like.

That I thought I'd best take him up on it. So I said yes and asked for a pint of mild. I were still a bit unsure like because this just weren't the Jim Booth that I'd come to know. The Jim Booth I knew and grew up around used to bully me and tease me and throw stones at me and punch me and kick me and push me over into cow pats and push me into the duck pond and push me into nettles and push me off the school bus when it stopped and push me over in the snow and put thistles down me trousers and call me thick and say things about me mum and laugh at me and... well, you get the picture. And yet now here he were buying me beer so you'll forgive me if I were feeling just a bit supiscus... subscrupulous... sispucuous...

...wary.

Anyway, he buys me one and then he says, 'Let's go and sit over by the window Joe. I need to have a word with you.'

'Right you are!' I replied but I were still ready to be on me toes if it were one of his blummin' schemes to get at me.

We sat down and before you know it he starts talking to me about fertilizer and how often to water young plants and all sorts of gardening stuff. Well, I answered him as best as I could and he even wrote down a few notes here and there. The next thing you know, Simon comes in, gets himself a pint and comes and sits with us and he starts asking all sorts of questions and all and they kept looking and nodding at each other and all the while I'm sat there wondering what were going on. I finished me pint and were going to leave but Simon bought me another one and then we all started talking again but this time we were talking about Meg and me and all sorts of stuff. Then Boothy got another round in even though I offered to pay and we talked some more about the village and what certain people were like and who were the gossipy type. I were starting to enjoy meself I were. Then Simon got 'em in again, then Boothy and then Simon and then Boothy and then Simon again and before I knew where I were I'd had about eight pints and it had gone right to me head. I decided that I'd best get home and go to bed because I had to be at work at seven to prune back Her Ladyships' lobelias. But lo and behold Boothy gets another round in and we carried on drinking and all the while Simon is calling me 'man' and 'dude' and prattling on about something or other called Gong and Caravan and early Genesis. Well, I don't know much about gongs and caravans but I do know all about early Genesis don't I? That's when God created the earth and Adam and Eve and then there were Noah and his ark. So I told him all about that, which made him laugh and say things like 'No man, I'm talking about Trespass and Foxtrot,' and I'd say things like 'Oh no, you don't want to go trespassing around here, especially when Her Ladyship's dogs are loose. Mind you the foxes do trot across the lawn now and then. You can see their tracks in the frost.' And then he'd laugh again and I laughed too because we seemed to be getting on so well and I were pleased that I were making someone laugh. And eventually I bought us all a pint and by the time I'd finished that one I were three sheets to the wind to be honest and that's when Bob called out 'Time gentlemen please!' and we all left.

Like I say, I were more than a bit tipsy and when I got out into the fresh air I felt even more so. I said goodnight to Simon and Boothy and I made me way home and I'm ashamed to say that I were staggering quite a bit by now. I don't remember too much about getting home other than Major Brimmish shining his torch in me face and saying 'Halt! Who goes there?' to which I replied 'Joe Wilkie sir! I think.' He switched his torch off and told me to get home or he would report me for breaking curfew.

The next thing I knew were me blummin' alarm clock going off and waking me up all of a sudden. I were lying on top of me bed with all me clothes on and me mouth felt like a rat had slept in it. Me heard hurt and I were farting for all I were worth. So I got up and went downstairs. The old man weren't up yet but that didn't matter. I made meself a cup of tea but I couldn't face any breakfast. Especially since all we had in were bread and dripping. I mean, I love it normally but I couldn't even think about it that morning. I looked at meself in the mirror and I looked blummin' awful.

'You've got a hangover you daft beggar' I said to meself and I started to remember what had happened the night before and told meself that I were a right blummin' fool for drinking so much on a work night. Mind you, I got meself to work on time. That's one thing I can be proud of, I've never been late to work. Scared to be if truth be told.

I got to work on the lobelias but I were feeling rough I can tell you. I'd been at it about twenty minutes when Her Ladyship turns up with all them blummin' dogs leaping around all over the place. She had her twelve-bore cocked in the crook of her arm and I hoped she weren't going to let it off anywhere near me because me head were splitting.

'Morning Wilkie!' She snapped. 'A fine day!'

'Yes Ma'am.' I replied, but I were feeling far from fine.

'Make sure you do a first-rate job on my lobelias Wilkie. You wouldn't want my boot up your arse now would you?' She said with that scary cackle of hers.

'No Ma'am, I'll do me very best.' I said and do you know what I were feeling proper queasy I were and I were hoping she wouldn't hang around too long because I were sure I were going to be sick.

'Lovely colour on the lobelia when it comes out. Don't you agree?' She said.

'Oh yes, Ma'am, lovely.' I said feeling me guts churning.

'Yes, right, get on with it then Wilkie and don't give yourself cause to rue the day by doing them badly.' She said.

'I won't Ma'am.' I said and were now desperate to spew.

'Good day then Wilkie,' she said turning away, 'I'm off to see if I can't get myself a nice plump woodcock for my tea.' And with that she started walking away and I felt relieved that I could throw up at last behind the bushes. But she only went half a dozen steps when she stopped and turned back.

'Oh, there is one other thing Wilkie.' She said walking towards me and pointing at one of the dogs. 'Cromwell here has got an upset stomach and unfortunately has sprayed liquid shit all over the back steps. Leave the lobelias for ten minutes and go and clean it up.'

That were it. I couldn't hold it back any longer. I dropped onto me knees and out it came. Came pouring out of me it did. A big pile of spew right in front of Her Ladyship's feet. She stared at me for a few seconds and then at the spew and then back at me. You can probably guess what were coming.

'WHAT THE FUCKING HELL IS WRONG WITH YOU WILKIE! She roared. 'HOW DARE YOU HEAVE YOUR STINKING INNARDS UP IN FRONT OF ME? HOW FUCKING DARE YOU I SAY! BY GOD I'VE NEVER KNOWN THE LIKES OF IT. A MEMBER OF MY OWN STAFF PUKING BEFORE ME. SUCH IGNORANCE, SUCH IMPERTINENCE, SUCH INTOLERABLE FUCKING INSOLENCE! YOU VILE CREATURE. YOU DRIBBLING EXCUSE FOR A HUMAN BEING. YOU'LL PAY FOR THIS WILKIE. I'M GOING BACK TO THE HOUSE TO FETCH A RIDING CROP AND IF YOU'RE STILL HERE I'M GOING TO THRASH YOU RAW WITH IT. NOW BE GONE AND LEAVE MY PROPERTY WHILE YOU'VE GOT THE CHANCE.'

'Please Ma'am,' I begged through tears, 'I didn't mean. I couldn't help it.'

'DIDN'T MEAN IT? She bellowed. *COULDN'T HELP IT?* PAH! WHY IT'S QUITE THE MOST DISGUSTING DISPLAY OF... OF... WELL, IT'S JUST QUITE THE MOST DISGUSTING DISPLAY. WHAT DO YOU THINK YOU'RE PLAYING AT WILKIE?'

'I, I don't feel very well Ma'am.' I said getting back to me feet.

'DON'T FEEL VERY WELL! WHY? WHAT'S FUCKING WRONG WITH YOU?' She demanded and I'd never seen her look as mad as that since that day when I were stuck on the roof.

Well, the last thing I wanted to say were that I'd had a skinful of ale the night before so I'm afraid I lied and said, 'I think the tripe and onions I had for tea last night must have been off Ma'am.'

'TRIPE AND ONIONS? YOU MEAN TO TELL ME THAT YOU EAT THAT FUCKING MUCK?' She were still right mad. 'I'M NOT SURPRISED YOUR ILL, EATING THAT SORT OF SHIT. WHY, IT'S A COWS GUTS FOR CRYING OUT LOUD. BY GOD WILKIE, I KNEW YOU WERE A BUMPKIN BUT I DIDN'T REALISE YOU SCRAPED THE FUCKING BARREL JUST TO EAT!'

'I'm so sorry Ma'am,' were all I could say, 'I'm ever so sorry.' And she stood and glared at me for about a minute before she carried on in the awful low voice of hers which I reckon is just as bad as when she shouts.

'And I suppose you'd like to go home wouldn't you Wilkie?' She growled.

'Well, I...' I began.

'Yes, yes. Go snivelling off to your filthy, little hovel with your tail between your legs and spend the day sitting on your scrawny arse doing fuck all. That's what you'd like isn't it? That's what you're after Wilkie!' She said sarcisticly... carcasticly...arsetastically...

...sneering like.

'If I could just...' I said.

'Oh no Wilkie! You're not pulling that one on me. I wasn't born yesterday. If you want to go home you'll clean up that dog shit first my lily-livered, weak-gutted, offal eating, puking little friend.' She pointed towards the back steps as she spoke. 'And you'll be in tomorrow morning to finish off the bally lobelias as well.'

'Oh, but I'm putting out the hymn books in church tomorrow Ma'am.' I said.

'Really? Is that a fact? Well I'm afraid the good vicar is going to have to do without his little helper this Sunday Wilkie. You'll be here working on my lobelias and if you should choose to defy me I'll come down to that church and drag you out by your fucking nostrils and ram the shears up your arse for you. Do I make myself clear? Or shall I just go now and fetch the riding crop instead?' She said through gritted teeth.

'I'll be here Ma'am.' I promised. 'I'll be here first thing.'

'You'd better be Wilkie.' And with that she spun on her heel and strode off.

I put all me tools in me wheelbarrow and took 'em back to the potting shed and then I got out the long hose and washed all the dog muck of the back stairs, of which there were quite a lot. Cromwell must have felt as rough as me. To tell you the truth though, spewing up had actually made me feel a bit better but I'd had enough for one day and I went home feeling proper sorry for meself. On the way I stopped at the vicarage and told Nick all about it. He made me a cup of tea and spoke to me about the perils of the demon drink and about making better choices about the company I keep. He said that I ought not to have anything to do with Simon as he seemed like trouble to him. At the back of me mind I knew he were right but I'd already made a promise to Meg about the herbs and I just couldn't go back on that now could I? Especially with all them kisses that were going to be coming my way. So, I promised Nick that I wouldn't sit drinking with Simon and Boothy again like that but I didn't mention anything about the herbs. I thought that if the only time I saw Simon were at the vegetable garden then that would be enough.

Well that time soon came. Her Ladyship went off to London for a few days. She seemed to have forgotten all about the spewing episode and as it were now well into Spring I were as busy as could be. While she were gone Meg arranged for Simon and Boothy to come round and sow their plants in the cold frames which they did. I'd agreed to keep an eye on 'em but they were going to look after 'em proper like, when Her Ladyship were either out for the day or in her study. When she's writing she sticks at it for hours on end you see and Meg said she'd come to a sort of deal with Harvey to make sure them blummin' dogs were locked up as well. I don't know what the deal were exactly but I overheard her say to Simon that Harvey had quite a big shaft and he certainly knew how to ram it in. I think she must have meant his walking staff that he carries to keep the dogs in check. It's quite a good one, got a ram's head carved at the top. Anyway, all the plans were in place and the herbs were soon growing and sure enough Simon came to the vegetable garden whenever Her Ladyship were out.

As for the herbs 'emselves I didn't give it too much thought after a while. They grew well enough and they had leaves that reminded me a bit of the maple tree that were in the middle of the flower bed in the back lawn except they had seven leaves on each stalk and they were dark green. They had a funny sort of smell too that reminded me of that night in the pool room when Simon were going on about his mate Floyd. I made sure they stayed fed and watered and didn't dry out and Simon or Boothy or both did the rest and as the months passed I got busier and busier with everything that were going on at the hall and in the village and the Summer soon came around and with it July and preparations were being made for the open day. And that's when things really took a turn for the worse.

11
The Open Day

It were one of the hottest July weeks on record they say. I say, who wants to make a record about July. No one's going to listen to that, are they? Anyway, dead hot it were and Her Ladyship had me watering everything regularly, even the lawns. Rushed off me blummin' feet I were. And by 'eck she weren't half barking some orders at me.

'FORK THE CROQUET LAWN WILKIE!' she'd say, and *'FEED THE ROSES WILKIE!'* and *'GET THOSE WEEDS OFF THE FRONT PATIO WILKIE!* and *'BY GOD WILKIE IF I SEE YOU ANYWHERE NEAR MY RED-HOT POKERS WITH THAT HOE I SHALL DRIVE A WHITE-HOT POKER UP YOUR WRETCHED LITTLE ARSE!'* That kind of thing you know.

But it were going well really. Everywhere were looking good and Her Ladyship even gave me a compliment. She said 'The grounds look quite adequate Wilkie. Carry on!' Beaming with pride I were. No one ever called me work a posh word like 'adequate' before. She must have been right pleased with me.

And then the big day arrived and I were told to 'look smart for a change.' So I wore me Sunday best trousers and shirt that I normally go to church in. Her Ladyship had some important guests coming, you see, and she didn't want me looking like 'some bally scarecrow!' as she put it. She had old woman Horton and Lord Elppus coming of course and the former mayor of the town who goes by the name of Councillor Elders and how could I forget her good friend Constable Saywane? Or rather Chief Constable Saywane to be precise. He's in charge of the police force in the town and they became friends through her supporting the retired police officers' home and him supporting her camp-pain to bring back the death penalty. I don't like him though. He's the one that started all this nasty business off in the first place.

Anyway, all the staff were given jobs for the day. Kennedy were taking the car parking money at a cost of £3 per vehicle. Mrs Partridge, Meg and Roger were to take kiddies on horseback rides up and down the drive at a cost of £2.50 a time. Polly and Peggy were to serve cups of tea and coffee at a cost of £1 a time, £2 for cucumber sandwiches and £2.50 for cakes in the marquee on the front lawn. A marquee is like a big tent that gets very hot in the sunshine and smells like the scout hut. Mrs Franks were to keep making the sandwiches Harvey were to patrol the perry-meat-err with a couple of the dogs to keep undesirables and low-life out. Mr Franks were to oversee everything, and I were told to remain in the vegetable garden and stop anyone from stealing fruit off the trees. 'Some damned underhanded people about Wilkie.' Said Her Ladyship. 'They'll not think twice about helping themselves to my plums and pears. Bastards! Damn their odious livers! I despise the very air that they breathe. It's your job to make sure it doesn't happen. Stay vigilant Wilkie. Vigilant now I say.' I didn't know what vigilant were, but Mr Franks explained it to me. He said I had to keep me eyes open. I did me best but after five minutes I couldn't help blinking because they were getting sore. So I thought it best just to watch the fruit trees and make sure nobody nicked anything off 'em. She's very keen on her plums, you see, is Her Ladyship. 'They, and the humble pear, maintain regularity, promote lubrication and free up the bowels.' She always says.

As for His Lordship, he were told to 'Just keep out of bloody sight, you tiresome and annoying little piss-quick.' So he stayed indoors and fell asleep in his favourite armchair with the newspaper over his face. Besides, it were a very hot day and he don't take too well to the sunshine.

And busy? Why, it were one of the busiest open days we'd ever had. There were loads of people in the vegetable garden and I reckon I saw quite a few eyeing up them there plum trees. But I stuck to 'em like a crumpet and made sure nothing got stolen. I did have one nasty little moment when some kiddie threw a fallen plum at me that had a wasp in it. By 'eck, I were tempted to give him what for around the ear 'ole. I know Her Ladyship would have done. His folks were as bad because they just laughed and said he were' high spirited.' I don't know about that, but I know what old Rodwell would have done with his high blummin' spirits.

Other than that though it were alright. I heard quite a few people say how nice it all looked and how well the brassicas were coming along and such like. And the tomatoes in the big greenhouse drew huge gasps of ambidration... emulation... ammunition...

...folks were amazed at how big they were.

Now, about them blummin' tomatoes. That were a right old palaver and all. You see, a week before the open day Her Ladyship had got the idea for me to stand and sell 'em to the public in brown paper bags seeing as there'd been such a good big crop of 'em that year. It were a good idea I suppose but there were one or two problems with it though:

1. I weren't too good when it come to using the weighing scales.
2. I were even worse when it come to working out the money.

We had what they call a dry run, you see. Her Ladyship got the scales out of the kitchen and brought 'em down to the vegetable garden with a pound weight but I couldn't get the blummin' things to work properly despite her showing me about ten times and threatening me with all manner of things. In the end it were decided that I'd pick 'em, take 'em up to the kitchen and she'd get Mrs Franks to weigh 'em and bag 'em up. I just then had to sell 'em. But then when it come to the money side that were even worse.

'If a pound of tomatoes is sixty pence, Wilkie, and I give you a pound for them, how much change will I get.' Her Ladyship said to me.

'Oh no Ma'am,' I replied, 'They're *your* tomatoes. *You* don't have to pay for 'em.'

'No Wilkie,' she tutted, 'I'm not buying them.'

'Quite right Ma'am,' I said, 'you shouldn't have too.'

'Oh, for the love of God, man, it's a fairly simple exercise.' She groaned. 'Even for you.'

'Well, to tell you the truth Ma'am, I don't do too much exercise. I get enough working on the garden you see.' I said. 'Although I am keen on walking up on the...'

'Give me fucking strength!' She said through gritted teeth. 'I'll try one more time and then I might have to knock it into you thick skull with my fist. Now look, a customer comes up to you and asks for a pound of tomatoes. You give him a pound and he gives you sixty pence for them. Do you understand so far?'

'Yes Ma'am!' I lied.

'However,' she continued, 'here's another supposition, let us suppose, for just a moment now, that the customer doesn't have the exact money and gives you a pound, how much change do you give him?'

'Well that depends Ma'am.' I said.

'Depends on what?' She snapped and I could see her temper were wearing thin.

'Well,' I said, 'I give him a pound and then he gives me a pound so that's two pound right? Then he wants me to change it from tomatoes to something else because he ain't got the right money for tomatoes so I'd probably have to give him a cucumber or a lettuce or something else instead and I don't know how much they cost and in the meantime I've still got his pound and he's got mine and then there should be sixty pence somewhere as well but he ain't got sixty pence you say, so I...'

'Can I just stop you there for a moment Wilkie?' She said.

'Yes Ma'am?' I replied.

'WHAT IN THE NAME OF BLUE BLOODY THUNDER ARE YOU FUCKING DRIBBLING ON ABOUT?' She roared, and yes, as you will no doubt guess, I nearly pappered meself. 'YOU REALLY ARE THE MOST CONFOUNDED, BLOODY IGNORAMUS I HAVE EVER ENCOUNTERED

IN MY ENTIRE LIFE WILKIE! MY GOD, THERE ARE AMOEBA INVISIBLE TO THE NAKED EYE FLOATING IN THE LAKE THAT HAVE A GREATER I.Q THAN YOU! THERE ARE FLIES BUZZING AROUND THE HORSES ARSES IN THE STABLES THAT HAVE A GREATER UNDERSTANDING OF FISCAL MATTERS THAN YOU! I WOULD RATHER HAVE ONE OF MY DOGS IN CHARGE OF HANDLING MONEY THAN A HEAP OF SHIT LIKE YOU! HOW THE FUCKING HELL CAN YOU NOT KNOW HOW MUCH CHANGE IS NEEDED FROM SIXTY PENCE IN THE POUND? DID YOU ACTUALLY ATTEND SCHOOL WILKIE AND IF SO WHAT IN GOD'S NAME DID THEY ACTUALLY TEACH YOU? NOT SIMPLE MATHEMATICS THAT'S FOR SURE. I OFTEN WONDER WHAT THIS COUNTRY IS COMING TOO BUT BY GOD YOU TAKE THINGS TO A NEW LEVEL, MAN. FOR FUCK'S SAKE WILKIE. ONE POUND MINUS SIXTY PENCE IS FORTY PENCE. *FORTY PENCE! FORTY FUCKING PENCE!* CHRIST ALMIGHTY, IS IT REALLY THAT DIFFICULT WILKIE? I AM SO TEMPTED TO SMASH MY FIST INTO YOUR GORMLESS LITTLE FACE RIGHT NOW, I REALLY AM. AND YOU OUGHT TO THINK YOURSELF EXTREMELY FORTUNATE THAT I'M CERTAIN YOU'RE JUST AS THICK AS PIGSHIT AND NOT TAKING THE PISS. IF I THOUGHT YOU WERE TAKING THE PISS WILKIE, BELIEVE ME YOU'D BE LYING ON THE FLOOR RIGHT NOW WITH YOUR FUCKING FRONT TEETH MISSING. FORGET THE ARSING TOMATOES. I'M NOT GOING TO WASTE MY VALUABLE TIME STANDING HERE TRYING TO DO BASIC PRIMARY SCHOOL LEVEL ARITHMETIC WITH A FUCKING SIMPLETON. BY GOD BUT MY BLOOD IS BOILING. GET YOUR BRAINLESS CARCASS OUT OF MY SIGHT WILKIE AND GET ON WITH SOME WORK. DAMN AND BLAST YOU!' And with that she stormed out of the greenhouse and slammed the door so blummin' hard that a pane of glass fell out and smashed onto the floor.

'*THAT'S COMING OUT OF YOUR BASTARD WAGES!*' She said glaring at me through the hole that the glass had come out of. Then she stomped off muttering about how livid she were and how I should have been drowned at birth and what a pitiful state the education system were in and things like that. I were shaking in me boots I can tell you but I were glad I didn't have to sell tomatoes no more. It were just so confusing. People giving me pounds and me giving 'em pounds back and changing things and what-not. I were glad it were over to be honest. And Her Ladyship had calmed down a fair bit by the next time I saw her which were just as I were leaving for the day.

'Goodnight Ma'am!' I said as she watched me from the front door with her hands on her hips and a scowl on her face.

'Fuck off you useless, uneducated, halfwit!' She said without shouting, which believe me, is her calmed down. And sure enough, she were true to her word and the cost of that piece of glass came out of me wages. Fifteen blummin' quid! Fifteen quid for a piece of glass. Mind you, I reckon it were worth it to not have to sell them blummin' tomatoes.

Anyway, back to the open day. It got to about four-ish in the afternoon and I were feeling a bit tired from standing in the sun all day, because I'd forgot to bring a hat with me, and there weren't too many folks still wandering around. Half four were closing time you see. And as far as I knew no plums or pears or anything else had been stolen from the vegetable garden and I were dead proud to think that I had done me job proper like. It were at that moment that Her Ladyship walked into the vegetable garden with her guests. She were walking along with her hands behind her back, crop in hand and talking to Chief Constable Saywane about how the reintroduction of the iron maiden would more than halve the crime figures in the country overnight. Lord Elppus kept stopping every now and then to look at me onions or the strawberries under the nets and they all seemed in good spirits. Old woman Horton were wearing a bright yellow and blue dress with flowers on it and a sort of straw hat that looked like an upside-down birds' nest to me. And she were saying things like 'Oh, I'd simply love some plums like that in my mouth!' and 'Ooh, just look at the girth of that courgette! Why, it's positively throbbing with vitality and goodness!' and 'I say, what I couldn't do with those walnuts!' and other strange things about the fruit and veg. I thought I'd better keep out of the way and were going to go to me shed but Her Ladyship called me over to 'em.

'Ah, Wilkie!' She called. 'Come here. I want to introduce you to some people.'

Well, I felt right blummin' honoured I did. To be asked to go and meet her friends! That were a real prilavage... pearlavige... ripalage...

...I were dead chuffed.

So over I went with a big grin on me face like a cheesy cat. It felt like I were going up in the world meeting her posh friends, especially the Chief Constable and the former mayor. Wait until I tell Major Brimmish, I thought. He'd be proper jealous and no mistake.

'Gentlemen,' said Her Ladyship when I reached 'em, 'this is Wilkie, my gardener. Blasted, bloody nincompoop, if truth be told, when it comes to intellect but he knows his way around the garden.' Ooh, I didn't half blush with pride. 'Shake hands damn it Wilkie!' She demanded and so I shook hands with the first one of 'em.

'Saywane! Chief Constable Saywane!' Said Chief Constable Saywane. 'I must say young man you've done a first-rate job on these grounds. And the fruit trees look marvellous. Very tempting indeed. I wouldn't mind holding a nice round pear in my hands right now.'

'Ooh, Chief Constable, I say!' Said old woman Horton for some reason, waving her hand in front of her face and making an O with her mouth.

'Oh no sir,' I said, 'You mustn't take any fruit off of the trees. I'm guarding 'em.' This made Her Ladyship snort loudly but the others just laughed so I laughed too.

'It's alright Wilkie,' he chuckled, 'I won't steal any fruit. Lady Stark-Raven keeps you busy down here I see.'

'Oh yes,' I replied, 'I like growing vegetables sir.'

‘So I see, so I see.’ He said twice. ‘And I must say it all looks very esculent.’ Well, as you will no doubt know by now, I had no idea what esculent meant so I just nodded.

‘Councillor Elders!’ Said Councillor Elders, offering me his hand which I shook. ‘I wish my garden looked as splendid as this. You’ll have to be careful Lady Stark-Raven or I shall be poaching your gardener off of you.’

‘Well actually,’ I said, ‘it’s me old man what’s the poacher.’

‘Ahem! I think we should carry on.’ Said Her Ladyship giving me a bit of a glare. ‘Come Wilkie, you may walk along with us and explain to my guests what’s what in the vegetable garden.’ Well I knew what vegetables there were but I didn’t know what ‘what’ was but I followed ‘em anyway and we all walked around the garden. Every so often we’d stop and I’d get asked questions about rhubarb or raspberries or when were the best time to sow runner beans or when were the best time to start harvesting carrots and such like and I think I answered quite well. I mean, I don’t know much about most things but I do know about gardening and Her Ladyship seemed happy with what I were saying. I were feeling ever so good and best of all I were enjoying meself. So much so that I hadn’t noticed that we’d walked as far as them two cold frames that I’d given to Meg, Simon and Boothy, and it weren’t until the Chief Constable said ‘Ah! And what have we under here then?’ that I realised where we were. I weren’t too worried though because I were just going to say that those herbs were mine. Which is what I did.

‘Oh those,’ I said with a smile, ‘those are a couple of cold frames that Her Ladyship very kindly said I could use for meself.’

‘I see, I see.’ He said twice again. ‘And what are you growing for yourself Wilkie?’ He asked me.

‘Just some herbs sir.’ I said.

‘Ah! I’m rather interested in growing herbs myself.’ He said. ‘Is it easy?’

‘Easy enough sir.’ I said, ‘You just need the right soil, plenty of sunlight and water and feed ‘em regular like.’

'As easy as that is it? And what herbs are you growing under there?' He said.

Well, the last thing I wanted to say were 'basil' or 'foreign herbs' with Her Ladyship in earshot but I couldn't think of what else to say so I just said, 'Special herbs, you know.'

'Oh for God's sake Wilkie!' Groaned Her Ladyship. 'It's only parsley man! Lift the damned frame up so we can see!' And I gulped I did. Blimey, I thought, she were going to know it weren't parsley as soon as she saw it and I'd get an almighty rollicking for growing basil on her property. 'What are you waiting for man? Get on with it, that's a damned order!' She said shaking her finger at the cold frames. My guts turned to water, water I tell you, and it were with shaking hands that I lifted the lid off the first frame. They all leaned forward to have a look inside at the basil and I braced meself for a blast from Her Ladyship. But no-one said anything for quite a few seconds. It were the Chief Constable who spoke first.

'You say these are your plants Wilkie?' He said turning towards me furrowing his brow.

'Yes sir,' I said, 'I'm afraid they are. It's basil.'

'Basil?' He said straightening up. 'Are you trying to make fun of me, boy?'

'Oh no sir.' I said. 'I'd never make fun of anyone so important as yourself.'

'You know as well as I do Wilkie, what these plants are.' He said sounding very serious.

'Ain't they basil?' I said.

'No, Wilkie, they most certainly are not!' He said as sternly as old Rodwell would have done when I got me times tables wrong.

'Why? What on earth are they?' Asked Her Ladyship.

'My dear Lady Stark-Raven,' he said clearing his throat, 'I'm afraid I have to tell you that these are cannabis plants!' And then there were silence as they all stared at the plants inside the cold frame. As for me, I never heard that word before – cannabis!

The silence were terrible and it seemed to go on for ages, but then Her Ladyship broke it by turning towards me with the most fearsome look on her face and growling my name all drawn out like. 'W-i-i-i-i-i-l-l-l-l-k-i-i-i-e-e-e-e!' Then she drew in a big lungful of breath, shouted *'YOU BASTARD!'* and lunged at me, her hands wrapping around me throat. And for the first time since I were a young 'un I wet me pants and screamed.

'YOU HORRIBLE, VILE, SCABACIOUS LITTLE BASTARD!' She roared and she shook me by the throat as she did. *'YOU DIRTY, STINKING, LYING, CHEATING, FILTHY, LOATHESOME, DISGUSTING, DRUG DEALING, SCUM! YOU WALKING ABOMINATION UPON THE EARTH! PREPARE TO DIE WILKIE! PREPARE YOURSELF TO DIE I SAY!* And tears filled me eyes just as quickly as the pee had filled me pants. I really thought she were going to throttle me to death and I didn't know how anyone could get so mad about a few herbs. And then all blummin' 'eck broke loose.

The Chief Constable grabbed hold of her left arm and tried to pull it away while Lord Elppus gets hold of her other one and tries to pull that away and old woman Horton starts squealing 'It's drugs! Drugs! Drugs!' over and over again at the top of her voice and waving her arms about. And all the while Her Ladyship is squeezing me by the throat and shouting *'DIE, YOU FUCKING SWINE, DIE!* And I'm crying and being shaken around like a bit of wet lettuce and Councillor Elders is calling for everyone to calm down and then Her Ladyship let go of me throat for a second to elbow Lord Elppus in the nose and then her hand went back on me throat and started shaking me again as His Lordship sank to his knees with his hands over his bloodied face and making a strange sort of gurgling sound and The Chief Constable started shouting at Her Ladyship 'Let him go, let him go! You'll make matters worse.' And I didn't see how things could have gotten any worse and Councillor Elders started shouting at old woman Horton to 'Go and fetch help, woman, for God's sake!' and so she ran off and then The Chief Constable grabbed Her Ladyship around the waist like they do in the rugby match and managed to pull her to the ground even though she still had hold of me throat which meant I got pulled to the ground as well and I wanted to beg for mercy but I couldn't speak because she were throttling me and I honestly thought I were going to blummin' well die!

Well, the next thing I know is Mr Franks rushing into the garden with Harvey and old woman Horton trailing behind and they joined in with The Chief Constable in trying to pull her off with Mr Franks saying 'Ma'am, Ma'am, please, you'll be arrested for assault!'

'ASSAULT? ASSAULT? I'M GOING TO DO MORE THAN ASSAULT THE BLOODY LITTLE FILTH PEDLAR!' She screeched and I could feel her spit on me face and smell her breath and I could tell she'd eaten salmon sandwiches and pickled onions at some point in the afternoon and pickled onions don't half make her fart but she weren't farting then. The only thing she were blowing off were steam.

But between the three of 'em they managed to do it. They got her hands off me throat. They saved me blummin' life that day they did. '*GET YOUR FUCKING HANDS OFF ME!'* She screamed. *'I'LL HAVE YOUR FUCKING JOBS AND YOUR FUCKING ARSES IF YOU DON'T FUCKING WELL GET OFF ME!'*

'My wife has called the police sir.' Said Mr Franks to the Chief Constable. They're on their way.'

'Let's just hope we can hold her until then.' He replied.

But they did it. By 'eck it took some doing but they held her. Mr Franks got a black eye and Harvey got his lip all busted open and Lord Elppus had managed to join in as well even with his smashed-up nose but somehow, they held her. It were a magnificent effort on their part and the language from Her Ladyship were, well, I can't really repeat what she said she were going to do to me once she got free but it sounded very painful and it involved a roll of barbed wire, some pliers, a car battery, at least three of the dogs and the flagpole. And then about ten minutes later we heard the siren as the police car pulled up in front of the house and about half a minute after that Mrs Franks came running into the vegetable garden with two bobbies. Well, it all seemed really too blummin' much to me over a few herbs.

Anyway, The Chief Constable and the two bobbies led me away from the vegetable garden and up to the hall to where the police car were whilst Her Ladyship screamed blue murder at me. I'd never seen a police car close up like that before, it were quite interesting really with the flashing lights and everything. And then imagine me surprise when one of the bobbies says to me 'Joseph Wilkie, I am arresting you on suspicion of growing a class B drug. You don't have to say anything but anything you do say may be taken down and used as evidence against you!'

'Arrested!' I said. 'But I ain't done nothing wrong. All I did were grow a little bit of basil in the cold frames. I didn't know that were against the law.'

'He's doing it again!' Said the Chief Constable. 'He's taking the piss; he's trying to be funny. Get him down the station and get him charged.' So one of the bobbies opens the back door of the car, puts his hand on top of me head and helps me get in. Then he got in next to me. The other bobby got in the front and we drove off. We hadn't gone very far at all when I looked out of the window and saw that Her Ladyship had gotten free and was charging across the front lawn, with Mr Franks and Harvey trailing behind her, shaking both her fists above her head and shouting *'YOU'RE A DEAD MAN WILKIE! DO YOU HEAR ME? A FUCKING DEAD MAN! I'LL FIND YOU WILKIE, I'LL HUNT YOU DOWN AND FLAY YOU ALIVE!'* But I suppose the car were going too fast for her and soon we were going down the drive, then through the village and out along Market Road towards town. That were the last time I saw Blessham, and I remember that I felt so blummin' scared and confused by all that had happened that I cried all the way to the police station.

12
Legal Doings (Part 1)

Well, the first thing I noticed about the police station were the smell and I didn't like it I have to say. It smelled like a piece of knackered old farmyard machinery that's been left out in the rain and gone a bit rusty. It weren't a very cheerful looking place either. The walls were covered in funny looking posters, most of which I couldn't read but I did work out one of 'em which I think said something like – STOP CAR THEFT! in big red letters. I thought that were odd because even though no-one wants cars to get thieved, no-one's going to stop if one has been. You ain't going to catch it on foot now are you? Life goes on you know. Still, I did feel sorry for whoever's car had been stolen.

On the way to the police station, whilst crying me blummin', eyes out I had been thinking about what were going to happen once we got there. I knew I were in a bit of bother about the blummin' basil and I couldn't think why. Meg had told me that basil were an herb that them eye-ta-leons use in cooking. The only thing I could think of then were that basil must be against the blummin' law in our country. And if that were the case then it meant I were in big trouble. The problem were of course that it didn't really belong to me, that basil, and so me head were in a right muddle as to what to say. It were clear to me that growing basil were wrong and if I said it were mine then I would be for it. On the other hand, if I said it were Simon, Meg and Boothy who were growing it then they would be for it and I just couldn't bear the thought of me beautiful Meg getting into trouble with the bobbies. That were a horrible thought. And then I thought to meself I'd just better wait and see how it pans out and hope that it all blows over. I mean, surely a bit of basil never hurt anyone. Then again there were that other word that the Chief Constable had used. Canned-A-Bit or something like that. I never heard that word before.

Another little problem I had were wet trousers of course due to having pee'd meself when Her Ladyship had set about me, and on top of which me neck were chaffed a bit from where she'd had hold of me. But I hoped the bobbies would see to all that.

Like I say, we arrived at the police station which is right in the middle of the town and I remember that pretty much everyone who we drove past stopped and stared. Honestly, you'd think that living in the town they would all have seen a police car before. The two bobbies got me out of the car and led me into the station and as I said, I wrinkled me nose at the pong in there. I were then introduced to a very large bobby with a thick moustache and three sort of dog-legged stripes on his upper arm who introduced himself as the Desk Sergeant. Well I didn't know he were a sergeant but I could see he were standing behind a desk so that were blummin' obvious. Talk about a waste of time. Anyway, he asked me what me name were.

'Joe!' Said I.

'Joe what?' He said.

'Jo-seph.' I replied and he began to write that down on a form that he had in front of him but then he stopped and looked up at me again.

'You're first name is Joseph?' He said with a nasty stare that I didn't much care for.

'That's right,' I said, 'but everyone just calls me Joe.' He stared at me again and I felt right awkward and tried not to look him in the eye.

'Listen laddie,' he said, 'you'll be doing yourself a favour if you don't waste my time.'

'Ooh, I wouldn't do that sir.' I said. 'I'd never waste the time of the police. Nick says we should all do what's right and not break the law and help the police if we can. I wouldn't waste your time sir, not in a hundred years I wouldn't.' I called him sir because I thought that might go well with me and I were dead scared I were.

'Just tell me your name.' He said still staring.

'I told you sir.' I said. 'It's Joseph.'

'Your full name!' He barked, raising his voice. 'What is your full name?'

'Oh, why didn't you say sir?' I replied. 'Me full name is Joseph Wilkie. I'm called Joseph after the man in the bible. You know, the story of the birth of Jesus and all that? Joseph and Mary? They went to Bethlehem and...'

'Yes, yes, yes,' he snapped, 'I'm quite familiar with the nativity.' And he wrote me name down on the form.

'Address?' He then said.

'No sir,' I said, 'Sunday best shirt and trousers!'

He looked up again and this time it were more of a glare than a stare. He looked at the two bobbies who had brought me in and then back at me before saying 'Trying to take the piss, sunshine, will get you absolutely nowhere. You're in enough trouble as it is without acting the goat.'

'But I were never the goat sir.' I said, thinking I were going to cry again. 'I were always the donkey in the nativity. Miss Finchley never wanted any goats. Just sheep and a donkey. There ain't no goats in the nativity.' Well, I don't know what I'd said wrong but he smacked the palm of his hand down on the desk and stood up and I could see he really were rather a big chap.

'Listen to me lad.' He growled 'You're in deep shit. Really deep. So, you'd be doing yourself a really big favour if you started co-operating with me and stopped trying to be a comedian. Now, what – is – your - address?' Them words came out slowly but loud.

Well, you know what, I never have been much of a one for telling jokes so I don't know how he thought I were a blummin' comedian. The only joke I knew were the one about the dog who had no nose and couldn't smell anything but seeing how he were looking so angry I thought I'd best not tell it right then and save it for later. And besides, I'd worked out by that time that he wanted to know where I lived.

'Blessham sir!' I said. 'Poachers Cottage, Sheep Dip Lane, Blessham.'

'That's better.' He said and wrote it down.

After that he asked me all sorts of questions and we had similar problems. Things like date of birth you see. I said April Fools' Day and he got cross again until I said 1st of April 1965. Then he asked me what me occupation were and I said going to work kept me occupied and he started clenching his fists and blowing through his teeth at the same time, but eventually I worked out what he meant and told him I were the gardener at Blessham Hall which seemed to calm him down. There were a few other questions and then he asked me if I knew why I had been arrested and I told him I didn't really to which he replied that surely I must do to which I just shook me head.

'Alright Mr Wilkie, have it your way.' He said and I felt strange because no-one ever called me Mr Wilkie before. 'Cell number 2!' And he sort of jerked his thumb towards a corridor and one of the bobbies took me down it towards a cell. And a blummin' pokey little thing it were and all. Had a bed in it and nothing else. Anyway, the bobby made me take off me belt and me shoelaces which made me a bit miffed because it takes me best part of ten minutes to get me shoes done up in the first place and without me belt me trousers were likely to fall down. Then he goes off and slammed the door behind me and locked it. Two minutes later he came back and said, 'Right! Trousers off and put this on.' And he passed me a white bundle. Well, I didn't want to lose me best trousers but I did what I were told which was just as well I suppose with 'em being wet. And he dropped 'em in a black bin bag, screwed up his face and went again.

I thought I'd best look at the white bundle. It were a funny kind of thing. Felt a bit like stretchy paper. Anyway, I unfolded it and stared at it for a bit. The only thing I can say it looked like were a blummin' big kiddies romper suit with a hood on it. Funny looking thing it were but as I'd lost me trousers and the bobby had ordered me to put it on, I put it on. It were a bit too big for me but I zipped it all the way up to me chin and pulled the hood over me head. I weren't too sure about the hood to begin with but I didn't want to upset the bobbies and I were in enough trouble as it were. The next thing I knew a hole appeared in the door of the cell and another bobby looked through it.

'Oh, hello there.' I said, wanting to be friendly.

'Want a cup of tea?' Said this bobby.

'Ooh, smashing.' I said. 'I wouldn't mind one.'

'Ok, sugar?' He said. Well, no-one had ever called me sugar before either and I felt a bit embarrassed by it so I just smiled and said, 'Thank you, that's very nice of you to say.' It were only after he'd gone that I realised he were asking if I took sugar in me tea which of course I don't and I were going to call him back but thought better of it. I could have it with sugar this once.

So he brought me the tea and I sat on the bed and drank it and it were alright. Nice and hot. Took me mind off things for a while at least. Although that blummin' bed were rock hard and I weren't looking forward to sleeping on it. I finished the tea and I laid down on the bed, anyway, feeling very sorry for meself. I tried in me head to make sense of everything that had happened. It had been a lovely day up until when they had found the basil and then everything had turned really horrible. I closed me eyes and I could see Her Ladyship's face in front of mine with that look of rage on it and I could almost still feel her hands around me neck. I could still hear the sound of her elbow cracking into Lord Elppus' nose and see his blood come squirting out. I could remember how terrified I'd been, thinking I were going to die and I couldn't help but think I were in a right bigger heap of trouble here at the police station than I'd ever been in. And in the middle of it all I thought about Meg, sweet Meg, getting into trouble with the bobbies as well and I were demetrined... demented... returdminded...

...certain that I weren't going to let that happen.

I must have dropped off to sleep because I were woken up by that big metal door being unlocked and opened and the bobby who brought me the tea were standing there. 'On your feet lad.' He said. 'It's question time.'

I did what I were told and he led me out of the cell, down the corridor again and into another little room. This room were a lot nicer than the cell because it had chairs and a table in it. There were two men in suits sat on one side of the table and another bobby standing at the back of the room. On the table were one of them tape recorder thingies and an ashtray. I remember thinking it were a funny blummin' sort of set up.

'Sit down.' Said the bobby who had brought me in.

'Where?' I asked.

'There's only one chair spare. Where do you think?' He said. Then he turned to the two men in suits and said, 'Bit of a joker this one. Thinks he's funny.' But that ain't true. Like I said, I'm no blummin' good with jokes.

'Hood' Said the bobby, pointing to me head.

'What?' I said.

'Hood!' He repeated.

'I believe that's what it's called.' I said. 'I've got one on me old coat back home as well which comes in handy when it rai...'

'Take the bleeding hood off. Now!' He snapped. Ooh, he didn't half snap and I didn't much care for it. But I pulled the hood off though and the bobby told the two men in suits what me name were and what I'd been arrested for which again were something or other about something or other called drugs. I thought maybe that were another name for eye-ta-leon herbs. Then he handed one of the men in suits a piece of paper and left the room.

The two men in suits both sat and stared at me for a while and then one of 'em took out a packet of fags, knocked one out of the packet and said to me 'Cigarette?'

'Yes,' I said, 'I'm pretty sure that is one. Don't like 'em though.'

They looked at each other again and one of 'em shook his head. 'Got a right bleeding clown here haven't we?' He said to the other one. I thought he must have been talking about the white romper suit which to be fair did make me look a bit like a clown. I've seen the circus on the telly you see. Anyway, the other one leaned forward and switched on the tape recorder and I were told again, that whatever I say would be used in evidence against me. I still had no idea what that meant but I went along with it. They then introduced 'emselves. The one who had said I looked like a clown were a portly, grumpy looking man with salt-and-pepper stubble and a big bald patch called Detective Inspector Small and the other one were a much leaner, younger man with black hair called Detective Sergeant Finn and they told me that I were being interviewed by them. Well at least I understood that. I were going to be given a good going over by Small and Finn. And it were Finn who started asking questions first.

'Let's get straight to the point Joe. I can call you Joe can't I?' He said and I nodded. 'Ok, just tell us about the grass Joe.' He said with such a nice smile.

'Well,' I said, 'it's blummin' hard work, there's such a lot of it you see, but I do quite enjoy it actually, especially the smell.'

'I'm sure you do.' He said. 'And the taste as well I bet.'

'No, not really.' I said. 'Mind you I try not to get it in me mouth.'

'So, you're saying you're not a user, just a dealer.' He said.

'Oh no, I have to use something.' I replied. 'Because it gets quite high.'

'I see, I see. Got to get your fix eh?' He smiled again.

'Well sometimes,' I said, 'especially the big one but a man comes from town to do that.'

'Aaah!' He grinned, 'A guy comes to you from town does he? And he's your mule?'

'Oh no,' I said, 'there's no mules. I think. Only horses. And he don't fix 'em. That's the job for the farrier. The other chap does all the make-annie-call stuff because Her Ladyship says I'll be certain to balls it up if I even tried.'

'What?' He asked. 'What are you going on about?'

'The big lawnmower.' I told him.

'Lawnmower?' He said, without smiling this time. 'What's that got to do with it?'

'I use it to cut the grass.' I said. 'And I make a blummin' good job of it too. I have to otherwise Her Ladyship will...'

'Still being the funny fu... clown are we?' Said Small suddenly pointing his finger at me. I were a bit confused as I were the only one who looked like a clown, not them.

'No sir,' I said, 'you two don't look like clowns at all. It's just me.'

'You are digging yourself a very deep hole my friend.' He said.

'Oh yes, I have to do plenty of digging as well.' I answered.

Small sat back in his chair, shook his head again, snorted and lit a cigarette. I wish he hadn't because I really don't like the smell of the blummin' things.

'You're not making things easy for yourself Joe.' Said Finn, smiling again.

'No, I'm not.' I said. 'It's not easy at all. The soil is all clay you see, and...'

'Just making wise cracks and trying to be funny all the time isn't going to get us anywhere is it?' He said.

'No sir.' I replied. But I ain't trying to be funny.'

'How so?' He asked.

'Well sir,' I went on, 'you told me to tell you about the grass, so I did and then you asked me to tell you about fixing lawnmowers and I did and then you asked me to tell you about digging and I did. I don't see how I were being funny.'

Small and Finn looked at each other again and then Small leaned towards Finn and said something quietly into his ear. Finn nodded and then said something back into Small's ear and then he nodded as well.

'Ok, Joe, ok.' Said Finn. 'Let's start again and let's keep it nice and simple. We just want to know about the weed.'

'Ah!' I said. 'Depends which one you mean.'

'Which one?' Said Finn with a surprised look on his face. 'You mean there's more than one? What else are you growing down there?'

'Oh, there's loads of 'em' I said. 'There's chickweed, groundsel, goose grass, twitch, thistles you name it, we got it. Them nettles are the worst though. I get stung all to beggary by 'em, although I can usually find meself a dock leaf if I need to.'

'Not those bloody weeds and you know it.' Snapped Small. 'The Marijuana!'

'Oh, I see!' I said. 'But actually, it's just called marrow and they ain't weeds. I grow some absolute beauties as well. Her Ladyship has won prizes with 'em at the village fete. Why, she once won champion marrow three years on the trot she did. Of course, the secret is in feeding 'em and I've got me own secret recipe for that which I ain't telling. More than my job's worth that is. But I'll give you a clue, it's made up of sheep muck and...'

'It'll be more than your bloody life is worth if you don't start coming clean.' Small said angrily, his face starting to go red.

'Well, I wouldn't mind a good strip wash.' I said. 'I pee'd meself earlier and it would be nice to get cleaned up.'

'You little bast...' Small started to snarl and lean forward but Finn put his hand on his shoulder and stopped him from saying ...ard! Well I think that's what he were about to say. I hear that word off Her Ladyship almost daily and I ain't too keen on it because I think I know what it means and it ain't very nice.

'Why don't we try approaching this from another angle.' Said Finn. Now, I can remember trying to do angles when I were at the big school and I were neither use nor blummin' ornament at 'em. I mean, Mrs Beardsmore were very patient and did her best but I just couldn't get me head around it. Come to think of it, I were no good at any kind of maffymafic... methymitics... miffymottocks...

...sums at all.

So I said, 'What angle is that then sir?' Hoping he weren't going to test me on 'em

'Ok, take yourself back to the hall.' He said.

'Oh, that's lovely!' I said, 'Can we go in the police car again?' And I started to stand up.

'No Joe. Not literally go back to the hall.' Said Finn, gesturing me to sit down again. 'I meant figuratively, in your mind.'

'Fig-your-a-tiv-lee?' I asked, not knowing what the blummin' 'eck that meant.

'Yeah,' said Finn, 'I want you to cast your mind back to what happened at the hall today. You know, when those plants were found.'

'Oh right!' I said. 'Well, Her Ladyship tried to strangle me.'

'Ok, so far so good. Why did she try to do that Joe?' He asked.

'Because she don't like foreign herbs.' Were the only thing I could think to say.

'Herbs?' He said raising one eyebrow.

'Yes.' I said. 'You see, I'd been growing me own herbs in the old cold frames and she weren't none too happy about it. Can't say she hasn't warned me about it though.'

'Now we're getting somewhere.' He said, still smiling. He actually had quite a nice smile. Very straight teeth. 'You call them herbs do you? That's ok, that's ok. They're often known by that colloquialism.'

I have no idea what a collo... I can't even say it, is. But he seemed to know what he were talking about so I just nodded and said 'Yes.'

'So you're telling us that you have been growing these plants, erm... herbs, for your own consumption?' He asked.

'What's con-sum-shun?' I said.

'For your own personal use.' Said Finn. 'To get baked with.'

'That's it!' I said with a big grin, thinking that now they thought that I were probably going to do some baking with 'em and I would be going home and Meg would be in the clear. But then suddenly for some reason I thought about how they're always trying to raise money for the church roof so I quickly added 'Although, of course, I'd most likely make sure people in the village would buy some as well.' I thought I were being clever with that.

'So, you were planning on selling it then. Make your mind up Joe.' Said Finn.

'Well yes,' I said. 'If anybody wanted any, I would sell it to 'em and put that money in the parson's pocket.'

'I see,' said Finn, and his eyes went all narrow like. 'And this Parsons chap, is he the Mr Big in the village?'

Well I thought about this for a few moments. Nick weren't a big chap really, quite thin actually, but I reckoned that weren't what he meant. But Nick were closer to God than anyone else in the village and you can't get much bigger than that really, can you? So I said, 'Yes, yes, you could say that, I suppose he is.'

'And you're no doubt afraid of him eh Joe? Worried about what he'd do to you if you didn't line his pockets?' Finn said and he leaned forward with his head sort of tilted on one side and one eyebrow raised.

'Oh no, I ain't afraid of him.' I said. 'He's me friend, and it ain't his pockets that need lining, it's the church roof. Some of that lead is in a shocking state.'

'You scrawny little bastard.' Growled Small. 'Trying to fucking wind us up again.'

'No sir, I'm not, honest I'm not.' I said and the way he spoke made me feel even more scared than I already were.

'Let's worry about this Parsons guy later.' Said Finn. 'For now, just so that we can all get out of here, Joe, did you grow those plants to sell to the public?'

'Yes!' I said, without thinking too much really. I just figured that was what they wanted to hear and so I just agreed.

'I think that's all we need to know.' Said Finn, blowing out what I'd call a sigh of relief.

'Great.' I said excitedly. 'Can I go home now?'

They both stared at me and shook their heads and Finn weren't smiling anymore. In fact, he looked dead serious. 'Joseph Wilkie,' he said, 'I hereby charge you under The Misuse of Drugs Act of 1971 with growing an illegal class B drug with intent to supply. You'll appear in court on Monday morning. You are allowed to make one phone call. Do you have a solicitor?'

'A solicitor?' I wailed. 'No sir. I don't. But I'd like to phone me grandma if that's alright.' I were blummin' pappering meself and no mistake and I realised there and then that I weren't going home and were in the biggest trouble of me entire life. Ooh I were right worried I were.

'Take him out.' Said Small to the bobby. 'And get him his phone call.' Then he turned back to me and with his voice all sort of low said, 'You're going to get seven years minimum for this Wilkie. Seven long years.' Well, I didn't know what minimum were, and I didn't want whatever it were and I certainly didn't want seven long years of it. And to be perfectly honest with you I had to ask one of the bobbies if I could go to the toilet. That's how blummin' scared I were.

13

Legal Doings (Part 2)

I didn't sleep very much that night, I can tell you. Even though they made me a cup of cocoa. I did ring me grandma though and she weren't none too happy I can tell you. She wanted to know what on earth I'd been playing at and she gave me such a rollicking down the telephone, which didn't help the way I were feeling. She said I were a very naughty boy and it were me own fault I were in trouble. When I tried to explain she just started going on about how there were no such things as drugs when she'd been a girl and that I needed 'a bloody good hiding' for meself. Well, I'm sorry, but I believe there comes a time in life where you are too old for a good hiding off your grandma and I said as much to her. That didn't go down too well but she said she would come to the court in the morning anyway and take me back home by the scruff of me neck if they let me go. She's a hard woman at times is me grandma.

After that I had to wait in me cell again and had another cup of tea which I think had been made by someone else this time because it were a bit weak. I thought it best not to complain though, as it didn't have sugar in this time, and drank it anyway. Then about an hour later I were taken out of the cell by another bobby and into another little room. This time there were a short, chubby sort of man in it, with his hair all swept up over from one side to hide his baldness, sitting at a table with one of them fancy, posh little cases in front of him. The bobby said to me, 'This is your brief.'

'Oh no, it's not mine.' I said, pointing at the case. 'I ain't never had one of those before.'

'Not the bloody bag,' said the bobby, 'I mean this fellow here. He's your brief, your solicitor. He's going to represent you in court.'

'Why does he resent me?' I asked, and I felt a bit hurt by that. Well, you would be, wouldn't you?

'REP-resent!' Said the bobby. He's going to speak for you in court. He's your legal adviser. Jesus H! You really are as thick as they say you are.' And then he left the room and I were alone with this brief chap. He seemed friendly enough though and he held out his hand for me to shake.

'Wankel!' He said as I shook his hand. 'Jackson Wankel.'

Well I didn't know where to put me face. Fancy using that kind of language in a police station. So, I said, 'Come again?'

'Jackson Wankel, solicitor. I work for Fulsom and Cumley Legal. I'll be appearing for you in the magistrates' court tomorrow. See if we can't iron this little problem out eh! Get you back home.' He said.

'Oh, I'd like nothing better sir than to go back home.' I said. 'I ain't too good at the ironing mind you so me grandma usually does that for me.'

'No, what I meant was... never mind,' he said, 'I need to ask you a few questions Joe, I can call you Joe can't I?' And I nodded. 'The thing is Joe, you're in quite a lot of hot water here and the police are going to want to throw the book at you.'

'No,' I said. 'I ain't had a bath yet. And I ain't happy with the bible being thrown around, not by the police nor anyone else either. That ain't right.' At that Mr Wankel closed his eyes and pinched the top of his nose.

'Let's start again.' He said. 'You, Joseph Wilkie, are in very serious trouble and the police are going to want you to go to prison for it. Do you understand?' I nodded again. 'Good,' he said, 'now, I need you to tell me, in your own words all about how those cannabis plants came to be in the vegetable garden at Blessham Hall.'

Well I were in a right quantitty... quantits... quanderrity...

...me head were in a spin.

I still wanted to leave the bit about Meg out of it as I didn't want her to get into trouble and if I mentioned Boothy and Simon I reckoned I'd probably get a good doing over off him and his mates like so many times before, but if I said those blummin' plants were mine then I would go to prison. I couldn't decide what were the lesser of the two weevils. We had weevils one time at Poachers Cottage. Me grandma had to get this special powder to put down to kill 'em. That made a lot less of 'em that did. Anyway, I tried to think as fast as I could and so I said to him, 'Well, I planted 'em meself, Mr Wanker.'

'Wankel!' He said with a frown.

'Sorry, Wankel' I said. 'You see I thought they were basil plants and I really like eye-ta-leon food so I thought I'd grow meself some nice herbs for which to cook with.'

'Do you honestly mean to tell me that you believed those plants to be basil and that you merely expected to be preparing Italian cuisine with them?' He said peering at me. 'And if so, where did you acquire them from?'

What the 'eck 'ack-wire' meant I didn't have a clue, but I guessed he were asking where I had bought 'em. And as for eye-ta-leon cousins, I don't know of any. I'm sure I ain't got any of 'em. I just got Ruby and Pearl and they ain't eye-ta-leons. I think. But I could tell he didn't believe me, so I tried to think fast again.

'Well, you see, I grew 'em from seed.' I said. 'I'm a dab hand at that I am. You want to see the cucumbers I grow from seed, they're as long as....'

'Ok, ok, we're getting somewhere.' He said. 'Now, where did you buy these seeds?'

'Her Ladyship gets 'em from the gardening catalogue.' I said. 'They come through the post with a stamp on 'em and...'

'Not the bl... cucumbers! The cannabis!' He said and his voice went rather high pitched I thought. 'Where – did – you - buy – the – cannabis – seeds - from?' He spoke very slowly.

Well, that foxed me good and proper that did. The only shop I ever go into were the general store and I know for a fact that they sell packets of seeds in there, veg and flowers and all that. And I were just about to say that I got 'em there but then I had another thought that if I said that then I were going to get Mrs Byamile and Mr Goodnight into trouble. Then I had a brilliant idea although I'm afraid and very ashamed to say I told a complete lie. It were a right good idea though.

'I got 'em from this travelling fella who came through the village!' I said, and under me breath I asked the Good Lord for forgiveness for telling a lie. 'Yes, that were it. He were in the pub one night and we got talking, you know. Well, one thing led to another and he ended up selling me the seeds.' I thought that ought to do it. Hated lying though.

'I see, I see.' Said Mr Wankel. 'And you bought them under the misguided belief that they were, in fact, actually basil seeds?'

'Yes, that's it!' I said grinning. 'Of course, I know now that they ain't basil and that's what all this blummin' kerfuffle is all about.'

'It's a little bit more than a kerfuffle, Mr Wilkie.' He said in a serious voice. Anyway, he then started asking me all sorts of questions about me background and about coming from a broken home. Well, I don't know about that. One of the kitchen chairs is broken and one of the staves on the stairs bannister but the rest of it is alright. And he asked me about me friends and things, but I made sure I never once mentioned Meg's name. Eventually though, he finished up by saying 'Well, if what you've told me is the truth Joe, I think we can safely say you'll be home this time tomorrow.' Blimey, it were a relief to hear that, I can tell you. 'But,' he carried on, 'you'll probably be released on bail and have to attend another hearing but I'm sure that due to your, erm, shall we say - intellectual difficulties, this case will probably be dismissed.'

Well, that sounded just grand, especially that bit about the bale which reminded me of you-know-what, but, like I said, I didn't sleep well that night even though he said that. I kept thinking all sorts of things. I'd never been in blummin' court before. Me grandma were as mad as 'eck at me. Her Ladyship wanted me dead. I were confused by all them big words I heard like ma-jee-straight and ack-wire and marijuana but most of all I just wanted to go home. I couldn't stand the smell of the place for one thing and I wanted some fresh air. One of the bobby's brought some food in for me though. Fish fingers, chips and beans. Weren't very nice. I reckon they were them oven chip things and they weren't cooked proper. The fish fingers were cold in the middle and them beans were like chewing bits of blummin' rubber in tomato sauce. I ate it all though because I were ever so hungry by then.

I did get a bit of sleep here and there and at one point I had a bad dream that Her Ladyship were chasing me through the woods with her dogs and her twelve-bore shouting *'YOU'RE A DEAD MAN WILKIE!'* at the top of her voice and for some reason I didn't have any clothes on. Ooh, horrible it were. Naked as the day I were born. I woke up though before she could catch me. Never been so glad to wake up in me life.

Morning came eventually of course, and I were brought another mug of tea and some scrambled eggs on toast. Them beggars weren't free-range, I know, and I wouldn't have minded some brown sauce with it. Still, it were nice of 'em to give me some breakfast. And, I got me trousers back, so I didn't have to wear the clown suit no more, which I were glad about because it chaffed a bit in the night. The bobby who brought me 'em said I were due in court at eleven o'clock. I asked him if that were morning or night-time but he didn't answer and just shut the door behind him as he left. So, I thought I'd best put me trousers on and get ready in case it were eleven in the morning which it actually turned out to be anyway.

I had to wait a couple of hours or so, but I were taken out of me cell, placed in blummin' handcuffs (can you believe?) which I thought were a bit too tight, and put in a police car again and driven to the ma-jee-straights court. It were nice to be out of that place though and to get a quick breath of air. The court building were on the other side of town and it took a little while to get there so I made a point at waving to some of the people who were walking about, just to be friendly like. Well, until the bobby who were driving said to me 'Oi! Pack that in!' I reckon he must have had eyes in the back of his head that one. Anyway, I stopped waving and started thinking about the lie I'd told Mr Wankel and how what I'd told him were different from what I'd told the police. It had all seemed like such a great idea at the time but now I couldn't help thinking I had dug meself into a deep hole. The good book says… hang on, how does it go now… ah, that's it – 'The truth shall set you free!' And I really started to think about that. Shouldn't I have told the truth? But if I did then Meg would get done for it and, oh, I just didn't know what to think anymore.

By this time, we'd reached the court and the car went round the back of the building and parked up. It were a grand looking building and all. Big wooden doors like the ones on the church and nice stonework like the hall and I stood and stared at it for a while until the other bobby said 'Never mind the scenery, sonny. Inside!' And he jerked his thumb towards the door which I thought were a bit rude of him although I never said so.

So in we went and I had to go to a desk first where the bobbies gave me name and address and what I were charged with and I were told that I were due in court number 2 at eleven but that they were running a little bit behind due to a mass brawl that had taken place in one of the town centre pubs on Saturday night leading to several arrests. After that I were taken to see Mr Wankel again. We had quite a long chat and he reckoned that me best defence were to claim something called dee-mini-shed-riss-ponce-able-ee-tea. I had to ask him four times to repeat the words so I could say 'em right and I still had trouble with it. Then I had to ask him what that all meant, and he said that the bottom line were that I had learning difficulties and therefore probably didn't understand what I had been doing all along. Well, he were right there. I've always found learning stuff difficult, except gardening for some reason. And blimey, all this blummin' legal talk is ever so confusing. But, eventually, at twenty to twelve we were called into the courtroom by this chap called the usher.

It were a big enough room and all. There were chairs either side with one or two people sat on 'em including me grandma who gave me a very frosty look and at the far end there were a long table with three ma-jee-straights sat behind it. Two men and a woman. They all looked very smart I must say. The woman were a very thin looking fair-haired lady with the highest eyebrows I ever saw and not much of a chin. Funny looking sort she were. And the chap on the left had the reddest cheeks and the biggest red nose I ever saw. Didn't look at all well if you ask me.

We sat right at the front, Mr Wankel and me, with one of the bobbies and on the other side at the front were one of them detectives from the day before, that Finn fellow, and the Chief Constable. I smiled and waved at 'em but Mr Wankel pushed me hand back down and gave me a stern look. Then the usher asked us to stand and said, 'Joseph Wilkie, your honours', to the ma-jee-straights.

The man in the middle of the three, who were a large chap with short grey hair and a face like an old chamois leather and thick glasses, looked at some papers in front of him and then peering over the top of his glasses said to me, 'It says here that you are charged with growing cannabis plants Mr Wilkie with the intention of selling them to the local populace for financial gain. I must point out to you that the prosecution must prove its case against you. It is not for you to prove you are innocent but for the prosecution to prove you are guilty. Do you understand?'

'No sir,' I said, 'I'm sorry but I didn't really understand a word of that. Begging your pardon.' And that were no lie, I didn't have a blummin' clue what he meant.

At that point Mr Wankel coughed and asked for permission to speak which the man let him do and he explained that he were appearing for the defendant.

'I thought you were here to speak for me?' I said.

'That's what I mean.' He said with a hiss. 'You're the defendant.'

'Oh! I see.' I said, and that one were a lie because I didn't see really.

'Can we please continue?' Said the man at the front.

'Oh yes, you carry on sir.' I replied, and at that Mr Wankel put his hand over his eyes and drew in a sharp breath through his teeth.

'My client, err, the defendant, has a high degree of learning difficulty your honour and I respectfully ask the bench that this be taken into consideration during this hearing.' Said Mr Wankel.

Well, them three ma-jee-straights all looked at each other and mumbled a few words together and then the middle one said, 'Oh very well. Mr Wilkie, how to you plead?'

'Well,' I said, 'I usually drop to me knees and beg for mercy. It all depends on what I'm pleading for really.' I heard Mr Wankel groan at that.

'No Mr Wilkie,' the man continued, 'Do you plead guilty or not guilty to the charge brought against you?'

'Oh,' I said, 'what charge would that be? I didn't know I were going to be charged with anything, I ain't brought me wallet with me. Not that there's ever that much in it.'

'I've already said haven't I?' The man said sternly. 'The charge that you have illegally grown cannabis plants with intention to supply to the general public.'

'For the love of God, Wilkie, just say 'not guilty your honour' or we'll be in trouble before we've even started.' Mr Wankel sort of whispered out the side of his mouth.

'Not guilty your honour, or we'll be in trouble before we've even started.' I said the words exactly how Mr Wankel told me and then I heard him groan again.

'I see, we shall now hear the case from the prosecution.' Said the man and at that Finn got up and walked across the room to this little stand thing that looked a bit like a poor man's pulpit to me. Not like the one at church that's all carved and fancy with a big eagle on the front. This one were a bit of a plain looking thing. Anyway, Finn cleared his throat and began to tell his side of it. He began by saying it were an open and shut case, whatever that means, and then he went on about them blummin' plants and how the

Chief Constable himself had been the one to discover 'em and that I had reduced their inquiries to a farce at the police station by saying one thing and then another and that I had in the end confessed to growing 'em for both my own use and intent to supply to people in the village and an unknown local man, called Parsons, who simply goes by the name of 'Mr Big.' He said that it was the intention of the police to track down and apprehend this 'Mr Big' who clearly poses a threat to the local community and that it would be in the best interests of the defendant to help them to bring this man to justice.

'You never told me any of that.' Mr Wankel said to me in a hissed whisper again. 'What's all this about a confession and Mr Big? And intent to supply? Jesus Christ almighty! We're right in the shit now. What was all that nonsense you told me about seeds?' Ooh, he looked really cross at me.

'Well, I get confused you see and...' I started to say but the man in the middle told me off and said I weren't to speak whilst Finn were saying his piece. Felt dead embarrassed I did because I'm sure I heard someone behind us sniggering. Anyway, Finn finished by reading out me statement that I'd made to 'em and Mr Wankel pinched the top of his nose again like he did before. But then he had to stand up because the man in the middle told him to make a statement for the defence. Which were me.

'Erm... if it pleases your honours, he began, 'I would like to reiterate at his point that my client, the defendant, has severe learning difficulties and I believe that owing to his confusion in this matter he may have said certain things to the police that on the surface may not have looked quite as they are underneath.' Blimey! I thought to meself. That were a right load of old jargon that were. He continued though. 'My client claims that he bought the seeds for those plants from a new age traveller in his local public house believing them to be nothing more than common basil seeds that he intended to use for the preparation of Italian food. Furthermore, due to his aforementioned difficulties he has never even heard of the word cannabis and consequently finds himself in this situation as a result of, shall we say... ignorance? I therefore request that my client be freed on bail, pending further investigation into this traveller, and that this case, for now, be dismissed.'

Well at this, the three ma-jee-straights all had another little chat together and then the one in the middle said 'Mr Wilkie, would you take the stand please.'

'Certainly, you're on-her.' I said, remembering what Mr Wankel had called him. 'Where is it and where would you like me to take it?' And I heard Mr Wankel groan again.

'Mr Wilkie,' said the man in the middle, 'I can't decide if you really have, as your solicitor says, learning difficulties, or whether you're attempting to turn this courtroom into a platform for some sort of comedy act of yours. I'll give you the benefit of the doubt for now, however, but please rest assured I shall be paying very close attention to you. That, is the stand!' He pointed to the little pulpit thingy and I heard Mr Wankel behind me saying 'Go over there Wilkie, where the policeman stood!'

'Ah, righto!' I said, and I went over to the pulpit thingy. It felt a bit strange standing there and it made me wonder about Nick on Sunday mornings when he had to do it. Mind you, there were more blummin' people in that courtroom than we usually get at St Mildred's. Me grandma were still there and she had this awful frown on her face and were shaking her head at me. The usher chap came up to me with a bible and told me to put me hand on it and he said, 'Do you swear by almighty God that you solemnly, sincerely and truly declare and affirm that the evidence you shall give shall be the truth, the whole truth and nothing but the truth?'

'Certainly not!' I said proudly. 'I never swear, nor do I take the Lord's name in vain. It ain't right to do that. And that's the blummin' truth for you.'

Well the usher turned and looked at the ma-jee-straights and the one in the middle said 'Mr Wankel, your client is slowly but surely turning this hearing into a circus.'

'I ain't, honest.' I said. I wouldn't know how, I ain't never been to the circus. I only ever seen it on telly.' And some of the people who were watching laughed but the man in the middle shouted *'SILENCE IN COURT!'* or something like that, and then he turned to me and said, 'Mr Wilkie, either answer the usher or I will have you charged with contempt of court.' Well, as you can imagine, I didn't 't have a blummin' clue what he were going on about but Mr Wankel came to the rescue and asked if he could approach the stand which they allowed and he came over and explained what I were supposed to say. Which were 'I do!' And that made me sad because it made me think of mine and Meg's wedding when I'd say it to her, but I said it there and then anyway and the trial carried on.

And then all blummin' 'eck broke loose and me head were in a spin in no time. Horrible it were. The solicitor for the prosecution came up and he bombarded me with fancy words and questions. He went on about everything I'd told the police and he asked me about the old man who is 'known to the police' and he mentioned 'Mr Big' again and I'd forgotten who Mr Big were by then so I said 'I don't know' and he accused me of covering up for him and being part of his gang. Well I said I ain't never been in a gang and the only gang there's ever been in Blessham were the Bulls but that were years ago and they all just about were grown up by now anyway. And I wished to Heaven that I'd never even mentioned Mr Big in the first place. Then he went on about this 'supposed' new age traveller who had sold me the seeds and I had to think as fast as I could and said that 'he were actually quite old really' and then he said that I'd known all along what the plants were and that I were merely feigning ignorance all along and I had to stop him and ask what feigning were. Then he spoke about Her Ladyship and how her trust had been violated and I said, 'She don't wear one as far I know' and he said that the good and noble name of the Stark-Ravens had been sullied by me actions and so on and so forth and he finished by saying that the court should find me guilty and issue the maximum punishment allowed. I tell you I were dead worried and close to tears by the time he'd finished. He'd used all posh and fancy words that I didn't understand. And then he'd said he wanted to call a witness and that were none other than the blummin' Chief Constable himself.

So, the Chief Constable came over and I were told to go and sit back down and the solicitor asked him what had happened at the hall on open day and to be fair to the Chief Constable he told it exactly how it had happened. Even how Her Ladyship had gone for me and that when I were arrested I had tried to be funny and make wise cracks to the bobbies which to me weren't right, but I didn't interrupt because I didn't want to upset Mr Wankel again. Then, the solicitor called for something called 'Exhibit A' and the usher came over with this clear plastic bag and it were full of them blummin' plants. I recognised 'em straight away. So did the Chief Constable though, and he said that they were what he'd seen in the cold frames. And I noticed by that point that Mr Wankel were sat with his head in his hands. And when the man in the middle asked him if he wished to question the witness he just sighed and said, 'No questions, your honour.'

After that the three ma-jee-straights all talked together for a bit and they nodded a lot and the thin woman pointed at me a couple of times and there were more nodding and the red faced man made a snorting noise, like a horse fart, and I heard him say 'Oh absolutely, absolutely!' for some reason or other and then I were told to take the stand again. The man in the middle cleared his throat and started to speak.

'Mr Wilkie,' he began, 'this court has heard all the evidence we believe it needs to. I'm not sure how badly your learning difficulties are or whether it is merely a rather clever act on your part. I begin to strongly suspect the latter. The stories you have told the police and your solicitor do not match, and it is patently clear that somewhere amongst all of this that lies have been told and the truth distorted. Not only that but your behaviour in this courtroom today has been wholly unacceptable and it is our considered opinion that you have used it as a distraction, a ruse, carefully disguised trickery to make us believe you had no idea what your actions were.

Personally Mr Wilkie, I would like the pleasure of sending you to prison myself, however, we feel that that is a decision for a crown court judge. You are either a simple man with an incredibly low I.Q or a quite brilliant actor, which is what I firmly believe you are, and until further investigations are completed I'm afraid we have no other choice than to have you remanded in custody until a date for a crown court trial can be arranged, as it is clear that your actions in this case have posed a threat to the community of the village of Blessham and I, for one, sincerely hope that it concludes with you being prescribed a lengthy term of penal servitude which I should imagine will run to at least seven years. Do you have anything to say?'

'Well,' I said, 'there were some of that I didn't understand.'

'Which parts?' He asked.

'Please you're on-her,' I said, 'all of it.'

'Constable, you make the prisoner down.' Said the man in the middle.

'What's that mean?' I said turning to Mr Wankel.

'It means Mr Wilkie, that you're going on remand. To prison! And to be quite honest with you, after this utter shambolic bloody farce, I can hardly see how they could have reached any other decision.' And he flung his arms in the air and looked sort of belewdered… bewolfed… bewinded…

…flummoxed!

And the next thing you know the two bobbies have got the handcuffs on me again and I were led off out of the courtroom, past me grandma, who shook her finger at me and said 'Silly little sod,' and down to the cells that they had at the bottom of the building. I weren't in there for very long before the bobbies came back for me and took me out again. They led me upstairs and I could hear a lot of shouting and noise coming from above and I thought I knew the voice that were shouting. So I asked one of the bobbies what were going on and he said, 'We're taking you out the back door because there's a really large woman up in the reception area brandishing a horsewhip and demanding to be given the right to thrash seven shades of shit out of you.'

INTERLUDE

Pause for thought.

Take a walk in the countryside.

Listen to some folk music.

Wang a welly or two.

Then come back and see how Joe gets on.

14
Liberty and Justice
(6 months later)

Blummin' 'eck, I've got so much to tell you that I don't hardly know where to start. Me head's still in a whirl so much has happened. I reckon I'd best start at the beginning. As you know I were looking at going to prison for a good long while and I were fair worried about that I were. To think I'd never see me beautiful little home village of Blessham for years were blummin' frightening but what do you know, I'm here! I'm home again and it's all been a bit mad I can tell you. Actually, I've been at home since well before Christmas and it were the best Christmas I've had ever. But I'm getting ahead of meself. Like I said, I'll start at the beginning.

Well, that ma-jee-straight fellow had told me that I had to go to the big court and that I'd be looking at jail time and I were taken to the prison in that big van, you know, the one that smelled like a khazi. That's where I met Rufus and Wendy and I settled in and all that and were getting meself ready for a pull of oats, or something like that. And to be honest, I were starting to come to terms with it. I mean, how bad can seven years inside be? Anyway, there I were in me cell one day telling Rufus how to milk cows by hand when Mr Riddle comes in and says, 'On your feet, Wilkie lad. The governor wants to see you. Quick smart now!'

Blimey, I thought, I'd not seen the governor since that first day they brought me here and I started to think that I must be in trouble or something. But I jumped up and apologised to Rufus and said I'd see him later to which he replied, 'Dread man, truly dread!' He were right and all. I were dreading it. Anyway, I did what I were told and followed Mr Riddle out of the cell and along the landing and then down a corridor. It took us a few minutes to get to the governor's office and when we got there we had to wait outside until his recpectionist... reperferist... reprefferist...

...his female helper, who answers the telephone, told us we could go in.

I remember thinking that apart from me grandma visiting me, that were the first person of the opposite you-know-what that I'd seen in ages. I were hoping that Meg would have visited but then I suppose I wouldn't really want my future wife in a place like that with all them blokes gawping at her, what with her being so blummin' beautiful and all. But the governor's helper were a nice enough woman. Not pretty like Meg but nice enough. Name of Barbara I think it were and she told us that we could go in to see the governor.

His office were better than our blummin' cell that's for sure. There were a window with a view and nice, comfy chairs to sit on and paintings on the wall and pot plants here and there and carpet and even a fish tank with bubbles going through it. I had a goldfish once you know. Got it from the hook-a-duck stall at the fete. I called him Goldie. I loved that little fish; he were the only pet I ever had. Died the next day like but there you go. Anyway, we got in there and Mr Riddle said 'Wilkie, to see you sir.'

'Ah yes, Wilkie,' said the governor, pointing to a chair on the other side of his desk, 'do sit down.' So I did. He were a nice chap really and it put me more at ease. He's got a friendly sort of face has the governor. Reminds me a bit of a comedian that I saw on the telly. He were doing this funny dance and singing about sunshine with this other funny little man. The comedian I mean, not the governor.

'Thank you sir,' I said sitting down, 'I hope I ain't in any trouble.'

'Trouble Wilkie?' He said looking at me from over the top of his glasses. 'Oh dear me no, quite the opposite in fact.' And he gave me a smile so I gave him one back.

'Tell me Wilkie, do you know what the most satisfying part of my job is?' He asked.

'No sir, I'm sorry sir, I don't.' I said. Well how could I know? I'd only just met the bloke really. I were hardly likely to know stuff like that.

'It's when I get to release people.' He said. 'It's when I get the chance to send them home, hopefully rehabilitated.'

'What's bilitated mean sir?' I said. I never heard that word before.

He gave a little laugh and said, 'It's when someone has changed their ways through being in prison and are leaving here as a better person.'

'Oh I see.' I said. Well, I think I did at any rate.

'Have you learned anything from being in here Wilkie?' He said.

'Oh yes sir, loads of stuff.' I said. 'I've learned how to slop out and I've learned how not to grass on anyone and I've learned how not to pick the soap up in the showers if someone drops it although I don't know why. There's nothing wrong with being helpful is there? Or clean?'

'No,' he smiled again, 'that's not what I meant. Wilkie, I'm not sure how to tell you this although I'm pleased to do so but I'm not sure I can put it in a way you'll understand. The thing is, it seems you've been wrongly accused.' He were dead right; I didn't understand and I think he could tell so he carried on. 'What I mean is, you're innocent Wilkie. You've done no wrong, you've committed no crime. Unless simply being unbelievably gullible and immensely naïve is a crime these days but I'm pretty sure it's not. The bottom line is, you're free to go Wilkie. You're free!'

Now, I know I'm a bit slow even at the best of times but it seemed to take ages for that word to sink in – *free!* I looked at the governor who was smiling from ear to ear and then I looked at Mr Riddle who closed his eyes and nodded at me saying 'It's right lad.'

'So what you're saying is, I don't have to be in prison anymore?' I said very slowly.

'That's right Wilkie. you don't. And I have to say how personally glad I am.' Said the governor, leaning towards me.

'Then I'm... I'm free to go? Free to go back home? Back home to Blessham? Oh sir, sir, can it be true?' I were starting to fill up I were.

'Yes indeed my good man.' Said the governor. 'There are one or two things that you need to know, however, and I'm afraid it may all come as a bit of a shock to you.'

'Oh, ok then.' I said, but blimey, that were a shock in itself. I nearly peed meself again I felt so happy.

The governor had one of them cardboard folder file things in front of him which he opened up and took some papers out of. He cleared his throat and pushed his glasses up to the top of his nose and began to tell me all about it. And he were right and all, it were an 'eck of a blummin' shock. But he spoke slowly and clearly and in small words that I could understand. I could scarcely believe me ears what he told me and I'll try and tell you what he said to the best of me abletility... atelbiliby... analtinity...

...as best as I can.

Well, it seems that Meg had gone to the police station and made one of them full con-fesh-uns. She'd told the police that it were nothing to do with me and that it had all been her idea along with Jim Booth and Simon. She told 'em that I were a plain and simple man who had no interest in drugs and didn't even know what they were. She were right enough there. She said that they had taken complete advantage of me and had fooled me into growing the drugs. She said she didn't care what happened to her so long as I were free because I were as innocent as the day is long. Well, I seem to remember at the big school that they told us the day were twenty-four hours long or something like that so that's how innocent I were then. Which were great, however, the governor then told me that Meg and Boothy were both in custard-ee but that Simon were nowhere to be found. The police suspected that he would have gone underground but I can't imagine him digging a big hole like that.

Oh I felt odd I can tell you after hearing all that. I mean, it were blummin' brilliant being told that I were going home but the thought of Meg being in custard-ee were too much to bear. Then again, the thought of Boothy being in custard-ee made me feel happy. But Meg though, oh my sweet,

sweet Meg. What would happen to her I wanted to know. The governor told me that there would definitely be a prison sentence for both of 'em and Simon too if they got hold of him but that Meg were being very helpful and that would go well with her and that the judge would most likely be lenient with her, whatever that means. I didn't know what to think for the best. I wished Meg were there so I could hold her in me arms and tell her it were all going to be alright and that I'd be there for her. I didn't care that they'd tricked me and she were involved. I were so madly in love with her I could've forgiven her for blummin' murdering me. And I reckoned that blummin' Boothy and that other beggar, Simon, would have put her up to it. I started to cry and the governor very kindly gave me a man-size tissue from the box on his desk.

After that it were all a bit of blur. I were taken back to me cell until some paperwork or something were done, and I said goodbye to Rufus and Wendy. They were both sad to see me go. Well, Wendy definitely were, because he gave me a great big hug and patted me on the bottom as he always did and said that if I ever wanted to hook up then he was me man and he'd show me a real good time. I never knew he was into fishing. Sounds like he really enjoys it though. Rufus just made me bump our fists together and said 'Ya alright, country boy!' I'll miss those two. I told 'em both to come and visit me in Blessham when they got out. I hope they do. Wendy said he'd love to come and have a roll in the hay so I think he's planning on coming over in the Summer.

Then I got given back what few belongings I had and were escorted outside of the prison whilst all the other inmates cheered and clapped. I felt very special I did. Me grandma had come into the city to pick me up. She'd had to take two buses to do it, bless her, but I said I'd pay her back. But the best bit were when I stepped outside them blummin' gates and took a great deep breath of fresh air. The good book tells us that love is sweeter than wine. I don't know about that. I ain't never drank wine, but I should think it don't taste any better than that air did to me. It were like neck-tar and I took quite a few lungs full of it. Me grandma were there, and she gave me a hug as well which weren't something she normally did really. She normally just cuffs the back of me head with her hand and tells me off. And then we got the bus back to the town and then another bus back to Blessham.

I enjoyed them buses I have to say. It were the first time I'd been on one since leaving school and of course we sat right at the front so we could see everything. But the really amazing thing were when we got to Blessham. You see, the bus shelter is right opposite the Pig and Whistle and when we pulled up there were most of the blummin' village standing outside and they all had glasses in their hands. I figured there must be a party going on or a wake or something. Then the bus pulls away and I heard someone say, 'There he is!' and the whole crowd started cheering and raising their glasses in the air and calling my name. Ooh I didn't know where to look. Then Ernie O'Dyan comes over the road to me and puts his arm around me shoulders.

'Alright Ernie?' I said.

Ah boy, not so bad.' He replied with a grin. 'It's bloody good to see you Joe. Come on, let's have a pint.' And then he led me back over the road and into the pub and everyone were slapping me on the back and saying nice things about me. I'd never known anything like it. Nick were there and Mrs Byamile and Mr Goodnight and old Mr Cummings and everyone I knew from the village. The old man weren't there though, but I suppose he'd taken the chance to go and do a spot of thieving while everybody else were down the pub. Farmer Bull weren't there either which I didn't mind. I just wish that you-know-who had been there. That special lady of mine. They led me into the pub and there were a great big sign over the bar that said WELCOME HOME JOE! In big red letters. And then Bob passed me a pint of mild over the bar and said, 'Here you go lad.' I had to tell him I'd got no money on me of course which were a bit embarrassing but he said it were on the house and would be all night. I tell you what, that were the best pint of Fartleberrys I ever tasted. I'd waited a long time for that. And then they all started singing 'For He's A Jolly Good Fellow' and then shouted 'Hip-Hip Hooray!' three times and I never felt so special in all me blummin' life. Well, apart from that day in the haystack with Meg.

The party went on for hours. There were a buff-hay meal for everyone and Mr Cummings played the piano and people sang. Blokes were shaking me hand and the women were kissing me on the cheek. It were smashing and I right enjoyed meself. A proper good knees-up it were. Every time me glass were empty there were someone there to take it to the bar for a refill and everybody were all being so nice. Then I looked up and who should walk in but Mr Franks. I were dead surprised because he never goes to the pub normally.

I've got to be honest when I say that I hadn't given the hall and me job much thought other than that it were all gone and I'd have to find something else. But Mr Franks came up and shook me very firmly by the hand and said 'Good to see you Joe. How are you? The rest of the staff will be along after work.'

'I'm fine Mr Franks.' I said. 'How are you and how's Her Ladyship? I bet she still wants to lay her hands on me throat.'

'She's the reason I'm here Joe.' He said raising his voice over the noise because a load of folks had started singing. 'She wants to see you tomorrow, midday sharp, if you're up to it.' He said looking at me pint with a laugh.

'Oh no.' I said. 'Please no, I don't want her to finish where she left off.' And I rubbed me neck with me hand as I remembered the last time I had seen her and felt them great big mitts round me throat trying to squeeze the very life breath out of me.

'Don't worry about that lad.' He said. 'She's calmed down from all that now. Mind you if she ever gets her hands on that Jim Booth or that hippie shyster he were in cahoots with I wouldn't have much hope for either of 'em. But you just take my word for it and get yourself over there tomorrow, alright?' And he gave me a little wink which somehow made me think everything were going to be alright.

Well, that party went on for hours it did and I were getting fair tipsy. And I lost count of how many sausage rolls I'd had. Everyone were having a grand old time and I were too, but deep inside me, I couldn't stop thinking about Meg. My poor, beautiful Meg. Locked away in that awful place. I hoped that maybe there'd be someone like Big Donny in there to protect her. Of course, not exactly like Big Donny because he's a bloke and blokes ain't allowed in women's prisons no more than women ain't allowed in men's prisons. At least I think so. I don't know. I just hope there's a female Donny to look after her. But oh, the thought of that pure and lovely girl of mine slopping out and eating that awful food and the blummin' smell of the place. I couldn't put it out of me mind. At one point Nick came and had a long chat with me about how I were feeling and how pleased everyone were that I were out and all that. But seeing him in that white collar just made me think of the church and that made me think of our wedding one day and I felt really sad. It weren't long after that that I thought I'd best be making me way home so I got up and thanked everybody which got another great big cheer and I left the party.

I stood outside the pub for a minute while I waited for Nick, who'd gone for a pee, as he were going to see that I got home alright. It were dark and the sky were so clear you could see all the stars and there were a bright half-moon up there and I just stood and gazed up at the heavens as I have done many times before, but they never looked quite so beautiful as they did right then. I took in a deep breath through me nose and I could smell Blessham. I could smell woodsmoke and the faint whiff of manure and the breeze blowing off Blessham Hills carrying the smell of the sheep. And I could smell the trees as they turned and the brown leaves on the ground and the damp grass and even the night itself and I knew... I knew I were home.

'Beautiful isn't it?' I heard a voice behind me say and I turned round. Nick was standing there looking up as well. 'God is in his Heaven.' He added with a smile.

'I've missed it.' Were all I could think of saying.

'We've missed you Joe.' He said and then he patted me on the shoulder and we walked back to Poachers Cottage.

It were lovely walking through the village and seeing all the old familiar places and Nick and I chatted about what had been going on at church and he made me laugh when he told me about Major Brimmish bringing a live chicken to the harvest festival and how it got loose and ran round the church. And then he'd lectured everyone about how rationing were likely to continue after the war and that if he became aware of any black marketeering he were going to report it. I wish I'd been there to see that. He's a laugh a minute is Major Brimmish.

I don't know what time it were when I got home. I invited Nick in for a cup of tea but he said that he had a meeting with the parochial church council in the morning and needed to get to bed. We said goodnight and I went inside. The door were unlocked and there were no lights on but somehow I knew the old man were in there. Sure enough he were laying fast asleep on the couch, snoring his blummin' head off. There were an empty half bottle of scotch lying on the floor. He grunted and farted and scratched his rump as I shut the living room door and then he opened his eyes and sat up.

'Whah? Who's zat? Who's there?' He said and his voice were all slurry like it always is when he'd had a drink.

'It's me dad,' I said, 'It's Joe. I'm home.' And I hoped that he were going to jump up and hug me and welcome me home like the prodigal son in the bible…

But he just grunted again and said 'Keep the bleedin' noise down will ya. I were fast asleep.' And then he laid down again and within a few seconds were snoring like I don't know what once more. So I went upstairs and into me room. It were just as I'd left it on the morning of the open day except that the bed had been made with nice clean sheets. That must've been me grandma, I thought.

I were dead tired by now so I got into the bed, me own little bed, and set me alarm for eight so as I could have a lie in but not so late that I would miss going to the hall and seeing Her Ladyship, and I were feeling nervous about that. The very last time I had clapped eyes on her or heard her voice she were screaming that I were a 'dead man' and had tried to throttle me. And by 'eck there's many a man who wouldn't have set foot in the place after that, I know. But Mr Franks said she were over it and I trusted him so I lay me head down on the pillow and I reckon I were asleep about five seconds later.

Before I knew it, it were morning and the alarm were ringing. Do you know what, that were the best night's sleep I'd had in years. Deep and dreamless it were and I got meself out of bed and went for a pee. It were funny because I half expected to see Rufus and Wendy there in the bedroom. I remembered how Rufus always blew out a huge great fart when he woke up and Wendy would say things like 'Please, do we have to wake up to that every day? The stench makes my nostrils burn' and Rufus telling him to 'Shut ya mouth batty boy.' Oh, we did have some fun the three of us.

I got dressed and went downstairs. The old man were still on the couch and he were snoring loud enough to wake the whole blummin' village up. Sounded like a blummin' great big pig wallowing in mud he did. And I reckoned there'd be no waking him so I went into the kitchen and made meself tea and toast. I were lucky and all. There were one slice of bread left, the crust. But I love the crust I do and I found a jar of me grandma's damson jam in the cupboard to put on it. I had to scrape some mould off the top first and there were a couple of damson stones in it but it were delicious. I mean, it weren't much but it were better than the stuff they used to serve in that prison. And the tea were much, *much* better. Even if I say so meself. But apart from the crust of bread and the jam and an out of date tub of gravy granules and an old jar of English mustard that had changed colour and a box of salt that had gone hard and an almost empty bag of flour there were nothing else to eat. Me grandma had said she were going to get some shopping in later for us though so that were alright and I'd asked her if we could have a steak and kidney pie with chips and gravy as a treat. She said we could and I were looking forward to that I can tell you.

I put on me coat and shoes and went out of the house without waking the old man up and went for a walk around the village. I wanted to see it in daylight. It were a bit of a misty morning but that didn't matter to me, I were just blummin' glad to be back in Blessham. It were a Friday morning and there were quite a few folk about and I chatted to a few people here and there and some of 'em had thick heads from the party I can tell you. And I were really enjoying wandering around the village when all of a sudden I walked past Blackthorn Farm and I saw a blummin' police car parked outside. I got scared I can tell you. I were worried that they had come back for me but then who should come walking towards me but old Mr Cummings.

Morning Mr Cummings, you alright?' I said.

'Ah boy, not so bad. It's alright Joe,' he said with a laugh, 'they ain't come for you.'

'Blummin' 'eck Mr Cummings!' I said. 'You must be one of them mind readers like you see on them magic shows on the telly.'

He just laughed again and said I were looking so worried that it were obvious that's what I were thinking. He's a clever chap is Mr Cummings. He's won the pub quiz quite a few times. I don't go in for it meself down to the fact that I'm, you know, blummin' useless at things like that. But anyway, he then went on to tell me that the bobbies were there because Farmer Bull had gone missing. He hadn't been seen since Mrs Bull had left for the party the afternoon before. Now, I've got to be honest when I say that I really never liked Farmer Bull. I used to call him Farmer Bully. Not to his face of course. But I never forgot the way he kicked seven bells out of me that day and got me and Meg into trouble that time. They reckon Mrs Bull were terrified of him and that he leathered both her and Desira regularly. Mind you, Desira left home when she were seventeen the day after all that ginger beer business and went to live in some place called Ma-wreck-ish or something or other. Still, I would never wish any harm on anyone no matter how much of a blummin' so and so they've been. I told Mr Cummings that and he laughed again and said, 'The trouble with you Joe is you're too forgiving.' But that's what the good book tells us to be, don't it? And that's what me mum said I should do.

Anyway, it were time that I got meself to the hall and Her Ladyship so I said goodbye to Mr Cummings and made me way there. I thought back to that day when I first went to ask for a job and how scared I'd been and I felt the same way now. I were sort of half excited and half blummin' terrified. The look on Her Ladyships face when she had her hands round me throat will always stay with me. And feeling her spit and smelling her breath right in me face. Ooh it were horrible. I tell you what, I were trembling a bit as I walked down that drive towards the hall.

Someone at the party had told me that Her Ladyship had taken on a firm of landscape gardeners to keep things in check. She'd advertised me job in the local paper, asking for someone who wasn't 'cloth-eared or as dense as a rain forest.' Her actual words so it seems. But there'd been nobody answering it at all and so she got them people in. Now, I ain't boasting but as I walked up that drive I could tell that them lawns hadn't been done proper like in a good long time and I reckoned I could use that to my avtandage... antavage... antacid...

...I could use it as a good point to make.

As I got nearer the hall I could see a wagon at the front with wheelbarrows and a lawnmower beside it and two men loading gardening tools into the back of it. I guessed they would be them landscape gardeners, so I went and introduced meself. One of the men were an older chap with a flat cap on his head and by the look of him he weren't no stranger to the old bread and dripping. He had some belly on him. The other one were a young lad with ginger hair and a lot of them zit things that looked all red and angry.

'Hello there!' I said.

'Ow do?' Said the older man. The other one just sort of sniffed a couple of times and rubbed his nose on his sleeve.

'You the landscapers?' I asked.

'No mate, we're here to polish the silver!' Said the older one.

'Oh really,' I said, 'I thought by looking at your tools you were gardeners.'

'We are the bloody gardeners!' He said, a bit too sharply I reckoned, and he pointed to some writing on the side of the wagon which I couldn't read but I'm guessing it probably said 'Landscape Gardeners' or something like that.

'Oh right,' I said, 'so you ain't here to polish the silver then?'

'No!' He said, sharply again and went back to loading up his tools.

'Righto! Only, I used to be the gardener here. In fact, I've come to see Her Ladyship and ask if I can get me job back.' I told him.

The man stopped loading, slowly turned to me and said, not so sharply this time, 'Are you Wilkie?'

'That's right.' I said. 'But you can call me Joe.'

'It's him, it's Wilkie!' He said to the other one with a laugh. 'It's Wilkie! We're free at long last! *Free!*'

The other one laughed as well and the older one took his cap off and grabbed me hand and began to shake it. 'By God boy, are we glad to see you! You've absolutely no idea how glad we are.' He said, and he really did look very happy.

'Why's that then?' I asked.

'Why, he says, why?' He said to the other one whilst jerking his thumb towards me. 'I'll tell you why my friend.' He turned back to me. 'Because she's off her soddin' rocker mate, that's why! I've never known the likes.

Constantly shouting and screeching and going on and on about her precious bloody roses and what she'll do to us if one of them gets damaged and marching around with those dirty great big dogs. One of them went for me. Fuckin' rottweiler! Backed me into a corner it did. I were fearing for my bloody life. Then she calls it off and starts petting it and saying, 'Did the nasty man give you a fright Maggie?' Give *it* a fright? I nearly bleedin' shit myself. And she's not happy unless you're shovelling tons of horse manure around the place and she's parading around making sure it's spread properly. She threatened to horsewhip Andy here because he accidently knocked a bleedin' peony over whilst shovelling shit. You can't do that! You can't go around threatening people in this day and age. No, mate, we've had enough. Heard you were coming back so we're packing up and getting out. You must have a hide like a soddin' rhino to put up with all that. Would've gone sooner but she threatened to blacken our name throughout the county and I reckon she would've done and all.'

'Right.' I said. 'Well, I suppose you have to get used to her.'

'Fuck that.' He replied, 'We're off. Ta-ta mate and the best of British luck to you.'

And with that they both got into the wagon and drove off down the drive. Quite fast actually. I suppose in many ways he were right. Her Ladyship can be a hard taskmaster and no-one else I know has had more tongue lashings off her than me. But so what? I love them gardens and I'm blummin' good at what I do even if I do say so meself. What interested me most about what he said though were that bit about he'd heard I were coming back. Did that mean I were certain to get me job back? Anyway, I took a deep breath and walked up to the door and rang the bell. Mr Franks opened it of course and bid me to come in telling me that Her Ladyship were in her study and that I should follow him.

He knocked on the door of the study and I heard that familiar booming voice.

'COME!' She said loudly and Mr Franks entered.

'Wilkie is here Ma'am.' He said.

'Is he, by God?' She said and then added. 'Well don't just stand there Franks like some bally statue waiting for pigeon target practice to begin. Bring him in damn it!' And Mr Franks beckoned me in.

Her Ladyship were sat at her desk writing and she looked up at me and stared at me for what seemed like ages before pointing at the little stool and saying 'Be seated Wilkie. That will be all Franks and close the damned door behind you.' Mr Franks left and I tried so hard to not tremble. 'Be with you in a minute Wilkie!' She said and carried on writing. At least she hadn't tried to throttle me so that were a good thing. I just perched meself on that stool and waited. It occurred to me that in all the times I'd been in that study, mostly for a dressing down, I'd never really had time to have a good look at it. Now, as I sat and waited, I looked around and saw what were really in there.

There were her huge great desk of course and the leather armchair but there were also one of them big wooden globe thingies on the floor and paintings on the wall. The one above her desk of a stag were quite magnificent I thought.

There were others as well though, of country scenes and an old map which I think were of England and that. There were a drinks cabinet with all sorts of bottles in it and next to that were a bookcase but not like the ones in her lie-brie that were full of dusty old books, the ones here were new and modern looking. I don't know what they were about but I'm sure she would have put 'em to good use. In the window there were a glass case with a stuffed pheasant in it which reminded me that shooting season had started and of course you know what that meant. But what I liked most were that the walls were all wooden. I suppose the ones at Poachers Cottage are in a way. Well, they're covered in woodchip wallpaper at least. But then she finished writing, put down her pen and got up and stood in front of the fire. This was it then. The moment of truth I think they call it.

'Good of you to come at short notice Wilkie.' She said with her hands behind her back and her legs apart. 'I was just writing a letter to that left wing lackwit that's currently ensconced in number 10 at the moment. I've called it 'Execution, Execution, Execution!', I think it's got quite a ring to it don't you?' I nodded although I didn't have a clue what she were going on about but she gave one of them loud cackles of hers so I figured nodding was the right thing to do.

'Right, Wilkie!' She said. 'I'll come straight to the point. I'm a busy woman and I don't have time to fanny about with triviality. Neither have I ever been in the business of issuing apologies, so I won't start now. You see, what you have to understand Wilkie, is, that on the open day I was quite understandably under the impression that you were growing disgusting drugs in the vegetable garden. Which of course you were but not for your own use. I know that now. It was that butcher boy scum from the village and some other stinking drop out who I'm hoping the police will apprehend soon. And of course, unfortunately, the Morrison girl who used to work here. Anyway, my reaction at the time as you'll no doubt remember was to launch a physical attack upon your personage with the express intention of ending your existence on this earth. In short, I wanted to kill you there and then Wilkie. Naturally, I believed at the time that you were a drug dealer, the worst, vilest and lowest possible piece of sputum on this earth, and the discovery that something such as that was going on right underneath my nose, especially in front of my esteemed guests, brought out quite a rage in me and well, you know the rest. I can't imagine how things were for you in prison Wilkie. I'm not a great advocate of the penal system. Far better to string criminals up by the neck or impale them on spikes and leave them to the crows in my opinion and save the taxpayer a bally fortune. By God! If I were prime minister there'd be a gibbet in every city, town and village in the country. That's by the by though. Unfortunately, we currently live under a Labour government and therefore it's the namby-pamby, soft-as-fucking-axle-grease approach. Bastards they are! But I digress. Wrongly imprisoned you were. Your only crime being that you are devoid of even basic intelligence and didn't have the foresight to see what this gang of reprobate lowlife were up to. You should have come to me Wilkie, you should have come to me. That's where you went wrong. By Christ I would soon have rooted them out. Nevertheless, the real culprits have now been unearthed. Morrison at least did the decent thing I suppose and made a confession of their crime so that an innocent, albeit imbecilic, man could be set free and it will no doubt go well for her, although a damn good thrashing and a few days in the stocks would serve her a sight better, I feel. Booth on the other hand can rot in jail for the rest of his miserable days as far as I'm concerned. And as for this other freeloading pile of shite that was involved, by God I'd like to have ten minutes alone with him in a locked room. I'd never get tired of kicking the fucking bastard. But the past is the past Wilkie. We cannot change what has gone before and nor can we adequately atone for it. Nor do I even hope to attempt to. What I am more than prepared to do Wilkie is to offer to reinstate you as the gardener here at Blessham Hall. Do you accept?'

Well, I'll be honest with you. The biggest part of all that went right over me head and I think she could tell because she rolled her eyes and quoted the shortest verse of the bible under her breath before saying 'I'm giving you your bloody job back man!'

I couldn't believe it. After all I'd been through, I were getting me job back. I jumped to me feet and thanked Her Ladyship over and over again.

'Yes, yes, that's all very well Wilkie.' She said. 'You'll start Monday morning. Usual time. See Franks for the key to the potting shed. Now! I must get on. I'm writing to our local MP next to see if we can start using the stocks on the village green to deter vagrancy. He'll probably say no, being a limp-wristed, she-man, ponce of a liberal, but you've still got to try haven't you?'

And then she did something that she'd never done before. She held out her hand for me to shake it. Ooh, I felt right proud I did. I shook her hand

and said thank you again and turned to leave. As I got to the door she stopped me and said. 'Oh, and I'm giving you a ten pound a week pay rise Wilkie, for your troubles.

'Thank you Ma'am.' I said. 'Thank you very much. I won't let you down.'

'You'd better not Wilkie. You'd better not. Or by thunder...' Then she turned, sat down and started writing again, so I left.

Well, as you can probably guess, I couldn't believe it. Me job back and an extra tenner a week. Just for spending a couple of months in prison. Blimey! It were too good to be true. I were so excited that I thought I would run round to the stables and tell Meg. And then of course I remembered that I couldn't and that brought me back down to earth a bit. But blummin' 'eck what a turn up! I'd only come out of prison the day before and I'd had a grand party at the pub and got me job back. I just wished I could get me girl back.

I wandered back into the village whistling a tune I'd heard in the prison and feeling chuffed with meself. Can't remember the words to the song but it were something along the lines of things getting better and I thought that for me they really were. I couldn't say the same for Farmer Bull though because as I went past Blackthorn Farm again there were now one of them ambeelances from the hopsital outside and another police car and all the lights were flashing and there were quite a few local folk gathered about looking. Well, I don't like to stand and stare and I would probably have been told to clear off so I did just that, I cleared off. The pub were open by now and I went in to see who were about and tell 'em the good news about me job. Then I were going to go round the vicarage and see Nick. It were a bit early for me to have beer so I thought I might have a glass of lemonade. Maybe even some ice, and perhaps even a slice of lemon just to be a bit dedicant... decatint... tecadont...

...to push the boat out a bit.

Imagine me surprise when I got in there and there were no-one else except Bob drying some glasses. Drinking ones that is. Not the sort you wear for reading. He's got a pair of them too. I ain't though, on account of the fact that I can't blummin' read. Anyway, I walked up to the bar and said, 'Alright Bob!'

'Ah boy, not so bad.' He replied. 'How you feeling today after your do?'

'Oh fine!' I said. 'I had a smashing time. Thank you.'

'That's alright Joe. You're welcome.' He said and I noticed he were looking dead serious in his face.

'Everything ok Bob?' I asked. 'You look a bit serious.'

'You ain't heard then?' He said.

'Heard what?' I said.

'Old man Bull.' Said Bob. 'They found him dead in his slurry tank this morning. Drowned in a thousand gallons of shite he was.' Bob shook his head. 'That's no way to die. Not even a prick like that.'

'No.' I said. 'I suppose not.'

'Don't get me wrong,' said Bob, 'the man was an absolute bastard. Treated that wife and kid of his something awful. There's going to be a lot of other folks around these parts who won't be sorry to see him go either. Even so, drowning in effluent...'

'Oh!' I said, 'I thought you said he drowned in shite a moment ago.'

'That's what effluent is, you daft bugger.' Bob said, trying not to smile, I could tell.

Well, it were a shock I can tell you. Farmer Bull had died. They reckon he'd had a good pull at the old rum bottle, gone up to check the level on the slurry tank, slipped and fell in. Blimey! It makes me shudder to think about it. But try as hard as I might I just couldn't find it in me heart to feel sorry for him and that bothered me. It were Mrs Bull that I felt sorry for, having to live with him for so long and now having to run the farm on her own. But I still couldn't feel sorry for him. Oh, I had forgiveness for the things he'd done to me in the past but when it came to sympathy, I'm afraid I were sorely lacking and I didn't like that feeling at all. So I threw back me lemonade as quick as I could and made me way to the vicarage. I knocked and Nick let me in.

'I'm sorry Joe,' He said, 'I can't talk long. I'm on my way to Blackthorn Farm. Have you heard what's happened?'

'I have Nick, and that's what I've come to see you about.' I said. Nick looked at me inquissantly… enquazziently… inquasimodo…

…odd like.

'You see,' I said talking as fast as I could because he were on his way out, 'Farmer Bull were a cruel man who's done some horrible things to me in the past and been right unkind to his wife and child. Now, I've forgiven him for what he's done, but I just don't feel sorry for him and in a way…'

'Go on.' Said Nick kindly.

'Well, in a way, I'm sort of glad he's gone.' I said. 'And that's a terrible thing to think of somebody ain't it?'

Nick stood and looked at the floor and I knew he were thinking because he always did that when he were thinking. Then he looked up at me and smiled and said. 'Joe, the whole village knows what kind of a man Terence Bull was. He wasn't liked and he upset a lot of people for no good reason. Perhaps you more than anyone.'

'But it's wrong to think ill of the dead ain't it?' I said. 'And aren't we supposed to love our neighbours and all that?'

'Our Lord told us to 'Love thy neighbour' Joe.' He said nodding. 'But He didn't say anything about liking them. And right now, it's Mrs Bull who needs help and support. You've done no wrong in having those natural feelings.'

And that were it. Bull the bully were dead. They had a funeral for him a week later and including Nick, Mrs Bull, old Mr Cummings on the organ and meself, because I said I'd help out, there were seven people in the church. I know because I can count that far and I counted 'em all. Bit sad really. He didn't have many friends did he?

Anyway, the next week there were a sign outside Blackthorn Farm saying 'FOR SALE' on it. They reckon it went to one of them orc-shun things and sold for over a million quid including all the land. Blimey! Imagine that. A million quid. That's more than... well, more than I'll ever blummin' see. As for Mrs Bull, she moved out of the village and went to live in some place called the Bee-Harm-Us and as I know only too well, bees can harm you so I hope she'll be alright. Still, the last I heard she were very happy, so all's well that ends well I say.

And that were it. Farmer Bull were gone, and Blackthorn Farm got a new owner. A rather nice chap by the name of Giles. Her Ladyship has him round for the croquet seeing how he's blummin' loaded with money. But like I say, a nice chap. Much nicer than old man Bull at any rate.

15
Family Values

So back to work I went and everyone there were pleased to see me. And I were pleased to be back and see all of 'em but I were heavy hearted about not seeing Meg every day. Worse still were that Her Ladyship didn't hold her job open for her and brought in a new stable hand to replace her. Some lass called Marguerite. She's from somewhere called You-Crane. I don't know where that is but it must be abroad somewhere because her voice sounds funny. And she ain't like Meg either, all shapely and pretty with lovely lips and shiny brown hair that smells of flowers. No, Marguerite is well over six-foot-tall, has blonde, plaited pigtails, she's built like a shit-brickhouse and she's into something called body building where you lift weights and things to get bigger muscles. It must be working as well; she can lift a bale in each hand and throw 'em around like they were lumps of polytes... poltystry... stryopoloy...

...that white stuff that's really light.

A strapping big healthy lass she is. She calls Roger 'Little man' and she's often grabbing his back end in that friendly sort of way that Wendy used to do to me and she says things like 'Hey, little man! How about me and you among the hay bales? I show you a thing or two. Let Marguerite get physical with you. I make you hard, hard like rock, like trunk of tree. Show you good time, sexy time, da?' And she smiles all wide-eyed and nods her head as she says it. I think she means she wants him to get big muscles as well. As for Roger, he looks very pale these days. Very wan. And he's started trembling a lot of the time. I hope he's alright

I get on quite well with Marguerite though. She calls me 'Joey' which I don't mind, and she says things like, 'I look after you Joey. Nobody mess with you when Marguerite is around. I kick them in balls for you.' Oh, she's a laugh a minute is that one. But, she ain't my Meg and I miss seeing her.

There were other changes at the hall too. Mrs Partridge got sacked for what Mr Franks called 'an indiscretion.' I weren't sure what an indiscretion were, so I asked Mrs Franks and she said Mrs Partridge were caught 'in-flagrante' with a young lass from the village when she were meant to be getting the General ready for Her Ladyship's morning gallop. Well, I had no more idea what 'in-flagrante' meant no more than I did indiscretion so I asked Polly and Peggy but they just tittered and giggled at me like the daft beggars they are so I waited until after work and asked Bob in the pub and he said that Mrs Partridge were found in the stables stark-bollock-naked in the sixty nine position with this other lass. Honestly, I gave up after that. I always thought her position were being in charge of the stables. And she's nowhere near sixty nine, as far as I'm aware she's only in her forties. And why would she be working in the nude at that time of year? Too blummin' cold. Unless she'd got a sweat on. Mind you, that's a sure-fire way to catch the flu that is. Anyway, she's gone now and Marguerite is in charge of the horses and all that. Her Ladyship reckons she can 'trust her more than that sex-addicted harlot' Her words, not mine. And no, I don't know what a harlot is and after all that I ain't none too bothered. And as for sex-addicted... well... I wouldn't know anything about that.

Harvey left soon after as well, saying that if 'Veronica was going then he was going too.' So Her Ladyship told him that were fine and that he should 'pack his bags forthwith and be gone before sundown or she would drag him off her property by his scrotum' (don't know what one is). Well, rather foolishly, Harvey tried to stand up to Her Ladyship and told her he weren't going to be 'sodding well ordered around no more' by her and that he would 'leave when he were good and fucking ready.' They reckon he eventually came round later that night although he never did find his missing back tooth. Last I heard, he'd asked Mrs Partridge for her hand in marriage, but she said no and went to live with her sister down south, somewhere called Tore-Key, and got a job at a nearby zoo, feeding the elephants and what-not. As for Harvey, he started drinking a lot, got barred from the pub for trying to start a fight with old Mr Cummings and got himself arrested for showing his, you know, his thingy, when it were perfectly normal, to a couple of young ladies in the car park the same night. Apparently that kind of behaviour is what's known as in-dee-scent ex-pose-sure. Got himself on some kind of register, whatever that is. Silly beggar. He don't live round here no more now either.

Now, as for Her Ladyship's dogs I'll give you a guess who has to feed 'em these days. You've got it, me, that's who. I have to feed 'em and muck 'em out, but that's all. Her Ladyship exercises 'em herself and we have a new gamekeeper called Stan who does everything else. It's alright I suppose but it means I'm busier than before and them dogs eat an awful lot of meat and that means they make an awful lot of mess. And there's a big difference between the smell of horse muck and the smell of dog muck, believe me. Especially when you've stepped in it or got it all over your hands. Blummin' dogs.

But other than all that life went on as normal at the hall. Her Ladyship were writing like never before and I didn't see too much of her at first. She gave me the odd rollicking of course but that were only to be expected. Like the time I dropped the log basket on the carpet of her study leaving bits of bark and sawdust and stuff all over it and she roared at me, *'I KNEW IT! I FUCKING WELL KNEW IT!* IT WAS ONLY A MATTER OF TIME BEFORE YOU DID SOMETHING UTTERLY BALLY WELL IMBECILIC WILKIE! FOR CHRIST'S SAKE MAN, ARE YOU INCAPABLE OF CARRYING OUT SUCH A MENIAL TASK WITHOUT TURNING MY STUDY INTO A FUCKING LUMBERJACK'S YARD? JUST LOOK AT THE MESS WILKIE! LOOK AT IT! GET OUT! GET OUT OF MY SIGHT BEFORE I TAKE THIS LETTER OPENER AND...' Luckily, the phone rang at that moment, so I scarpered out of there sharpish.

And so it were, I were happy again, apart from Meg of course, but then the most amazing thing of all happened and I still can't believe it to this day.

It were a week before Christmas, a Saturday, and there'd been a light snowfall overnight, so I made me way up to the hall good and early to sweep it all off the paths and I got there just before the light were coming in. I cracked on with it as fast as I could as I knew I'd have a right good tongue lashing from Her Ladyship otherwise. But, do you know what, she must have been in a really good mood that morning because she came out whistling a tune and spoke to me whilst I were doing it.

'Morning Wilkie! Damned cold one, by God!' She said.

'Morning Ma'am, it is, but don't worry, I'll have this done in no time.' I said.

'Just make sure it's done properly. If my foot should slip then rest assured it's going to slip all the way up to your arse.' And she gave that scary cackle of hers.

'Righto Ma'am.' I said.

'Come to think of it Wilkie', she said, taking a big deep breath, 'There's no point in you hanging around in the cold this morning. Nothing much to do. Get the paths finished and you can go!'

'What? Go home?' I asked.

'No Wilkie,' she groaned, 'Go to Hades. What do you think I bally well meant?'

'I'm not sure Ma'am. I don't rightly know where Hades is.' I said scratching my head. And the truth of the matter were that I really didn't. I'd heard her mention Hades many, many times but I'd never been brave enough to ask her where it were.

'Of course I meant go home you bloody simpleton. I was being sarcastic. God give me strength!' She said through gritted teeth. And with that she stomped back inside the hall muttering to herself about how she'd 'tried to do one of the serfs a good turn and all you get in return is bloody idiocy', or something like that.

Well, that were just grand. I were finished by half past eight and I got to go home and have the rest of the morning to meself. I were well chuffed although I think I know what sarcastic means and that made me feel a bit daft. Never mind though, I had the rest of the morning off and that were all that mattered to me.

I rushed home as fast as I could, although I did fall over once on the snow, but I thought better me than Her Ladyship. Didn't half hurt my hip bone though. Made me limp for a while. Still, better me hip than her foot up me rump. Anyway, I got home and made meself a nice, big mug of tea to warm up. The old man were still in bed and snoring the whole blummin' place down. Like a great big, old bear, he is, you know, when they're himbervating… hyperventing… imberdimber…

…sleeping for the winter.

Anyway, I'd just sat down and had a slurp of me tea and had a bite from the one digestive biscuit that were left in the cupboard when there came a knock at the door. Who could that be? I wondered. Then there were another knock. So instead of just sitting there wondering who it might be I thought I'd best go and see who it were. Well, I jumped up off the settee, spilling some of me tea, and went to the door with me mug in me hand. I opened the door and there were a very well-dressed couple, a short little man and a very attractive woman, stood there smiling at me. I thought that I recognised the woman for a moment or two and then she spoke.

'Hello Joe!' were all she said.

And with those two words and that soft, gentle voice all the years seemed to suddenly fly away as if they'd never happened and I felt like I were a kid again. I knew that face, it were still as beautiful as I remembered, just a bit older that were all. I dropped me mug on the floor and it broke into bits, but I didn't care I rushed forward, threw my arms around her and shouted *'MUM!'*

I hugged her as tight as anyone as ever hugged anyone else before in their life and she hugged me right back. 'Mum, Mum, you're home, you're home.' I said, several times in fact, and tears came to me eyes and rolled down me cheeks.

'Let me look at you.' Said Mum and we stared into each other's faces. Then she reached up and brushed my tears away with her hand. 'My Joe, my little Joe, oh God I've missed you.' And with that we hugged again and I held onto her as if I were holding on for dear life. Then we looked at each other again and Mum turned to the chap who were with her and said, 'Joe, I'd like you to meet my husband, Seamus.'

The man called Seamus reached out his hand and said, 'I'm pleased to meet you at long last Joe.' He had a funny accent, which I later found out were Irish, but he had a nice, friendly face and sort of twinkling eyes. He reached out his hand and I shook it but then a thought came to me. 'Hang on,' I said, 'if you're Mum's husband, Seamus, then what about the old man?'

'We've got a lot to talk about Joe.' Said Mum. 'Are you going to invite us in?'

'Oh, sorry Mum.' I stuttered, 'Come in, come in.' And I held the door open for 'em. They came in and Mum sort of looked around the living room and said 'Well, this place hasn't changed much has it? Here, sit down Joe, we've got an awful lot to catch up on.'

'Alright,' I said, 'but can I have another hug first please Mum?' She laughed gently at that and we had another great big hug. It were lovely. I had missed her so much and now here she were back in the living room at Poachers Cottage. I could hardly believe it. 'Here,' she said, at long last, 'Sit next to me Joe.' And we both sat down on the settee. Seamus made himself comfortable in the armchair. Well, as comfortable as he could I suppose because most of the springs and stuffing were well past their best and it had a few stains on it.

'Gosh.' Said Mum, 'I don't quite know where to begin.'

'Why did you go away Mum?' I asked, not nastily like, but it just seemed like the right question to ask if you know what I mean.

'Oh Joe,' she said, 'it wasn't easy, please believe that. It was the hardest thing I've ever done in my life. And there's not a day gone by that you haven't been in my thoughts. Honestly Joe. You were the apple of my eye. It's just...' and she looked down at the floor at that point as if she were trying to find the right words to say and she wiped away a tear from her eye.

'It's ok Mum,' I said, 'don't cry, you don't have to tell me. I'm just glad you're here.'

'The lad needs to know the truth, Sarah.' Said Seamus in his funny accent. 'It'll be fine.' Well I think he said 'fine,' it sounded more like 'Foin!' But anyway, Mum looked at me and told me her story right from the very beginning.

'Joe, the man you call dad, and I, were never married. I was pregnant at the age of seventeen and although he said he'd marry me, he never did. And to be honest it wouldn't have been right anyway. You see Joe, Amos Wilkie isn't your real father. And I think, at the back of his mind, he always suspected that. But I needed somewhere to live and to bring you up and we got this cottage. It isn't much I know but it's all we could get. As you know, you were born here Joe and you made me so happy. But seventeen is no age for a young girl to be a mum. Blimey, you're not even a woman at that age, and I struggled Joe. I had a lot of help from your grandma and a few others and I loved you with all my heart, but I struggled. And it wasn't long after you were born that Amos started to hit me. He knocked me down the stairs one time. And he drank heavily whenever he had any money. Used to come home in all sorts of states. I had to ask your grandma for money to get you clothes and things and I was a girl Joe, just a girl. But you grew up fast and had needs and I realised that I was the only person who could meet those needs. He was never going to provide. And your grandma and granddad weren't made of money. So, I went out to work

Joe, remember? I went out to work in the evenings. I... I... I provided a service, shall we say, for men in the village, and through that I was able to buy you the things you needed. Oh, it weren't much but I kept you clothed and fed. Sometimes Amos would take the money off me if I couldn't hide it soon enough and more often than not I'd get a few punches or kicks thrown in as well. Not that he cared where I'd been, he just wanted the money for drink. And then, one night, he came home early from the pub, reeking of drink and demanding that I give him money so he could go back and have some more. Well, I'd been saving up for a while to get you some new school shoes. I remember that awful Booth lad and his idiot friends had stolen the ones you had. Ooh, I hope he gets the living daylights knocked out of him in that place. Anyway, I weren't going to give Amos Wilkie money for drink when you wanted new shoes and I told him that to his face. Well, he slapped me, hard, as I knew he would but I'd expected that. What I didn't expect was for him to throw me on the floor and hold the bread knife against my throat. He said things to me, awful things. He called me a... well, it doesn't matter now, but what he did say was that if I didn't give him money he was going to kill me. And I believed him Joe, I believed he would have done it. So I said, 'Alright I'll give you money, let me up.'

More tears rolled down Mum's face as she spoke and I could hardly believe what I were hearing I felt meself getting ever so angry. I wanted to run upstairs and punch the old man in the face. Oh my, I never felt like that before in me whole life. I tell you I could feel meself burning with anger. But mum put her hand on me arm and continued her story.

'So I got up' she said, 'and asked Amos to put the bread knife down. But he said, he'd put it down when he got the money. I had to think fast Joe. I was fearing for my life. 'There's some money in the cupboard above the sink.' I said and he turned around and opened the cupboard door and that's when I took my chance. I got hold of that old heavy bottomed frying pan and I brought it down on top of his head with all the force I could muster. I hit him hard with it. As hard as I bloody well could. Made a noise like the church bell it did. The odd thing was, he never made a sound, he just fell to the floor. I thought I'd killed him at first so I put my hand in front of his face and I could feel his breath. But I panicked, oh how I panicked. What was I going to do? I thought it would be seen as attempted murder. My mind was racing. But then I thought about Seamus, we'd become... very close friends you see, he was so kind to me, and he had been talking recently about going back to Ireland very soon. Well, in my panic, I ran upstairs, threw my best dress on, packed a few things and then I came in to see you Joe, do you remember?'

I nodded at this. I couldn't say anything because for one I couldn't think of anything and for another I were crying and all choked up.

'And that was when I left,' she continued, 'I ran to the stud farm and found Seamus. I told him everything and we left Blessham that very same night.' And with that Mum covered her face with her hands and began to sob loudly. Seamus got up and put his hands on her shoulders and patted her.

'Don't cry Mum!' I said, crying meself. 'I don't blame you for running away. I didn't know how bad things were for you. I love you Mum, I always have. Please don't cry.' And then we hugged again. And then all blummin' hell broke loose, if you'll pardon the phrase. The living room door flew open and there stood the old man. He looked as rough as a badger's back end and in his hand he were holding what I always called his 'poaching stick', a piece of old hazel wood with a large knot at one end. He used it for knocking rabbits and birds on the head with once he'd snared 'em.

'So you've come back have you? You little bitch!' He said with a growl. Well, I jumped up and said, 'Don't you dare talk to her like that after all you've done to her!'

But he just ignored me and then glared at Seamus and said, 'And this must be your paddy lover boy then! I've waited a long time for this and by fuck I'm going to enjoy it.' And he started swapping his poaching stick from one hand to the other and back again. But Seamus, faced him and said, 'I'm not afraid of you, Mr Wilkie, or of that there shillelagh you be carrying.'

'YOU IRISH CUNT!' Roared the old man, and he raised the poaching stick up as if to strike Seamus with it. Seamus put his fists up to defend himself but before they could fight, I jumped in-between 'em, grabbed the old man's arm that held the stick and I shouted *'NO!'* as loudly as I have ever shouted at anyone in me entire life.

Then something strange happened. This really funny look came into the old man's eyes as if he were trying to find something that weren't there. Then the stick fell out of his hand with a clatter onto the floor. Then he opened his mouth to speak but the words that came out made no sense, just sort of grunts and groans. Then it seemed as if the whole side of his face started to, well, drop is the best word I can think of to describe it. And then he clutched hold of me jumper and sank down to his knees and then onto his face on the floor with this little gurgling sound.

I turned to Mum and said, 'What's happening, what did I do?'

'The man's having a stroke be-Jaysus!' Said Seamus, 'we need to call an ambulance.'

'We ain't got no phone.' I said and I were close to pappering meself, I don't mind telling you. In me mind I'd killed the old man. And I dropped to me knees and wailed 'he's dead, he's dead, I've killed him, they'll put me back in prison now.'

'No Joe, you've done nothing, but we need an ambulance.' Said Seamus. 'Get round to your neighbours and use their phone. Go on, now!'

Well I fairly sprinted round to old Mrs Catchpole, our neighbour, and I banged on the door shouting her name. The door eventually opened and old Mrs Catchpole didn't look none too happy at being disturbed like that. She can be a right funny old so-and-so even at the best of times.

'What do want to go about banging on old folks' doors like that for you daft bloody idiot?' She said scowling at me.

'Please Mrs Catchpole, I need an ambeelance. It's the old man.' I said and I were shaking too, and not with the blummin' cold. Anyway, she were good enough to call an ambeelance which arrived quite quickly and the old man were taken away to the big hopsital in the city. They said that Seamus were right. He'd had what's known as a stroke, and the two ambeelance men reassured me that it weren't anything to do with me. That were a relief I can tell you. I mean, I don't know exactly what a stroke is and a few people have tried to explain it to me, something or other to do with the brain, but what I do understand were that it were brought on by the way he lived. All that blummin' booze and fags and all that.

It were strange to see him being loaded into the back of the ambeelance on a stretcher with this plastic mask thingy on his face but at that moment I didn't feel any sympathy for him, just like when Farmer Bull died. All that kept going through me mind were what a horrible man he were and what he'd done to me mum. And I'm not ashamed to say it but right there and then I were glad that he'd had a stroke and it wouldn't have bothered me if I never saw him again as long as I lived.

I have seen him though, just the one time. He's been put in one of them nursing homes that's run by the council in town and has to be looked after all day. Not a very nice place either. Smells like me grandma's cabbage soup in there. Pee-ew! Anyway, I went to see him about a month or so ago but I didn't stay very long because he just sat there in a tatty old armchair and stared out of the window and drooled a lot out of the corner of his mouth. Then this nurse came over and said he needed changing so I left. And, I thought to meself, he needed to blummin' well change years ago and I ain't seen him since.

Anyway, after all that happened on that Saturday me and me mum started to spend a lot of time together, although she wouldn't stay at Poachers Cottage but at the fancy hotel in town. Never mind, they had a motor car and came into Blessham every day to see me, and she told me what she'd got up to in Ireland. You'll never believe it but her and Seamus are very well off. I mean really well off. Rich, for want of a better word. You see, it seems that Seamus did very well at breeding the racehorses. And they sell 'em all over the world. They're very popular with some people called Arabs apparently. So much so, that they are what's known as millionaires which I think means they've got about as much money as Her Ladyship, maybe even more, who knows.

And we talked a lot about Ireland and she told me how beautiful it were and how friendly people were and then she asked me if I'd like to move over there and live with her and Seamus and that I shouldn't want for nothing in me life ever again. Well, I thought about it mind, I thought about it long and hard. Seeing me mum every day and spending time with her sounded lovely and I very nearly said yes. But in the end it came down to this. I ain't never left Blessham in me life, apart from the prison. It's all I know. I love this blummin' village. I love the people, well, most of 'em. I love me job, well, when Her Ladyship ain't giving me what for. And I love Meg Morrison with all me heart and soul and I'm going to be here for her when she gets out of that horrible place. I tell you I'm going to marry that girl if it's the last thing I do.

So, I said no to me mum's kind offer and she just smiled sweetly at me and said, 'I think I knew that Joe, but I had to ask.' But we agreed that I would visit Ireland as often as I could and I'm looking forward to that. I've never been on an airyplane and I'm excited and a bit nervous about it. Seamus says he'll show me Dublin and The Ring of Kerry and Cork City and all these other amazing sounding places I never heard about before. Imagine that, a whole city made out of cork! And I can't help but wonder who Kerry is and what's so special about her ring. There were a lass in my class at the big school called Kerry but I don't think it's anything to do with her. No, hang on, I'm wrong, her name were Kelly. But here's the most amazing thing of all...

We spent Christmas together and it were the best Christmas ever. Me mum paid for us all to have Christmas dinner at that posh hotel they were staying in, ooh it were ever so fancy. All the knives and forks matched each other. And it made a nice change for me grandma to not have to cook for everyone. Grand it were. We all gave each other presents of course and I gave me mum a new pair of gloves because I remember the only pair she had when I were growing up didn't have fingers on 'em and I wanted her to keep her hands warm. I didn't know what to get Seamus but he just said it were 'foin and grand' and that there were nothing he needed so that were alright. Anyway, everyone had got their presents me mum turned to me and said, 'I've got one more present for you Joe.'

Well, she'd already given me a gold watch and a thick winter coat and a pair of them fancy training shoes, called Reeby-something-or-other, so I wondered what on earth else she could have got me. Well, she reached into her handbag, dead posh one it were, and she brings out an envelope with my name on the front.

'Oh,' I said, 'you didn't have to get me a card mum.'

She laughed and said, 'It's not a card Joe. Go on, open it.'

So, I opened it and took out the papers that were inside and I stared at 'em for a minute or two. Now, as you know, I ain't too good at the old reading. And there were an awful lot of words on the top piece of paper. Dead confusing it were. The only words I could really make out were me own name, Poachers Cottage and the word 'DEEDS' in big letters at the top. I didn't have a blummin' clue what it were all about. And I must have looked a bit daft sat there just staring at that bit of paper without saying anything.

Then Seamus gave this little chuckle and said, 'You best tell him Sarah.'

'Tell me what?' I said.

'What it means Joe,' Said mum, 'is that Poachers Cottage now belongs to you. You are the legal owner of that house. It's yours son, I've bought it for you. I knew you'd never leave Blessham and I knew you wouldn't want to live anywhere else, so a week ago I bought you the house. It's yours Joe, it's all yours.'

Well I stared at her for a moment, although gawped would be a better word as me mouth fell open like a blummin' dead trout, and I've seen plenty of them over the years, and her words started to sink in like.

'You mean…' I started to say and then me eyes filled up with tears and I started crying. Like a big blummin' baby I were. I couldn't believe it. Me mum had bought Poachers Cottage for me. I owned me own house. No more blummin' rent to pay. It were like a dream and I hugged her close and said 'thank you mum' about ten times. And everybody cheered and clapped and I felt dead special again like I did at the party in the pub only more so because me mum were there and I owned a house.

Best. Christmas. Ever!

Me mum and Seamus stayed until just after the new year because they had to get back to the racehorse business but before they went, they opened a proper bank account for me and put £250,000 in it. Now, I'm not great with figures and sums as you know, but I'm led to believe that it's a lot of money and that if I didn't want to then I didn't have to work anymore. Nick told me that me needs were always simple and that I weren't too extremenant… excavernment… exteramignant…

…I didn't spend a lot of money like.

But you know what, I, am the head gardener, at Blessham Hall, and I'm blummin' well proud of it. I reckon I've got a job for life there and that'll do me. And besides, I'm going to need that money to set up home for me and Meg after the wedding. So, I'll carry on working and keep hold of me money thank you very much. Blummin' 'eck, gardening is all I know, what else would I do with meself?

And that's what I've done. Nick says that my money will earn interest. Well, I couldn't care less who's interested in it, good luck to 'em whoever they are.

One other thing, I should mention were something that happened in the butchers' shop. Now, to tell you the truth, I'd been keeping out of the place on purpose after what happened with Jim Booth but me mum said I were to go in and see Mr Booth and tell him that me mum said to say hello. So, one lunchtime, I went in and I thought I'd best get meself some of their best sausages or something as well seeing as I could properly afford to buy 'em now. Old Mr Booth were in there serving and do you know what, I felt sorry for him. He weren't himself; I could tell. I reckon all that police business with Jim must have taken a toll on him. But when he turned and saw me he smiled and said, 'Hello there Joe, what can I do for you?'

'You alright Mr Booth?' I said.

'Ah boy, not so bad.' He replied.

'I've come for some sausages and me mum asked me to say 'Hello' for her.' I told him.

Mr Booth smiled again and nodded, and then said, 'I would have liked to have seen her myself, just for old times' sake. Lincolnshire?'

'No,' I said, 'She's in Ireland.'

He laughed at that and said, 'No, you daft apeth, I meant the sausages. How many?'

'Oh, ah, yes please.' I said. 'About four, I reckon.'

'Righto!' He said and he started to wrap 'em up, at which point I thought I really ought to say something about Jim.

'Mr Booth, I… I'm sorry about Jim.' I said staring down at the floor.

'That's alright Joe, my boy,' he smiled again. 'Not your fault. Stupid bugger has got what he sodding well deserved. It'll teach him a lesson. And if that bloody hippie mate of his ever shows his face around these parts again I'll… well, I'll have him, that's what. They should never have done to you what they did and folks in this village won't forget that in a hurry. I won't forget it, and neither should you my lad.'

'Oh, I believe in forgive and forget Mr Booth. How much for the bangers?' I said.

'Have 'em on me.' He said shaking his head. 'You're a good lad Joe, you've turned out alright you have.'

'Thanks Mr Booth,' I said. 'I'll see you later.'

'See you later son,' he said with a smile and a wink, 'see you later.' And I had bangers and mash with peas and gravy for me tea that night.

16

Loose Ends

So that's me story for you. Me life so far, so to speak. You know, I remember someone once said to me, can't remember who, but they said, 'You have to take the rough with the smooth in this life.' Actually, it may have been me granddad. Anyway, I suppose that's what I've always done. And you know, if you put your trust in the Most High, he'll come through for you. I mean, look at me. I'm healthy, wealthy and, I think, a lot wiser these days. Oh, I know what you're probably thinking. You're thinking what a rough life I've had. Born thick as pig muck, lost me mum, knuckled by the old man, leathered by old Rodwell at least once a week at school, beaten up by Boothy and his bullies regular, screamed and sworn at daily by Her Ladyship, strangled and wrongly imprisoned and so on and so on. But that's all in the past. You see, what you have to understand is this. Life ain't about what happens to you, it's about what happens inside of you. You have to find out what makes you happy inside and live for it. And for me, I've learned a thing or two about what it takes to make you happy, and you know of course what's going to make me happiest of all. Marrying Meg.

But what about Meg? Well, things went quite well for her really. She got three years inside but they reckon she'll be out in eighteen months. Apparently she really stood up for me when she went to the police and told 'em the truth. Nick went with her you see, and he told me all the good things she said about me. She said that, 'Joe Wilkie is the kindest, sweetest man I ever knew. He wouldn't hurt a fly. All he tried to do was to protect me and keep me out of trouble. But he's innocent, he's as innocent as a child and I'm ashamed to say that we took advantage of that innocence and I don't think I'll ever forgive myself for it as long as I live.' That's what she said.

Well, I don't know about that but I blummin' well forgive her. You know, if someone asked me to make one of them list thingies about the things I love the most in this world I'd say, me mum, the village, me job, the smell of cut grass, the sunrise, the sunset, the church, me friends and me little home. But right at the very top of the list I'd put Meg Morrison. Me best girl. And as soon as she gets out of that place and comes home I'm going to be there waiting with a bunch of roses and an engagement ring and I'm going to ask for her hand in matron-money and make her Mrs Meg Wilkie! That's what I'm going to do, you'll see.

I wanted to visit her of course, in prison, but she said she doesn't want anyone to see her in there, not even her folks, so I'll just have to wait. But I'll be there, when she gets out.

As for Jim Booth, well, I forgive him for what he's done to me. Not just the basil thing but for all the horrible things he's done to me throughout me life. They reckon he'll never be able to show his face in the village again, poor beggar. I just couldn't imagine that. Five years he got. Five blummin' years in that place. I wonder if he's in with Rufus and Wendy. He'd get on well with that pair. And Mr Riddle wouldn't half keep him in check and on the straight and narrow I know. Blimey! A lot of people down the pub say things like, 'He wants the shit kicking out of him in prison' and that they 'Hope he gets what's coming to him inside.' But, to me, never seeing Blessham again would be punishment enough. I know. And I were only away for a short while from this little village, the best little village in the whole blummin' world.

They never did catch that Simon fellow, well, not yet. But I don't reckon he'll ever show his face in the village again either. By 'eck, I wouldn't even like to think about what Her Ladyship would do to him if he did. That last time she mentioned him she said, 'Scum like that should be purged from the face of the earth, Wilkie, purged I say!' I had to go and ask Mr Franks what purged meant and when he told me it don't sound like anything Simon would enjoy, that's for sure.

Life goes on though and I decided to do something good with some of me money. I paid for the church roof to be fixed. Five thousand quid it were, but I didn't mind paying that for the Lords' house. It were great though. I had me photo in the local newspaper standing in front of the church with Nick and the new bishop. Nice man is the new bishop. Comes from somewhere called Samoa, and no, before you ask, I don't know where that is. Bishop Tapawnfri is his name. Lovely fella. We had a nice chat about Samoa over tea and cakes at the vicarage afterwards. He said I really ought to visit there sometime. I said, 'I'd like that but the only foreign place I really want to visit is Ireland to see me mum and take a look at Kerry's ring with me stepdad.'

Of course, that means getting one of them pissport thingies with me photo on and flying in an airyplane. I don't know how I'm going to get on with that, flying. I reckon I'd probably mess meself up there in the blummin' clouds. Seamus says I could always take the ferry but I ain't never been on a boat neither and that takes even longer than the airyplane, so I reckon I'd be just as worried about that. You know, if it hit an iceberg and sank like that Titty-tonic boat I saw on the telly. I don't know, I've still got a few months to make me mind up. It'll be nice to see 'em again though, mum and Seamus.

I tell you what, them blummin' landscape gardeners didn't do much of a job at the hall. It's taken me a long time and a lot of hard work to get it back to its best. Her Ladyship seems happy with me efforts and all and I even get the odd compliment off her now and again, which never happened before, so all's well that ends well you see. Mind you, she still gives me an earful from time to time as well, so some things never change I suppose.

As for Blessham itself, well, nothing much changes around here. Mr Booth took someone on at the butchers to replace Jim and there's a new barmaid at the Pig and Whistle. You'll never guess who. Marguerite! She works there in the evenings. Bob seems to get on alright with her. He reckons she could come in very handy if there's ever anyone who's had too much to drink and needs chucking out.

And I still walk a lot in me spare time. I wander round the village and I walk over the hills or through the woods, thinking about Meg or praying to God or sometimes just stopping to admire the view and marvel at all of creation and what a beautiful place I live in and how thankful I am that, overall, life is pretty...

...good.

In fact, if anyone ever asks me if I'm alright I always answer 'em in the same old honest way. I say, 'Ah boy, not so bad.'

THE END

Printed in Poland
by Amazon Fulfillment
Poland Sp. z o.o., Wrocław

60041298R00150

Alan Stevenson learned to write at the age of 5 (thank you Mrs Burroughs). Since then he has written extensively – letters, emails, postcards etc. His first published work was a poem on a cubicle wall of the gents lavatory in the Bricklayers Arms public house (sadly, out of print). Now, however, at the age of 53, he feels he is sufficiently grown up enough to write novels. His literary influences include Tom Sharpe, Jerome K. Jerome and the Carry On films.

Ah Boy! is Alan Stevenson's first novel and is a comedic and bawdy farce set somewhere in rural England. Joe Wilkie is a simple country lad, immensely likeable but oh so incredibly naïve and totally innocent of the ways of the world. In fact, the world to Joe doesn't much exist beyond his home village of Blessham. Life hasn't been kind to Joe, at all, but he retains an attitude and optimism that would put most people to shame. However, things get much, much worse for him when both the woman he loves and his arch enemy convince him to grow something at his place of work that isn't, shall we say, legal, and when those 'plants' are discovered Joe's world is turned completely upside down. Join Joe in this hilarious and ribald romp through English country life where molehills, welly wanging, Morris men, rugby match brawls, excessive flatus, monstrous nobility, sexual promiscuity and cannabis cultivation (it would seem) are just a normal way of life.